THE MAN FROM GADARA

Abdalla Hawatmeh
with
Roland Muller

The Man from Gadara

Copyright © 2000, 2003 Roland Muller

This story is true. However, in a number of cases the names of individuals and locations have been changed to protect the people involved. Nevertheless, Abdalla Hawatmeh is a real person and the events in this story really happened. We trust that you will enjoy this book and that through it you will be drawn closer to the Lord Jesus. We also trust that you will be spurred to pray for the Middle East and other lands that are under Islam's influence.

Printed in Canada   2003

This book is dedicated to all those who are involved in sharing the message of Christ's love with those from a Muslim background.

Also by Roland Muller

- **Tools for Muslim Evangelism**

- **Honor and Shame**
  Unlocking the Door

- **Missionary Leadership**
  By Motivation and Communication

- **Missions: The Next Generation**

- **The Message, The Messenger and the Community**

Acknowledgments

This story spans several decades and touches the lives of many people. We would like to express our thanks to those whose names or stories appear in this book and would like to acknowledge the many others whose names do not appear here for various reasons. Some names have been changed to protect the individuals involved. Others have simply asked that they do not appear in the story as they continue to minister in difficult and, sometimes, dangerous places.

Special thanks must go to those who have helped in proofing this book, both for historical and literary accuracy.

Roland Muller
Abdalla Hawatmeh

Preface

My first meeting with Abdalla Hawatmeh is indelibly etched on my mind. Afterward, I commented to my wife that when I met Abdalla, I had met with a man who was wonderfully transparent. I saw Jesus in him in a way that I haven't experienced in a long time. From that moment on, I was interested in writing Abdalla's story, but I decided not to pursue the matter until the Lord brought it into being. Several years later, Abdalla mentioned to me that he had often thought of writing a book that would be an encouragement to others working with Muslims and would help stir the church around the world to pray for Christians in the Muslim world. When he discovered that I was a published author, he invited me to work together with him in recording the events of his life. As we explored the ministry God has given Abdalla, I discovered an incredible story sprinkled with a wealth of spiritual insight. I trust you will enjoy this book as much as I have enjoyed researching and writing it.

I have tried, as much as possible, to preserve Abdalla's mannerisms and forms of speech. While some editors have objected to this, most readers who know Abdalla personally have appreciated being able to hear him tell his own story in his own way. We apologize if this makes the reading of some passages a little more difficult, but if you ever meet the real Abdalla Hawatmeh, we hope you will be able to recognize him as the same person who is telling his story in this book.

I have divided this book into two parts. The first section recounts Abdalla's story beginning from his childhood and ending with his release from prison. The second part is a collection of stories and events gathered from Abdalla's ministry after his release from prison.

Roland Muller

PART ONE

CHAPTER ONE

Jesus entered the district of the Gadarenes. Matthew 8:28

THE PRISON DOOR CLANGED SHUT BEHIND ME, the sound echoing down the empty halls. The prison guard slid the bolt into place. I was alone. I stood staring at my prison cell. The furniture consisted of a bed, a small table, and a chair. A door on one side led off to a small toilet. It wasn't bad but, still, it was prison. Self-pity and anger welled up inside of me. I had been here for several days and I might be here for many more. Maybe I would never leave. In despair I threw myself onto the bed and began to sob. I felt so frustrated, so sad, and so angry. All night long, for several nights now I had faced my accusers, answering their questions and hearing the taunts in their voices. Would I ever be released?

As I faced what I knew would be long hours alone, questions formed in my mind. How did I get here? How did a nice Jordanian boy from a good Muslim family end up in this awful situation? During the days before my arrest, government agents had been following me and listening to my telephone calls. My mail was read, and people I knew were approached and sometimes threatened. There had even been threats against me by persons unknown to me.

Now I was here, locked up in jail, facing my accusers as they tried to find some crime to charge me with. As I lay on the

13

bed, my mind drifted back to how it all began. I remembered my village, the old farmhouse and, especially, my father. Father had been a good man. He had been kind and gentle and always concerned about his boys, and we boys loved him and tried to please him as best we could. But I had changed. I had disappointed my father, and I had hurt my mother. I was different than I had been as a child. I had been born a Muslim and raised as a Muslim. Now I was a Christian, and people were angry and upset. Nevertheless, in my heart I knew I had met God, and I would never turn back, no matter what happened to me.

I GUESS IT ALL STARTED WITH FATHER and the stories he told us about his youth. As a young Arab teenager, my father had traveled to Haifa in Israel, where he found work with a Jewish man named Shlown. In those days, before the 1948 war, Arabs and Jews lived peaceably side by side. Shlown owned two businesses, one in Haifa and one in Jaafa. Father worked as a laborer for fifteen years for Mr. Shlown and the two of them became good friends. Those years left a deep impression on my father as he discovered that Muslims, Jews, and Christians all worshipped one God and were all good people. After fifteen years, my father was loved and respected by the Shlown family, but he wanted to return to his home country of Jordan and raise a family.

Father moved back to Jordan, bought some land, and settled down. Then the wars began and the Shlowns and my father lost touch. Many long years later Jordan signed a peace treaty with Israel and as soon as the borders were open, old Mr. Shlown sent one of his sons across the Jordan River to look for my father. He found us, but Father had already died. Of course, Mr. Shlown was now very old himself and a short time later he died. When we received the news, I traveled to Israel to represent our family at his burial.

Right from the beginning of my childhood, I knew my father had been affected through his contact with people other than Muslims. Most of the people in our village had never met a Christian, let alone a Jew. Village life was simple, and everyone in the village knew everyone else's business. Our world was small, and we were happy raising our crops and interacting together with friends and family.

My father's life experience was broader than most in the village and because of that many people looked up to him. Before the troubles in 1948, there were no enemies. The Jews and Arabs lived side by side like any other people. However, after the war, even the people in our little village began to think in terms of enemies and friends but my father never saw it that way. Although he was a simple man, he grasped that there were far greater things involved and that given the right circumstances, we could all live in peace again.

When my father came back from working with the Shlowns in Israel, he had a pocket full of cash. It wasn't a great amount of money, but compared to others in the village he was rich. With this money, he purchased land on the edge of our village, which is known as Um Qais. This village is situated on the top of a hill in the north of the Hashemite Kingdom of Jordan. In ancient times, our village was known as Gadara. Christians around the world know of this ancient town as the place where Jesus cast demons into pigs. While we knew that our village had a history, most of us knew nothing of this Bible story. Um Qais was simply home, and we lived in a house my father built with the money he brought back from Israel.

Our home had some very peculiar characteristics. My father located a large cave on the land he purchased. The entrance to the cave was simply a large hole in the ground, with ancient stairs descending down to an ancient stone door. The inside of the cave was huge. It was over one hundred feet long and almost thirty feet wide. The cave had a hard packed floor. Scattered around in the ancient dust of time were various pieces of pottery, most of them dating back to Roman times. We kids didn't know anything about pottery, and we would often play with the old pots and clay lamps. Sometimes we would simply break them when we were finished playing.

The Man From Gadara

My father built his house on the rock above the cave. He marked out a central courtyard and around this common space he built a series of rooms, each with a door opening into the courtyard. One room was the kitchen, another was the reception room, and others were bedrooms and storage rooms. Over the years, he added rooms until there were eight in all.

I WAS BORN IN 1957 and my father gave me the name Abdalla, which means "the servant of God." I was the fifth child in our home but only the second son. My older brother, Abdul Karim, and I became very close. When we were not busy with our studies, we would play in the fields or try our hand at basketball. We made a simple wire hoop and the village boys would gather at our house to play on the rocky ground.

We were not wealthy, but we never considered ourselves poor. My father had used all his money to buy land and to build our home. After this, we lived as farmers. We worked the fields and lived off the land. The atmosphere in our home was usually good, and we children loved our parents and they loved us. While we lived very simply, we were well known in the area. Our last name was Hawatmeh and we were part of the larger Hawatmeh tribe, and the leaders of the tribe respected my father.

Each day life in our village was much the same. We would rise at daybreak and, shortly afterward, we would sit down to the inevitable breakfast of olives, olive oil, yogurt, and freshly baked bread from our oven. Mother would rise early in the morning to make the dough and fire up the old clay oven. She would rake away the ashes from around the oven and place hot coals against the clay walls. Then she would pack hay over the coals, and in a short while the oven would become very hot. Next she would roll out the dough and place it in the oven. After a few minutes, it would become soft bubbly bread. Using a long wooden fork she would retrieve the bread and serve it to the family.

After breakfast, we would fetch our cows and wait near the road for the village shepherd to pass by. As the shepherd walked through the village he would gather cows from each home and take them to the surrounding hills. In the evening, the shepherd would again pass by our home and return our cows.

As soon as the shepherd gathered our cows in the morning, my mother started shooing the children out of the house. Abdul Karim and I would head off into the fields to play for two hours before we needed to head for school.

After school was out, we children would rush home to see what Mother had cooked for our afternoon meal. We never grumbled over our food because we always thanked God for what we got from the farm.

Our home always had a religious atmosphere. We were Muslims but not fanatical Muslims. We children worshipped like my father and mother did. Islam was our religion, and everyone we knew in the village was Muslim.

Islam is a religion of works. Every good Muslim has many religious things that he does, such as praying five times a day. We, however, took our religion in stride. We were faithful at the mosque for Friday prayers, but since we were often at school and my parents were busy with the farm, we usually only prayed the morning prayers.

Most people did their religious duties without question but, at an early age, I started to ask my father questions. My father was not a very scholarly man, but he could read and write. His schooling had been minimal and now that he was old he didn't bother much with books. "Son," he would say. "There are many things we should not understand in the Qur'an. We just have to believe. If we believe in God, then He will help us understand."

To be honest, I never really believed in some of the things I heard at the mosque. They were hard to understand, especially for a ten-year-old boy. Most of the other boys around me simply accepted Islam as their religion and went about being boys, but I wanted to know and understand what we believed and why we were doing what we did. Now as I look back on those days I can see that the Lord was with me, even when I was young. My questions at that time set the foundation for the search for truth that was to consume me in later years.

The Man From Gadara

Despite my curiosity about religious things, no one else in our home seemed interested in learning more about religion. We were Muslims, we did our religious duties, and that was enough. Then something happened in our home that was to change the course of our lives.

It all started very innocently when my father decided to build a special room onto our house. When the room was finished, Father announced that this room was to be a place of refuge. It was to be used for whoever might come through the village and need a place to rest. We were to welcome people who were in hunger or in need and make the room available to them. In the years that followed, a number of people came to our home because this room was available.

That room is still there to this day. Some years ago, my brothers demolished the old house so they could build a new home, but none of us wanted to demolish that room and so we left it standing. It was a special place for us, although sometimes when the room was occupied, my mother would grumble about baking more bread or preparing extra food for these strangers. However, my father always insisted that these people were our guests. If they were our guests, they were part of our family.

ONE DAY, MY OLDER SISTERS CAME RUSHING HOME from school and announced that they had met two Christian ladies who wanted to use the room. However, they did not want the room for only one or two nights. They were looking for a place to stay for three years. My sisters were so excited that they brought these Christian women to our home and the next day they were discussing arrangements with my parents. We younger kids were very curious to see these women. We had never had many dealings with Christians and certainly had never had them in our home before. They were in their late twenties, and they seemed like nice young women. They were sisters, and they had come to our village from the city of Irbid to teach school. Irbid was about thirty kilometers away and there was limited public transport. Back then, there was one broken down old bus that came in the morning and then again in the evening. Since this did not suit their schedule as teachers, these women wanted to stay in the village during the week and only go home on weekends. We kids were happy about this, but my mother said that since three years was such a long time they would have to cook for themselves.

"Of course," they answered, "we are going to rent the room."

My father firmly shook his head. "No," he insisted, "we don't rent it for money. Not that room. That room is free for whoever needs it."

In no time, these two women moved into the room. My sisters were very excited. They felt like they had two brand new older sisters and they were so happy. It didn't take long before these two women became part of our family. They slept in our home and, occasionally, my sisters would sleep with them in their room. Many times these two women would eat with us and my sisters would eat with them. We never felt like these two women were only using the room; they became part of our family.

The special thing about these women was that they were Christians. Since we kids did not know any Christians, we had simply believed the rumors we heard about how Christians acted. We had heard that Christians were often immoral, that they drank liquor and were awful people. However, my sisters and my family testified many times about how honest these two women were and how morally upright they acted. In addition, we heard the same report from their school where they also had a good reputation. Somehow, in their simple humble way, they left a profound impression on us all. I didn't realize it at the time, but they were a living demonstration of what it meant to have a servant heart. My sisters were very much affected by these two teachers and, to this day, they still have a close relationship with them.

So my father also told us about Jews and how good they could be, and those two women influenced our attitudes towards Christians.

Finally, the sad day came when these two women finished their teaching contract and had to leave. We all said good bye and our home seemed empty after they had gone. I still remember how my sisters didn't want to eat or sleep that night. It was like they had lost their own sisters. They cried all night and, in the end, my father became very upset. As a result, we all took the bus to Irbid the next morning. You can imagine how astonished those two women were when we all arrived on their doorstep the next day for a visit.

Those two women really touched our family. Their kindness meant so much to all of us. Moreover, the more I thought about those women, the more questions I had. Why were they like that? Why had we heard such bad things about Christians when we had seen only good things? Why did our Muslim leaders tell us that we should call them *kufar* or infidels? If they were *kufar,* then why did they act so much better than we did? That question became a major issue in my heart, which kept me looking for an answer for years afterwards.

A short time later a man came to stay with us. He was from the Hijazeen tribe in the south of Jordan. He had been appointed by the Ministry of Agriculture to our village to work as a forest ranger in the woods. When he arrived in our town people directed him to us. They told him to go to the Hawatmeh family who had a room that they let out for free. He rushed off to find us and ended up staying for a year and a half. He was from a nominal Christian background and this time we boys developed a friendship with a Christian.

SOON AFTER THIS, I FINISHED MY CLASSES at the village school and started attending a secondary school in the city of Irbid. I was now a teenager and every day I traveled by bus back and forth to the city. The trip would take me about an hour since the roads were not good and the bus was even worse. However, as the cost was low and my time was expendable, it was arranged that I would travel to the city to get a better education. The school I attended was a large government school for boys. In my village, there had been no Christians in my school but now in Irbid there were three Christian boys in my class. We sat in desks wide enough for two students and a Christian boy named Fendi was my desk mate for three years. And for three years I tried to ask him questions about his religion. Fendi was from a nominal Christian background so he didn't know that much about his own religion. I don't think he cared that much about it either. Nevertheless, I was interested in learning more. In my tenth year in school the idea came to me that I should get a Bible and read it. I looked in vain in the school library and then I thought of asking Fendi.

One day I finally got up the courage. "Where can I get a Bible?" I almost whispered.

"I don't know," he replied carelessly, "maybe from a church."

I was taken aback when he said the word 'church.' I had always heard bad things about churches. We were Muslims and we didn't have any dealings with churches. Our country was a Muslim country, so there were only a few Christians around. We didn't know much about them. The boys in the village used to talk in hushed whispers about the things that went on in churches. People would act wrongly there and do sexual things. There was alcohol in churches for people to drink and maybe, it was whispered, there were guns and people got killed there. Although we thought churches were definitely dangerous places, all the village boys secretly wanted to see the inside of one. Consequently, it took some time to work up the courage to ask Fendi if he would take me to church. When I finally asked him, he didn't seem too concerned and readily agreed to take me to a church close to our school.

At first I was very afraid. Just walking up to the church was frightening. We passed through the big wooden doors into the cool interior. Inside we sat on a long bench and watched what was going on. The church was very different from our mosque. In the mosque, we sat on the floor but, here, in church, there were seats. In the church, there were also pictures of people on the walls. We Muslims had no pictures of people because images of any kind were forbidden.

The Man From Gadara

At that time, I didn't know what kind of church it was, but some years later I learned that it was a Catholic Church. As I watched, I didn't see anyone doing anything wrong. We were just sitting in our seats and a priest was at the front doing things. No one bothered about two boys sitting at the back so we just sat there. After a while, my fear passed and I started to think.

"Oh my God," I said to myself, "What were we thinking about? This is a very peaceful place. It even seems kind of godly."

As we sat there, people looked at us with kind faces and, afterward, they greeted us although they didn't know who I was. From that time on, my opinion of churches started to change. I realized that the things I heard in my village were only rumors told by people who had never been in a church. Thankfully, in modern Jordan today, most of these rumors have disappeared but, somehow, many people still consider churches as dangerous places.

My opinion of Christians was starting to change. The kind faces of those two women clearly reflected Christian love. I saw something in my friend, Fendi, and in Mr. Hijazeen, who stayed in our home. They were all Christians. They all demonstrated kindness. Therefore, I began to equate Christianity with kindness. I knew that somehow they were linked together but I didn't know how.

Soon after this, my friend Fendi and I started looking for a Bible. The only name I knew it by was 'Injil' or Gospel, so Fendi and I started asking all the bookstores for an Injil. After much searching, we found a storekeeper who could get us a copy. It was a very small book and he wanted half a dinar for it. Since I had no source of income, I had to save my daily sandwich money. Instead of a full sandwich, I would buy only half a sandwich and I would save the other 2 1/2 piasters so I could buy my Injil. I saved my lunch money for a whole month before I had enough.

Finally, the day came when I could return to the store to buy my Injil. However, when the storekeeper put the book in my hands, I was disappointed.

"Why doesn't it have the word Injil written on it? What does 'New Testament' mean?" I asked.

The storekeeper looked puzzled. "I don't know," he replied and turned back to his work. He was simply a storekeeper and didn't care. Over his shoulder he said, "This is what you wanted and I got it for you. I have nothing other than that."

"OK," I replied tentatively. "Thank you." I was a bit disappointed but when Fendi, who was waiting outside, saw my face he soon had words to cheer me up.

"The New Testament," he explained, "means 'after Christ.' After Christ was born this Gospel was produced." So I accepted that and started reading in it that very afternoon. However, I also decided that I should tell my father what I had done. That evening, I waited until Father was home from the fields and was sitting alone.

"Father," I said carefully, "I have been saving for a whole month, and today I bought an Injil."

Thankfully, he didn't seem too concerned. "I guess it's better than buying some other books," he replied. "You can read it, but don't read magazines that could spoil your schooling, OK?"

I don't think my father ever realized how much impact that book would have on my life or the lives of our family. If he had, he might have taken it from me that day and destroyed it.

CHAPTER TWO

And they searched the Scriptures day after day. Acts 17:11

THE NEW TESTAMENT WASN'T ANYTHING LIKE I HAD EXPECTED. Lots of things in it puzzled me. Right from the beginning, I found it a simple book with simple language. Our Muslim Qur'an is written in difficult ancient language. It took a lot of thinking to understand the Qur'an. The New Testament was different. Not only was the language understandable but the subject matter was easy as well. It seemed more like a storybook than a religious text. I was expecting God to be speaking directly like he did in the Qur'an. What I found, however, was a nice story of how Christ was born and the places he went and the things he did. Everywhere he went there were people around him who saw what was happening and they simply wrote the events down.

As I read, lots of questions formed in my mind. I had heard things about Jesus that weren't in this book. No matter how much I searched, I could not find anywhere that Jesus spoke as an infant. It simply wasn't there. I had heard that Jesus had performed miracles when he was a young child but that also wasn't there. The story of Jesus' birth was different. The Qur'an told us that his mother Mary fled from her family and went into hiding because she thought she had brought shame on her family when she was pregnant without a husband. I didn't find any of this in the Bible.

Instead, I found that Joseph, Mary's fiancé, was there. He stuck with her and, moreover, he got his instructions from God. The story in the Bible made more sense to me. If she heard the voice of the God, why would Mary need to be afraid? If she accepted God's will, why did the Qur'an tell us she felt shame?

Even at a young age I was becoming aware that there were conflicts and discrepancies between the Bible and the Qur'an. I was anxious to resolve these conflicts so I started to read little bits from both of them and think about them.

One day I asked my friend, Fendi, "Why was Jesus born in a cave? Why wasn't he born like any of us?"

Fendi thought for a moment and then replied, "Maybe his father didn't have any money to go to a hotel."

That made sense to me. I was a village boy. The cave beneath our house was better than a hotel. In the wintertime it was warm and in the summer time it was cool. The hay was always clean and soft. In fact, I preferred being in our cave to living in our house.

Soon I started debating in my mind between the things I knew about Islam and the things I was reading in the Bible. I realized that it didn't make sense to debate, however. In the Bible, the facts were clear. In the Qur'an, they were not.

I wanted to study more, but as a young boy my days were filled with schooling, working on the farm and activities with friends and family. In the end, it took me two years of occasional reading to complete the gospels of Matthew and Mark and half of Luke.

But the questions continued. Matthew's Gospel told me who Jesus' father was, who his father's father was, and so on. I was expecting that it would say God took Mary as his wife and had a son. After all, that is what Christians believed, wasn't it? However, the Bible didn't say this.

I was also puzzled about other things. Why would a great king like Herod want to kill a baby? It seemed to me that he could wait until Jesus was a young man and then simply put him in jail. After all, Herod was a Roman king. He could do anything.

Those questions were like seeds in my brain and my heart. "What am I reading?" I often wondered, "Is it a new truth?" I had always understood that the Qur'an was given to make the Bible clearer, but it seemed to me that the message in the Bible was already clear and complete.

This question plagued me for some time. I hadn't read very far, but everything I had read seemed so different. The more I read the Bible, the more the Qur'an seemed doubtful. The more I read the Qur'an, the more the Bible seemed doubtful.

One day I approached my father, "Father, if you wanted to judge what is in the Qur'an, who or what would you refer to?"

He thought for a minute and then replied "I guess I would refer to God. And perhaps the other books before, like the Injil or the Torah."

"Why," I asked, "are we judging the Bible through the Qur'an then? The Qur'an came later. The Qur'an is not the base; it's the last one. The Bible is the base because it came before. If that is true, why are we judging the old by the new?" Father never had an answer for this.

All during this time I never ceased praying as a Muslim, but I started thinking more while I was praying. "Is what I am doing the true way?" When I was a child, I never understood fully what I was doing, but I believed it to be true. Now that I was a teenager, I understood more, but I wondered if it was really true.

One day, I decided to talk to my oldest brother, Abdul Karim. He was a young man who used his mind a lot. He was studying to become a mechanical engineer and my high school was close to his industrial school. So one day I paid him a visit. I didn't know what to say or how much to tell him, so I ended up telling him that Fendi and I had visited a church together. He listened but he never commented. He simply told me to take care of myself wherever I went. He also insisted that I tell my father.

It was our family code. Every night we would sit with Father and tell him what was happening in our lives. I never talked much with my younger brothers because they were a lot younger than I was, but I could talk about this with my father. It was also helpful that my sisters spoke favorably of Christians. Whenever we would talk about people, they would say that Christians were better and remind us of those two women. My mother, on the other hand, never bothered herself with our questions. She would simply say, "Go talk to your father."

Talking with Father was easy. He was a kind man and he never rebuked us. Usually he would give us an easy answer, so I wasn't very afraid. When I told him that I had gone to church with Fendi, he simply thought for a while and then he looked at me and said words I will never forget. "If you go into a church, son, remember that it is a place where God is worshipped. You should behave as if you are in a mosque. Do what your heart tells you to do, but do it out of obedience to God. Don't go to church for any other purpose."

The answer relieved me. I could pursue my search. However, I realized that I could not find my answers from my father. He was a simple man, and I had never heard him comment about theology. He never told me that the Bible was corrupt or that Christ was not crucified. These things I heard from other Muslims in the village. My father simply wanted his sons to act honorably and be upright.

"If you are going to be around Christians," he told me, "then remember how you should behave in their midst. Make sure you don't misbehave or say anything immoral." That was the end of that.

WHEN I WAS A CHILD, MY FAMILY TAUGHT ME how to practice our religion. They told us how to clean and wash ourselves before prayer. Having a clean body is very important to a Muslim. One should never pray to God unless one is clean.

In the morning, we would rise and eat and then the men would go to the mosque to say the morning prayers. Muslims

27

pray five times a day, but life on the farm made it hard to attend prayers at the mosque. Sometimes Father would stop his work in the field to pray, but when we boys returned from school, we were usually busy and there never seemed time for prayers. Father would return from the fields at sunset, and mother would have a meal ready for us to eat, so there was no time for prayer then. My little brothers never prayed much at all. On Fridays, however, we males would visit the mosque for noon prayers and during the holy month of Ramadan, we would go to the mosque and pray long prayers in the evening.

My father and mother also taught us how to function as Muslims. We learned how to read the Qur'an and how to chant it. They tried to teach us how to love our neighbors, but we boys weren't very good at this. We were always in trouble with the neighbors. Islam was simply our religion. We didn't do it out of religious fanaticism; we just did it naturally as everyone else around us did. We believed it was right, so we did it together.

However, in my last year of high school, I was never sure if Islam was right or wrong. I was slowly becoming a skeptic. I took a lot of notes and started to compare them. I was troubled. I knew that the kindness I saw in Christians was somehow part of what I read in the Bible. It puzzled me, but I had to be careful that my Bible reading didn't interfere with my studies, especially my final exams. In Jordan, the final exams at the end of high school are very important. The grade I would get would mark me for life. If I did well, then there was a future for me. If I did poorly, then finding any work other than menial labor would be difficult.

During my last year of school, I read the Bible very little. My whole life was focused on studying and getting a good mark in my exams. I knew that if I did well, then I could go to university. If I did not do well, then people would think of me as a failure for the rest of my life.

Finally, the days came when I could start my exams. I was 17 years old and young for my grade because I had been promoted ahead when I was in seventh grade. I was very apprehensive about my exams but I felt I had done quite well in them. I had to wait though, as sometimes weeks or months would pass before the marks were released.

Then the day came when the government released our marks. All across the country on the same day, the marks of the students were publicly posted. Those who did well would be offered the chance of further studies; those who did not would stay in the village.

When the marks were finally posted, I was very happy. I had made an excellent grade in English. In fact, I was number one in the whole kingdom of Jordan in English that year. I always liked English, and I was proud of my accomplishments. My math marks were my lowest as I always struggled with mathematics. Overall, my scores were quite high and I was pleased.

A short time later, I discovered that there was a scholarship available for me to study in America. I was so excited. The Jordanian government received four scholarships that year for engineering students to travel to America, and I qualified for the defense engineering scholarship. It was a fantastic opportunity. I could go to America. Just think of it! America: where people robbed you of your money and rode horses and killed Indians. It was so exciting.

Two weeks later I received a letter to inform me that it had been arranged that I would study at a place called Mississippi State University. I was very pleased and my family was all excited and very proud of me. The future looked bright and promising, and with great excitement, we boys got out our maps to locate all the places that I would travel to.

CHAPTER THREE

Forgive the rebellious sins of my youth. Psalm 25:7

I HAD NEVER BEEN IN AN AIRPLANE BEFORE; I had never even been to an airport before. As a young boy, I had seen airplanes flying high overhead and I had stared at the long streak of white that stained the sky for an hour or so afterward. I had wondered what it would be like to fly. Now that I was leaving, I was so excited. I felt like an astronaut leaving for the moon. There was a lot to do to get ready. My father made sure that I had a new set of clothes. My mother sewed money into little sacks to put around my waist. We all knew that people in America steal your money.

When it came time to leave the village, a crowd gathered to see me off. Almost everyone was there. More than 30 men and women piled into cars and accompanied me to the airport in the capital city of Amman. People were excited that I was traveling. I was not just going to the capital; I was going to America! It was a big deal, for me and for them. I remember four or five cars in a convoy, traveling together to the airport. Everyone stayed for a long time to see me off. The men hugged me and the women kissed me, and all too soon I had to pass through the gates to board the plane.

Taking off and leaving the ground was exciting and terrifying all at once. Soon, however, things settled down and I had time to think a bit. Then a very strange feeling started to come over me. I was sad as I looked down from the airplane and saw Jordan dropping away in the distance. The words loomed in my mind. "I will not come back the same." It was a bit terrifying. I knew that my mind and heart would change. As I sat there, I wondered if my family would like me when I came back. How much would I change? My family wanted me to stay as normal as they were. I was a village boy and they wanted me to come back and fit into village life as their families had done for many years. However, I knew that I would not return the same. It was 1977 and I was starting out on a new venture in life.

When I arrived in John F. Kennedy airport, I wanted to see, touch, taste, and experience everything. One of the first things that caught my fancy was a candy store with a wonderful display of American chocolate bars and little boxes and rolls of gum and candy. I wanted to walk up and buy something using my English. I had learned all about English in Jordan. I had the best grade in the Kingdom. I could read and write and do grammar; I had studied Shakespeare and all of the best English writers. I could say many clever things. However, standing there in front of the candy shop, I realized that I hadn't learned how to buy a chocolate bar. All I could do was blurt out, "Give me this" in my heavy Jordanian accent. The high flying young student from Jordan had just crashed to the ground.

A few days later I registered at the State University of Mississippi. From there, it was arranged for me to travel to Indiana to do a three month course called Introduction to Engineering. Being in America was so exciting. Everything was new: the houses, the trees, and cars, the food and, especially, the people.

In the beginning, I had nothing to do except work on my English and explore my new world. At first, I was surprised to learn that everyone around me was actually talking English. It certainly was not like the English I had learned in Jordan. People used strange words like *gonna* and *wanna*. However, once I discovered what they were saying, I set out to copy them as best I could.

The Man From Gadara

I never went to church but I passed many churches traveling to and from school. I was so busy studying and enjoying life that I didn't have much time for religion. I made new friends and, with them, I started visiting the local pubs and the other places where the university students hung out.

SOMETIMES I WAS HOMESICK and I would seek out some of the other Arabs living on campus. Although I wasn't very religious, I did miss praying in the mosque. I also missed having fun there. Once during Ramadan, my brother and I had been sitting at the back of the mosque secretly eating peanuts during the prayer service. We were quietly cracking the peanuts and hiding the shells under the edge of the carpets. Sometime later, the Mullah discovered what we had done. He told my father that it had been his kids had had been sitting at that spot. My father simply replied, "They are just kids. What's the problem?" He didn't even punish us. As I thought about things like this, I missed my father. He was such a kind man.

The holy month of Ramadan was another time I missed my family. Ramadan is the Muslim month of fasting. During the daylight hours, Muslims refrain from eating food, drinking, or even smoking. Once the sun is down, however, everything changes. During the day, we would fast but when evening arrived, my mother would prepare a feast with specially prepared food. Every night, we would either have guests or we would visit others and eat with them.

At the end of the day, we would sit and wait for the Mullah to start the call to prayer from the mosque. At that moment we would begin to eat. Often we would sit around the table ready to pounce on the food as soon as we heard the sound from the mosque. Our home was some distance from the mosque, so someone would have to wait outside to watch until he or she saw the Mullah come out onto the roof of the mosque to give the call to prayer. Then we knew for sure that it was time to eat. No one wanted to fast one minute longer than was necessary.

The Man From Gadara

In America, there was no Ramadan and there was no fasting during the day and feasting at night. I missed this special part of our life. Once I even had to laugh as I remembered an occasion when we kids thought that the Mullah was late and we cursed his mother and father. My father overheard us and he became very upset with us.

As I missed my family, I thought back on all the good things that had happened to me. One time, on the 27th night of the month of Ramadan, something special happened. The 27th night of Ramadan is a special night of prayer when Muslims remember the revealing of the Qur'an. Every single member of my family would stay up all night and pray and ask God for something special. Islam teaches us that if, from a pure heart, you ask God for anything, on that night, it will be answered.

On one occasion, my mother was praying and asking God for good health. I was young, so I asked God for two and a half piasters (about 5 cents.) My mother rebuked me. "Son," she said, "ask for something more. Ask for good health; ask for long life."

"I don't want to do that," I protested. "I'm healthy and I'm young. All I'm asking God for is two and a half piasters." To her chagrin, I kept repeating it all night. I was a bit rebellious and stubborn, and once I had declared my wish I stuck to it.

The next morning before school, I lined up in the courtyard with all the other students. That day, I was at the end of the line. After the national anthem, we all marched into class. As we walked along, we passed a place where the rainwater from the roof drained into a container where it was collected. The bottom was covered with sand and stones and, as I passed by, I looked down. To my surprise, there in the water were five half piaster coins. I was the last student in the row to enter the class and I was the only student to see the coins. I picked them up and put them in my pocket. After school I ran home as fast as I could. "Mamma," I cried out, "God gave me 2 1/2 piasters." Everyone in the family was delighted and impressed.

The two Christian sisters were living with us at the time, and they were very happy for me as well. "Wow, why didn't you ask for more?" they teased, but I was happy. For me it was a lot of money. I kept my two and a half piasters for over a year before I spent them.

When I was in America, I missed those days and I missed my friends from the village, but I was young enough to make new friends. However, I didn't know enough to tell good friends from bad friends and so some of my friends had a bad influence on me. It also didn't take me long to follow the American custom of having a girlfriend. Soon I had a new circle of friends and we would hang out in bars drinking and smoking.

Occasionally, I would get letters from my father. "Abdalla," he would write, "live for God and stay away from adultery and drinking alcohol. Stay away from evil." Sadly, I never did. I appreciated my father a lot at that time, but I never responded to his wishes. I lied to him many times. "Father," I would write back, "I am praying every single day." It was all a big lie. The opposite was true. I was going to school every day and then going to the nightclubs almost every single night.

Although I was far from God, whenever I passed a church, I always felt strangely drawn to go inside. I would feel guilty. I would think to myself, "I should go in there." But I never did.

DURING MY SECOND YEAR AT UNIVERSITY, however, I started reading the Bible. I found a Good News Bible in the university library and I signed it out. I thought that the easy English would be good for my reading practice.

But a strange thing happened. When I began reading the Bible in my room, I started feeling like I was standing in front of a mirror and God was looking at me. God could see me and He knew what kind of life I was living. God knew about the sins I was involved in. From my Muslim religion, I realized that I had a lot of bills to pay to God. I had been smoking, cursing, and drinking. I knew I needed to pay them off some day and I was afraid of what this would mean.

In Jordan I had owned a New Testament, but this time I had a full Bible. I started reading from Genesis and discovered that much of the material was quite new to me. I knew that God made man but in the Bible I discovered that God made man perfect. Man was without sin when God made him. This was very different from what I had learned from Islam. "Oh my God," I thought. "Look at how I've acted. I now have sins. I have corrupted what God made perfect."

Suddenly I felt guilty. With Islam, I had never carried guilt. I had never felt guilty while I was in Jordan. I always thought I was fine. I always thought I could make up for my shortcomings tomorrow. If I failed today, I could succeed tomorrow. I could always pray a bit more or do more good works to balance any wrongs I had done. I had always had the hope that I could renew myself by myself, by doing and saying good things. Now I started to look at life differently. I began to see from Genesis that God had designed a way for humanity and that I wasn't living it. In fear, I continued to read the Bible.

During this time, I made two short visits to a nearby church. It was an evangelical church but I didn't know anyone there. I simply sat in the back, listened, and then left. But my reading and my listening made me start to wonder. I wondered about my feelings of guilt. Perhaps it was wrong for a Muslim to be looking into Christian things. I was having some trouble with my schoolwork and I wondered if God was punishing me through my studies. The two biggest challenges to me were the English language and my Math classes. As time went by, I improved in the language, but Math was a lot harder. Somehow I had never realized that engineering was mostly Math. As I struggled with Math, I began to wonder if Math was God's way of punishing me.

One night I lay tossing and turning on my bed. I couldn't sleep so I prayed, "God, whoever you are, I know you are there. Please lead me to the truth."

CHAPTER FOUR

He led them through the deserts. Isaiah 48:21

MY FIRST TWO YEARS AT MISSISSIPPI STATE
UNIVERSITY were pretty ordinary. I studied during the day,
and I enjoyed student life during the night. My third year looked
like it would be much like my first two years, but little did I
realize how different that year would be.

It all started one Saturday at a reception that the school
hosted for students and teachers. It was one of those events that
most students hated. However, since I enjoyed meeting people, I
happily clipped on my nametag and started mixing with the crowd.

During the course of the evening, one of the university
professors noticed my nametag and tried pronouncing my name.
"Abdalla Hawatmeh," he said with difficulty, "and from Jordan?"

"Yes," I answered wondering what was coming next.

"Well, Abdalla, how would you like to come to our church
tomorrow and speak to us?"

I was astonished. "Excuse me sir," I protested, "but I'm a
Muslim, and my English language is really weak."

The professor just smiled at me. "We don't want you to
speak about religion, just come, and tell us about Jordan. Tell us
about your country and your king." He paused and looked at me

with friendly eyes. "Tell us about your language and customs, whatever you want, but please come."

In the end I agreed and the professor, whose name I discovered was Mr. Charles Love, agreed to meet me in the morning.

The following morning, Mr. Love showed up at my apartment with his beat-up old pickup truck. It was rather strange but pleasant having a total stranger acting so warmly to me, but I was looking forward to getting off campus and meeting some new people. So we headed out, Mr. Love driving his truck with me following behind in my own car.

We began by driving down a highway, but after a short while, Mr. Love turned off the main road and started down a country lane. This road was narrow, and soon we started to pass through some deep pinewoods. It was then that I became afraid. All the old rumors about churches and guns and killings flashed across my mind.

"This man," I thought, "is taking me somewhere to kill me!" I was so shaken by the thought that I started to pray. I said, "God, I am sorry that I haven't been seeking you for the last two years. I've had the freedom to seek you. My weekends have been free, but I've squandered my time on pubs and friends and fun. So if this trip is the beginning of my search again, please help me."

My fear continued to grow, so I reached into my glove box and retrieved my gun. It was a black 38 special that I had purchased during my first week in America. Other foreign students told me that I needed to protect myself. After all, this was America. So I went out and spent $153 on a 38 special. And now I needed it.

A few moments later, we pulled up in front of a nice little Pentecostal church in a place called Ocean Springs, Mississippi. The place looked pleasant enough and there were other people around, so I put the gun away and tried to relax. Mr. Love parked his Ford pickup and showed me where I should park. Then we walked together to the church.

Mr. Love led me inside and he and I sat on one of the pews. It was a pleasant place, with nearly thirty people sitting and waiting for the service to start. As I sat there, I felt a sensation of peace come over me. It was a strange feeling. I felt like I had discovered all the peace that I had yearned for over the years.

As people were sitting waiting for the service to begin, Mrs. Love came and warmly greeted me. Only after this did I dare to look around at the other women. They were all dressed very properly and that impressed me. Many of the girls on campus dressed in such a way as to catch a man's attention, but these women were different and I felt at home.

A few moments later, the service began. As we sang and read the scriptures, the feelings of peace left me and I started to feel afraid again. It was the same feeling that I got whenever I had read the Bible and now it was happening here in church. I felt as if I was standing in front of God, and I was looking at myself in a mirror. I was seeing myself and I didn't like what I saw. As I looked at myself, I grew afraid. The fear was so bad that I started to tremble. Right there in that little church in Ocean Springs, Mississippi, I decided to renew my search for truth. If the truth was in the Bible, I would seek it out and follow it. If it was in the Qur'an I would seek it out and follow it. Whoever and whatever was right, I wanted to know. I would find the truth and follow it wholeheartedly.

Later in the service I had the opportunity to speak to the people about my country. After that was done, they had me speak to the children. I really didn't know that much about my country, but I talked about what I knew and mentioned the countries around us and a little about politics.

I enjoyed the service, but there was one thing that puzzled me. I enjoyed the songs. Some of them were beautiful and some were very lively. The puzzling thing was that some of the people spoke a language that was strange to me. I was quite taken back and somewhat offended. As I sat there, I kept wondering about it. "Is it a language? Is it just noise? Perhaps it is just a different kind of language?" After the service I had the opportunity to ask Mr. Love about it.

"What language was that lady speaking?" I wanted to know.

"We know you won't understand this," Mr. Love said, "But this is what we call 'tongues.' It is the language of heaven.'"

I was quite surprised and began to think these people were quite odd. As a Muslim, I had been taught that Arabic was the language of heaven, and this is why God revealed the Qur'an in the Arabic language. It was all very abnormal and new to me, that people might think that there was another heavenly language and that they would speak this language in church. In the meantime, the same people who spoke in tongues came and greeted me warmly and welcomed me like I was the guest of honor. It didn't take long until I warmed up and enjoyed their fellowship.

After that morning, I never doubted about churches again. That morning all the rumors I had heard in my childhood were erased. I realized that they were just rumors and people repeated them because they had never experienced otherwise.

I was about to return to my car when the Loves invited me to their home for lunch. I was very pleased and gratefully accepted their hospitality. I really enjoyed that meal. It was so nice to eat in a quiet home instead of a crowded school cafeteria. Besides, homemade food was so much better than cafeteria food.

After the meal, we had some time to relax and so I decided to ask Mr. Love a question. "Can you please take me through the Bible? I need someone to lead me through it. I've tried reading it, but I have many questions."

"Well, Abdalla," Mr. Love said very humbly, "I can study the Word of God with you, but I'm not sure I can answer many of your questions. However, with time, I think you will answer them yourself."

"OK," I responded to his challenge, "let's see."

Years later, Mr. Love told me that if he had announced that he knew all the answers, he would have been a liar. Moreover, he wouldn't have given me any chance to search. I then realized that Mr. Love was not only a very smart Electronics professor, he was also very wise.

That afternoon I started my first Bible study. Now I had someone who might be able to answer my questions. However, when I heard an answer, I usually had more questions and suddenly my mind was caught up in discovering what the Bible was all about. When we finished that Sunday, Mr. Love arranged to visit me on a weekly basis so we could open the Bible together. From that time on, every week we would sit together in my dorm room, around the Bible. I would get out my notepaper and diligently take notes. I was serious about learning, and I wanted to have notes so I could later review everything that was said. Whenever Mr. Love would say something I didn't understand, I would stop him and say, "Excuse me, but I don't understand this." Mr. Love would then try and find a simpler way to put things.

As I studied, it soon became obvious to me that the more I read in the Bible the more questions I had. Buried beneath the truth were more truths that I wanted to know about. In particular, I wanted to know about the personality of Jesus. I had read the gospels as a child but I had never grasped what it all meant. Now, as I read, I learned many new things.

For the first time, I realized that Jesus was a completely holy man. The harmony of the events in the Bible also caught my attention. I was fascinated with the way Jesus was born from a virgin. I carefully examined the story of how Mary conceived and how Joseph reacted to her being pregnant. There was a harmony in the Scriptures that I had never understood from my Islamic background.

As a young boy, I had heard all kinds of stories from my father about how Jewish people acted and reacted. We had heard that Jewish men treated their women worse than Muslim men did. But Joseph acted properly. He acted in love towards Mary. In the Bible, it all worked together so smoothly.

I was delighted with the story of John the Baptist's birth and the reactions of Zachariah and Elizabeth. As I reflected on these stories, I began to realize that the same voice that came to

Joseph also came to Mary and was involved in John the Baptist's birth. It was evident that one person was controlling the whole thing. It was God. There was a voice speaking to Mary, and the message proved to be true. There was a voice speaking to Elizabeth and that message also proved to be true. This made me sure that John the Baptist came for one reason only: to prepare the people for the coming of Christ.

From Islam, I had learned that no prophet on earth had ever served another prophet. As I thought about my own religion, I realized that in Islam we had prophets coming throughout history. When they came, they fought, killed, preached, and then left. When Mohammed came, he lived 63 years and did many marvelous things but, in the end, he died from some sort of sickness.

John the Baptist was different. He was a gift from God and a miracle to Zechariah. John came for only one purpose. He was to focus everything on Jesus. He preached repentance and that the Kingdom of God was near. When he approached Jesus, he always pointed to Him and not to himself. He identified Jesus as the Lamb of God. When they asked him by what authority he did these things, he replied, "I am not Christ." This was true, but he had Christ in his mind every minute of his life. He was born to proclaim this message and died proclaiming it.

John had a very difficult job. He came to prepare a people for the Messiah. These people claimed that they were close to God, and yet they were far away. They claimed their closeness to Abraham through their blood lineage. However, their hearts were far from God.

When I read this, I began to understand. Bloodlines are very important to Muslims. Arabs claim bloodlines back to Abraham. Many families and tribes are very proud that they can clearly trace their bloodlines back to the prophet Mohammed.

Another thing that impressed me was the miracles of Jesus. I was not just impressed with his commands of "Be healed" or "Be raised from the dead." No, it was not just that. I believed in

Jesus' miracles even when I was a Muslim. Islam had taught us that Jesus did His miracles "in the name of God."

When I read the Bible, however, I began to realize that no one could do these things except God Himself. In the Qur'an, there is a verse that says, "Who can raise these dead (bones) except the person who created them (God)?" I understood that only God could do these things. But Jesus did them.

It wasn't easy for me to link all these things together. I woke up many times in the night with a dry mouth and a trembling heart wondering, "What is going on in my life? This is wrong! I'm sure Islam is the way to God and by studying these things I'm doing something wrong.... I must repent." My mind would switch back and forth between the things I had learned as a child and the things I was discovering in the Bible.

FOR A WHOLE YEAR I ATTENDED CHURCH. I always looked forward to attending church services, even when I knew that in the night my mind would be tormented with doubts. I seldom missed Sunday services and I often went during the week for the Tuesday night Prayer Meeting. If I did miss a meeting, it was because I was struggling with a rebellious heart. Sometimes I would get so fed up with my search that I didn't want to discover any more truth. It wasn't that I hated the search; I hated the truth I was discovering. The more I learned about the Bible, the more it made me look ugly and repulsive.

Questions would torment me. "Oh my, what if...?" The list of 'what if...' questions grew longer and longer. "What if my family knew where I was right now? What if the people in my village knew what I was thinking right now? What if...?"

I was afraid, honestly afraid. But every Sunday I would head out for church, even though my mind was plagued with doubts and fears. Sometimes I would struggle in myself whether I should go to church or not. God settled this one morning when on the way to church my old car suddenly stopped in the middle of a bridge. I had never had a car in Jordan, so I had no idea what was wrong. The first thing that entered my mind was, "Oh, it must be God punishing me, because I am going to church when Islam is the way."

I got out of the car, opened the hood, and stared at the motor. Cars whizzed by me, and then I prayed the first prayer I ever prayed in Jesus name. I prayed, "Jesus if you really want me to go to church this morning, would you please provide someone to take me there. That's what I'm asking." I really didn't want to miss the service. I looked at the motor and didn't have a clue what was wrong, and I didn't have any idea what I should do next. But I didn't have to worry long because a moment later a car pulled up and an elderly man looked out of his window.

"Can we help you?" he asked.

"Yes" I replied, "Could you please take me to church?"

"Close the hood of your car and get in. Just leave your car there," he instructed. So I left my car on the bridge and climbed into the back seat of his car behind his wife.

"Where are you going?" the old man asked.

"There is a Pentecostal church in Ocean Springs..." I began.

"Oh," he said rather abruptly, "I do not agree with those people, but we love them anyway. They are our brothers. I'm sure they don't agree with us, but I'm sure they love us as their brothers as well. So, let's go to Ocean Springs. I've never been in a Pentecostal service before, but I want to be in one today."

It took us fifteen minutes to get to the church, and this dear couple came in with me I introduced them to my friends there. They left after the service and I never saw them again, but to me they were a miracle. I had prayed, and I got an answer. That was enough to break the idea that God was punishing me. I realized that my car had just broken down and needed repair like any normal old car.

As I studied the Bible and attended church services, God began to stir up my heart. Sometimes fear would grip me. Sometimes I would cry. Sometimes I would go back to drinking. I was never a heavy drinker, but when faced with this new fear, I drank.

Nevertheless, every week Mr. Charles Love would faithfully come to my door. Sometimes we would study together. Sometimes we would pray. Together we started praying for my Math studies. "Lord I hate Math," I would pray. "I want to study Arts or English Literature, but my scholarship is for Defense Engineering." So we prayed together for my Math classes and slowly my marks improved. Eventually, with God's help, I became one of the honor students.

Many times, however, Mr. Love came to my door and rang the bell and knocked and I didn't open it. I could see him through the peephole. It was our appointment time, but I wouldn't answer the door. Sometimes he would stand for more than ten minutes, knocking and ringing and I wouldn't open. I was never angry with him; I simply wanted to hide myself. The things I was learning overwhelmed me and I couldn't take anymore.

In the mornings, I often saw Mr. Love in class. After class he would stop to say a few words.

"Where were you, Abdalla? I came to your room last night."

"I was out studying somewhere," I would lie to him. He would just nod. There was never any discussion. Many times I lied to him, and every time he simply returned love. He never said, "Abdalla, I saw your car in the parking lot," or, "I saw your lights on." No, he never said that.

Several years later I asked Mr. Love to forgive me for those many times he came to my door and I didn't open it.

"I knew you were home," he said. "But I didn't want to leave too quickly. I wanted to communicate to you that I cared for you, even if you didn't open the door." I appreciated that. Mr. Love cared for me as a person. He didn't just focus his attention on evangelizing me. He was interested in me as a person. Many times the Loves had me over to their home. They fed me. We drove together in Mr. Love's old Ford pickup. He even let me drive it sometimes. We worked together, and he educated me about the church.

One time, we built a cemetery for the church. I was happy to be out of the classroom and out of the city. Together we built a fence and did the landscaping. Mr. Love was more than just a teacher to me; he was a model. He was an example and I tried to follow him. Years later, as I started my own ministry of evangelism and discipleship, I realized how much I had benefited from that relationship. I'm certainly not as patient as he was, and sometimes I think that I need to go back to him again and take another course in patience. I never saw him angry. Although his family passed through some hard times, he was always praising the Lord.

Once, in the middle of my search for the truth, I received word that a cousin of mine had been killed. He was a close friend of mine and had been a pilot in the Jordanian Air Force. One day while flying, his airplane just exploded. He was one of the best pilots in Jordan, and he really wanted me to become a pilot as well. My family called me from Jordan and told me the news.

Mr. Love saw I wasn't in school that day and so he came to my apartment to see what had happened. I told him about my cousin. To my amazement, he called the university and took the day off. He stayed most of the day with me and even took me out for lunch. After lunch, he helped me send some telegrams to Jordan. I was amazed at how he left everything and concentrated on me. With Mr. Love's help I booked tickets so I could fly and attend the funeral. When my flight was ready, he went to the airport to see me off. When I returned a few days later, Mr. Love was there smiling and waving. It was as if he had never left the airport.

Through all this, I began to see the love of Christ in Mr. Love. Christ was always there, and Mr. Love was always there for me. Sometimes he would say, "Leave your car and jump in the truck and come with me." We became the closest of friends. Through this time I continued to study the Bible and ask questions.

THE BIBLE WAS SO DIFFERENT from the things I had learned as a child. I had heard that the Bible was corrupted. At first, this was easy to believe. In the Qur'an, everything was written as if God was speaking. "I the Lord God tell you..." but in the Bible, everything was written as if it was a storybook. How could a storybook be the word of God? When I asked Mr. Love about this, he explained to me how God's Spirit moved men to write. They wrote from their perspective but through the inspiration of God.

That might be true, I thought, but the Muslims at home said that Jesus prophesied that another prophet would come after Him. As I studied this, I began to realize that there was something wrong with this idea. Jesus Himself said, "It is finished." In addition, Jesus did not give the name of the one who was to follow. He simply said that He was to be the Spirit and that He would be a comforter. If there was to be another prophet, Jesus could easily have said more so that people would have recognized Him.

Along with this, Jesus was always pointing to heaven, never to earth. He said repeatedly that the kingdom of God was here. The kingdom of God was like this and like that. He would use parables and proverbs in His teaching so that people could understand and relate to what He was saying. If all this was true, how could there be a new prophet coming afterward to bring a new religion? Jesus himself said that He was not there to start a new religion. He did not deny the law in the Old Testament; He came to complete it. Complete means to finish the mission. If this was true, how could a new religion follow? Logically, it seemed wrong.

How could the Bible be corrupt? When I looked at it from Genesis to Revelation, I could see a ladder coming from heaven and going back to it. God created Adam, and the love of God continued for man even after sin spoiled things. God never ceased communication with man even when man was living in the pit. As I read, I could see that God kept revealing Himself through dreams and visions. I could see that God continued to send prophets. God continued to tell the people how they could be redeemed. He repeated over and over again the promise that Christ would come and save the world.

The picture in the Bible was complete. God was taking man with his sins and saving him through Christ. As I meditated on these facts; I realized that salvation was complete. There was nothing to be added to the message of the Bible.

But Islam presented another way. Islam had another book, a new book. As I began to think about Islam, questions formed in my mind. Where did Islam come from? Who brought it? Why was it established? Why does Islam concentrate so much on the language that the Qur'an was revealed in? Why doesn't the Qur'an have witnesses like Matthew, Luke, and John? Why has it never been subjected to historical or analytical analysis? Why was translation of the Qur'an into other languages wrong? I had questions, but Islam taught us not to question the Qur'an, just to believe it.

The two books were very different. Even their messages were different. In the Qur'an, God gave rules and instructions for Islamic society to live by. In the Bible, God gave very simple instructions to Adam. "Don't eat from this tree. But if you eat…." I could see that the biggest obstacle in man's relationship with God was disobeying God. Yet God gave Adam the freedom to act as he chose. Even today, God hadn't changed. We all have a choice. God gave us the Word to believe, to obey, and to apply to our lives.

As I went over my notes, I asked myself the question, "Where is the corruption in the Bible?" My process for analyzing the Bible was like filtering water. If it was bad water, how can you get good water? To prove it, you get into your laboratory and test it. If you want to test the Bible, live with it a while and see if the Word of God does what it says it will do. Does it change you or not?

So the problem of corruption became clear to me. The more I read and the more I discovered the truths of God's word, the deeper I understood. The more I understood, the further I moved from the past rumors that I used to believe in. All this came from testing. I tested it and it stood firm.

The most amazing thing about the message of the Bible was that it is completely fair to all. All men, no matter what their skin color or their position in society could receive forgiveness from God. This was a message of hope for mankind.

In the Bible, I discovered for the first time that God is truly just. His anger is not against people but against what people say and do. In my own religion, I understood that God was mostly angry with people themselves and not with what they did. The Bible, however, told me that good works were fine, but they are not all that God wanted from me. From my own religion, I had learned that God focused on the things we do. That was why we prayed five times a day, gave money to the poor, and fasted during the Holy Month of Ramadan. God would someday weigh the scales, and He would judge the good things I had done against the bad things I had done.

In the Bible, however, I discovered that God loved me. It didn't matter if I did good works or not. If I did good things, that was nice and I needed to do them. But even if I didn't do them, God would still love me. What I needed to do was to hang around the Lord and be with Him and do the things He was doing. Everyone could do his own good works, but the question was: are they through Christ or not? This is what makes the difference.

At that point, I reached a conclusion. The question of the corruption in the Bible was put behind me. I hadn't yet become a believer, but I had decided that the Bible was the book that I wanted to concentrate on and learn more about.

My search wasn't easy. Sometimes my heart would get so stirred up that I hated Islam. And I hated Christianity. I even hated myself. Why am I doing this? Why did I mess around with Christians? Why didn't I stay as a simple Muslim? Back then, my heart was settled and I was fine. Sure, I didn't know a lot, but I was fine and having fun. Now, I knew more and I was having difficulties. Little did I realize that my difficulties had only begun.

CHAPTER FIVE

If you seek Him, He will be found of you. II Chronicles 15:21

IT WAS A HARD PROCESS, BUT THE LORD WAS INTRODUCING me to many concepts and changing my wrong ideas to right ones. In my discussions with Mr. Love, we came across many theological issues, like the deity of Christ, that were very hard for me. When Mr. Love said that Jesus was God, it was like a nuclear explosion going off in my heart. My heart rebelled. "God cannot die; God cannot be seen as a man! God cannot be touched! What is all this rubbish about God barbecuing and eating fish with a bunch of sinners like Peter and John? This is a cheap God. This is not God!"

But His features were the features of God. He had power over creation. He could raise people from the dead. He himself was raised from the dead. He was eternal because He is coming back again. Islam believes that. He was the Word of God, and Islam believes that He is returning. Oh, we twist things a bit to say that the Spirit of God is on Him, but in the Bible I discovered that if Jesus didn't leave, then the Spirit wouldn't come. When one left the other came. If the Spirit was God, was Jesus also God?

The Man From Gadara

In the middle of my search, something happened inside of me that had never happened before. I started to be convicted over my sins. I started to say, "Lord I admit that I am a sinner; I repent from my sin." I started to stop sinning. I still had the same friends, the same car and the same girlfriend, but I quit drinking and smoking and I stopped attending nightclubs.

As I started getting closer to Jesus as a person, I began feeling that I was a bad person. I realized that if I was going to be around Jesus, then I should be a better person than I was. I decided I had better repent.

The first thing I did was to write to my father. "Father," I wrote, "please forgive me. I lied to you during the last two years. I was not praying and I was not following the right way."

Several weeks later I got an answer from my father. "Son," he wrote, "I was so sad about the way you were, but I am glad that now you are out of it." I felt relieved, but I had not explained to him why I had changed. "Father," I wrote back, "I am still studying the Bible." His next letter contained a strange sentence. I'm sure he never realized what it would mean to me in my circumstances. "Son," he wrote, "If you learn a better way in life, grab it. Get it. That will change your future." He probably didn't realize what this meant to me. I don't think he ever thought that I might leave Islam.

Conviction over sin was one of the biggest changes in my life. Before, I had hated easily. I was angered easily. But when I became linked with Christ, even though I didn't accept Him as God, I started to back away from sin and to feel cleaner. I didn't want to mess around in the dirt any more. Not because I was a nice man now, but because it was wrong to God. Suddenly I realized that everything around me belonged to God. Even my schoolbooks belonged to God. I needed to take good care of them. My whole outlook on life changed. If something was sin, then it didn't belong to Jesus and I wanted nothing to do with it.

As I studied with Mr. Love, I was changing and, slowly, I started to think that maybe I was finding the right way. But one big question remained. If Christianity was the right way, then what about Islam? I found the answer about Islam in my Bible. There were many people in the Gospels who did not admit that Jesus was the Messiah. Many of them were Jewish people, who saw Jesus and did things like eating from the bread and fish he provided, or perhaps they were even healed, but they didn't believe this man was the Messiah. They believed he was a nice rabbi who healed people. "God bless him," they might have said, but they never took Him seriously. They didn't say He was the Christ. Nevertheless, a few people did say it.

The first time someone said it, Jesus was very humble and replied, "It is not you who announced it, it was the Father through you, who has blessed you." Jesus was laying down the foundation stones in a very logical way. He did not build with superficial things. Almost everything Jesus did was in public, with witnesses. Except for being with the woman at the well, Jesus was almost never alone.

My time of searching planted many seeds in my brain and I needed to know if these things were true. I wasn't researching a term paper for school; I was searching out truth itself. I had to be sure. For more than two months, I diligently searched in the Bible. When Mr. Love came to my apartment, I had questions primed and ready for him.

"Mr. Love, in the Qur'an it says that when Jesus returns He will preach Islam. What do you think of this?"

"Well, you know what, Abdalla," Mr. Love smiled, "If Christ comes tomorrow and if He preaches Islam then I will be a Muslim. Whatever He wants to do I will follow. But since He did not say what He would do, except what He says in the Bible, I will believe Him from the Bible."

He paused and looked at me. "If someone says Jesus is going to come back and be a blacksmith, OK; this is what they say. However, in the Bible, Jesus says He is coming back as the ruler of this world and I believe Him. If He comes back and wants to be a blacksmith that will be fine with me. It doesn't affect my faith."

AS I DISCOVERED MORE FACTS FROM THE BIBLE, bitterness started to come into my heart against God. "God, how can you allow this? Why do you allow people to think wrongly about you? There are millions of people in the world who believe something other than the truth. It is not fair. It is not right." However, as I continued to study the Scriptures, the Holy Spirit started working inside me. Slowly but surely the war that raged inside my soul was being won over by God. As I read and studied, I began to grasp the situation as God saw it, not as I saw it.

When I realized that God allowed the first two humans to sin against Him, I had thought that God was weak. However, through my studies, I began to appreciate that people are free to choose in life. In Islam we believed that God directs everything, both good and bad. However, through the Bible, I began to see that people are free to choose. God gave us a choice. Slowly but surely I began to see that I too must make a choice.

One day during my studies I made a promise to the Lord. "Jesus," I said, "if I find you are the way, I will never ever leave you. But if you are not, then I will go back to Jordan and do whatever others are doing and not think about all this anymore. I will just enjoy life and keep what I have learned simply as notes in a book. But if it really is you, then I want to be with you, and I will never leave you again."

It was a brave thing to say and the Lord challenged me with it. I had crossed many bridges but there were two more bridges I needed to cross. The first was concerning the death of Christ. Islam had taught me that Jesus had never died. It took Mr. Love over a month to wrestle through this issue with me. We spent more than six Bible studies concentrating on why Jesus had to be crucified. At first, we explored the Old Testament searching through the books of Moses to discover how the Jewish people put the blood of sheep on their doors.

Then we started on the crucifixion story itself. During these studies, I set up a court in my mind. I am a man who likes to take notes and to work my way through things. I appreciated the scientific way of doing things and wanted to work this problem through in a logical way.

First, I examined the facts, comparing the Qur'an and the Bible in a scientific manner. The Qur'an told me that Jesus was crucified, but yet he was not really crucified. The body that hung on the cross simply looked like Jesus. After all, no prophet of God could die such a dishonorable death!

But in the Bible, there were at least fifty witnesses. There were people like Joseph, who carried His body to the tomb. Mary Magdalene and other women prepared His body for burial. Even before His death, Jesus announced that He was going to be crucified. He foretold His death and then He raised Lazarus from the dead as an example of what would happen to Him. He taught His disciples that time was crucial. Right from day one, at the marriage in Cana, Jesus told His mother that His time was not yet. What time was He talking about? It was His death. At the very peak of His power, He was arrested. Humanly speaking, this seemed all wrong. He could have done anything with these people. Nevertheless, He did not fight back. He did not respond. He just submitted. Even in submitting, He thought of others. He told the soldiers to leave the disciples alone and to only take Him.

If He were just a human prophet, maybe twelve disciples would be hanged before they would catch Him. If He was a king or a president, the whole nation would suffer and He would escape until the very end. This did not happen. Jesus let His followers escape and He gave himself up. All this fulfilled His preaching that He would be crucified.

There were other witnesses in my court. Soldiers were there; people with minds and brains and hearts. They saw Jesus. They knew He was dead. There were many witnesses at the cross: the centurion, Mary, Jesus' mother, and John. I did not count the two thieves. They were dying and were probably both liars anyway. But there were the soldiers who pounded the nails into his hands and feet. What about them? Surely they weren't fooled.

The Man From Gadara

Slowly I took the pieces and assembled them together. When collected together the evidence seemed solid. It would be hard for the court to ignore evidence like this.

On the other hand, in the Qur'an, it said that He only appeared to be crucified. That doesn't stand in court. No witnesses, no defense, nothing. It all seemed so weak. When I was finished, I sat back and looked at the court case. There wasn't much of a contest. The answer was obvious. After Mr. Love left that night, I was in a daze. I drove to the beach and walked for a long time. It was late at night and I don't remember anyone else being on the beach, I was so lost in meditation, trying to fathom how Jesus so graciously died for us.

That night Mr. Love had said something very simple to me. "Abdalla," he said, "are you honest with me?"

"Yes, I'm trying to be honest."

"Do you believe Jesus? Do you believe whatever He says in the Bible?"

"Yes," I replied, "I do, because someone who does all these things...why would He lie? There's no reason for Him to lie. Either Jesus was a prophet or He was a liar. If He was a liar then His deeds would be bad. He would work hard, build a kingdom, have an army, and ten or fifteen wives. He wouldn't have direction and protection from God, and He would end up doing many sins. But Jesus was not sinful. Even in the Qur'an, it says He was perfect."

"Well," Mr. Love continued, "here in the Bible, Jesus said, 'I am the life,' and He gave people life. He said, 'I am the way,' and he taught the way to the kingdom. It fits. But what if Jesus says, 'I am the redeemer?'"

This was a powerful question for me. I am from an Arab background and I know what it means to redeem someone. In my culture, it means paying someone's debts, sometimes with blood. If I redeem someone, it means I put myself in the place of another. Sometimes we could redeem something small by paying with an animal. Sometimes we could redeem ourselves by paying money. We called it blood money. But if a person put himself in the place of another, then his life would be taken.

Mr. Love looked at me. "Abdalla, do you believe that an animal can redeem a man? Do you think that a sheep or a goat, a camel or even a donkey can redeem you or me?"

"No," I replied, "I don't think so. An animal is an animal. I don't think God replaces us with an animal. The sacrifice must be worth at least the value of what it is sacrificed for."

Charles Love looked me in the eye. "You are right, Abdalla; we are so dear to God and the relationship is so different that it couldn't be an animal. The sacrifice had to be more than an animal. A normal man couldn't pay for the sins of everyone; he could only pay for his own sins. So it had to be someone greater than a normal man."

Suddenly I saw it. I believed. Jesus must have been the Messiah, and He must have died for the sins of the world. As I grasped this new belief, my heart was filled with passion. Before this, I used to think of the Jewish people as having been brutal. They killed Jesus, an innocent man. Being from Jordan and having been at war with Israel, I had good reason to think that they were bad people.

But suddenly I saw it another way. The key to Jesus' death wasn't the brutality of the Jews but the love of Jesus. Jesus could have demolished all of Jerusalem in one command, just like He ordered the storm to stop. He talked to a fig tree and it withered. He talked to a leper and he was healed. He could have demolished Jerusalem, but He wasn't a man of anger. I understood that. Jesus was not a man of anger. He was a man of mercy. All that He did, even when He calmed the sea, was for the sake of those people around him. He was asleep; He didn't care; He knew what would happen. He knew His death would be by crucifixion. He knew that the storm would not kill Him because God had set His destiny.

It was out of mercy and love that He chose the disciples and told them to leave their things and follow Him. Afterward, He got into the boats with them and taught them and fed them. He saw the crowds around Him and was moved with love. He never thought of having a republic or a kingdom. Everyone else, including Muslims today, think that He should have set up a kingdom, but His kingdom was different.

Through my studying, I began to realize that as a young man, I had heard so many wrong things about the church and the Bible. We thought that Jesus was not crucified, but now I realized that not only had He been crucified, Jesus needed to be crucified. Thank God He was crucified. Through my studies, I began to understand why Jesus is alive now and why He is coming back again. Even Muslims say He will come again, but the Bible tells us how He will come and what He will do! In the Qur'an, things were fuzzy, but in the Bible it was all explained.

My eyes were opened to the love and mercy that was present in the death of Jesus on the cross. I appreciated His death, and I believed that He died. But I couldn't believe that Jesus was God.

CHAPTER SIX
And I will draw all men unto me. John 12:32

THAT YEAR, THE CHURCH IN OCEAN SPRINGS STARTED EARNESTLY PRAYING that I would be saved. Moreover, they didn't do it only in secret. Many times people would come and tell me that they were praying for me. Sometimes they prayed for my salvation in the mid-week prayer meeting, while I was sitting right there listening. This did not offend me. I was actually encouraged that they were praying for me. Whenever someone would tell me that they were praying for me, I would tell them that there was a little gap in my heart that was not yet filled. I wanted God to fill that gap.

However, the situation was a bit more complex than this. On the outside I wanted the Lord to occupy me as God. I wanted Him to own me. I wanted Him to enter every little part of life. I heard others talking of it and, consequently, I wanted the Lord in my spirit, in my body and in my thinking.

I understood all this and desired it, but I didn't want to accept Jesus as God. The desire was in my heart, but I couldn't bring myself to acknowledge that He was God. My Muslim upbringing had ingrained in me the fact that God did not have a son. Jesus could be the Messiah, He could have died on the cross for my sins, but if I acknowledged Him as God it would be the last straw in separating me from my past. So, although the church was praying for me, I resisted them and the voice of God.

Then the Lord found a new way to bring pressure on me. It came in the form of a Christian girl friend. She was a wonderful Christian, and soon we were thinking seriously about one another. However, she always resisted talking about marriage. Whenever the topic came up she would say, "Abdalla, I won't marry you if you don't believe."

Inevitably I would reply, "I don't blame you," and the conversation would stop there. It seemed my life was at an impasse. In order to accept Christ fully, I had to admit that He was God. But admitting that Christ was God would mean that I was admitting that Islam was wrong and that I had to break completely from my past. It was too big a decision to make on my own. Then the Lord did something special in my life to confront me with Himself.

It all started when my new girlfriend and two other people from our church decided to visit California during the summer break. Since I had no studies and I wasn't going back to Jordan, I was free to take them in my car. I was excited because it was a chance to see more of the United States. We planned to set out from Mississippi and pass through Texas on our way to California. We were all looking forward to a great time together and we even talked of going to Disneyland.

When the day arrived for leaving, I was very excited. I thought I was starting a great vacation. Little did I realize that God was planning something more.

IT HAPPENED SEVERAL DAYS INTO OUR TRIP. It was a beautiful day with good visibility when suddenly a car we were following went out of control. It started swerving back and forth and then it headed for the side of the road. As it tipped into the ditch it started rolling repeatedly. When it finally came to rest, it looked like it was totally demolished.

I was driving and as soon as I saw what was happening, I slammed on the breaks and we came to a stop near the damaged vehicle. We were the first people on the scene and we raced from our car to the overturned vehicle. We were terrified of what we might see, but we knew we had to look inside. Dropping to our hands and knees we discovered two elderly people trapped inside. As the dust settled, we could see that there was blood and shards of glass all over the place.

I rushed back to my car and called for an ambulance on my CB radio. The AAA responded to my call and asked me where we were. I had to think for a minute but eventually realized that we were almost at the Arizona border near Phoenix. The AAA then told me that an ambulance was on its way, and they asked us if we could gently get the people out of the wreck and onto the side of the road. They instructed us to keep them warm and to wait with them until the ambulance arrived.

"OK," I almost hollered into the mike. "The woman looks fine, but the man is in a very bad state. He has blood coming out of his nose, his mouth, and his ears."

"The ambulance is already on its way." The voice from the radio sounded remote and detached. Realizing that I could do nothing more on the radio, I rushed back to the wrecked car and we started working on getting the old man out of the driver's seat. It was a tough job as the man was quite badly trapped. The steering wheel had come up and crushed his chest. As he was quite a thin man, the steering wheel seemed to have crushed him badly.

The whole time we were trying to get the man out, the old lady was busy praying. "Oh Jesus, please save him; please help him. Give him strength; please stop the bleeding."

As soon as we had the old man out of the car, we all started to pray with her. I too began praying with everyone else. We were pouring out our desires to God with our whole hearts. "Lord," I said, "I know I don't believe in you as God, but I believe you as Jesus. Can you please help this man and help us to know what to do?" I didn't know what to pray and I remember thinking that all these others could pray better than I could.

The Man From Gadara

After what seemed like a very long time but was probably only a short while, the ambulance arrived. They put the old man on a stretcher, and the woman got into the ambulance. The ambulance attendant came over to us and thanked us and told us we were free to go. We looked at each other and knew we wanted to go to the hospital with them. When we told the ambulance attendant, he didn't object. We then followed the ambulance to a small medical center. It was more like a first aid station rather than a hospital. They took the man and his wife inside, and we sat outside waiting and shaking.

A little while later a doctor came out and told us that the man was in very bad shape. Two or three ribs were broken, and these ribs had punctured his lungs and his heart. He was bleeding internally and slipping away by the minute. He was dying and they didn't want to open him up. There was nothing the doctors could do. It would only be a matter of minutes before he died. He was in a coma.

We sat in silence, shivering from fear and the effects of shock. As we sat there an idea suddenly came into my head. "What if I die? What will happen to me? Am I a believer? Am I a two-thirds believer? Am I even a half a believer? Am I half a Muslim and half a Christian?"

In the middle of these thoughts, another doctor came outside and said, "He wants to see all of you."

We were a bit confused, but then we realized that the old man must have come out of his coma and was talking. So we went with the doctor and entered the emergency surgery room. A group of doctors were standing around the room with nothing to do. It seemed that they were waiting around and watching the man die.

No one said much, so we drew closer to the old man on the bed. The woman was praying and seemed not to notice us. Then suddenly the old man opened his eyes and looked at us. His eyes were clear and sharp. He must have been over seventy years of age and he looked all beat up, but suddenly he seemed as sharp and clear as ever. Then he spoke to us.

The Man From Gadara

"You should accept the Lord as your Savior," he said. Those were his last words and his eyes were clear and knowing as he looked at us. I was the only one of our group who was not a Christian. I knew my friends were praying for me. When the old man spoke, all three of them looked at me. I could feel their eyes on me. My eyes met those of my girlfriend.

"Abdalla," someone said, "did you hear that?"

I nodded but said nothing. The doctors were amazed that he even spoke. Most of them seemed more interested in the fact that the old man spoke than what he had said. A few moments later the old man died. His last words had been directed at me. I knew it was God speaking to me.

As we left the room, one of the doctors followed us out into the hall. "Well, young man" he said, "that man inside gave you a very important message didn't he?"

"Yes," I agreed with a slight nod of my head.

"Well you'd better believe in that," he said and turned to go back into the medical center.

A few minutes later we got into our car to leave. I wanted to go back to Ocean Springs and tell all this to Mr. Love, but the others wanted to go on. In the end we did travel on, but later that night we called the Loves and told them the story.

"Abdalla," Mr. Love said over the phone after he heard our story, "If you don't want to accept Him, I don't want to push you to accept Him. I'm going to leave it to you."

Inside my heart a war was waging. Part of me wanted to accept and part of me fought back. It was a war that wouldn't be won that night. The step was too big. If I admitted that Jesus was God, then I would have to admit that Islam was wrong. I would have to admit all my upbringing was wrong. I would have to admit that much of what I learned as a child was wrong. It was too hard. I just couldn't do it. I knew in my heart that although I was going to church and even paying tithes, I was not a true Christian.

CHAPTER SEVEN

And their eyes were opened. Luke 24:31

FOR SIX MONTHS I CONTINUED TO RESIST the Lord. Now the whole church was praying for me. Many more people openly told me that they were praying that I would come to Christ. I guess they realized that my time in America was ending and that after my graduation I would have to return to my home country of Jordan.

One Sunday evening, a dear woman by the name of Mrs. Dye prayed for me during the church service. "Dear God," she prayed, "I'm asking you to give more time to Abdalla. Lord, don't let him leave until he accepts you as God and Savior, even if it means keeping him here longer."

After the service I approached this lady. "Mrs. Dye, you're crazy!" I exclaimed.

"Why?" she laughed. I knew she loved me like a grandson, and I loved her, but I think I loved her cookies more. "Abdalla," she said, "why am I crazy?"

"How can you pray that I will have more time? In one week I am leaving for Jordan." I was proud of the fact that I was leaving. I had obtained my Bachelor of Science degree in three and a half years. I had done well in my studies and now I was returning to Jordan to see my family. I had already booked my plane tickets. I was now buying gifts for my family. My brother, Abdul Karim, had arranged his visit to Jordan so he could be home when I was at home. My father had bought three sheep to kill and eat. Everyone would feast and celebrate our return. Many people were invited for the welcome-back party that my family would host. There was no way I was not leaving America.

Mrs. Dye just smiled. "I asked Him and now God won't let you leave until you have accepted Him."

The following day was Monday. Graduation was less than one week away and I had only a few things to do in order to wrap up my studies. I needed to do some last minute shopping for a gift for my sisters, confirm my flights, and I was ready to go. The big job for Monday morning, however, was to fill out a report on how my studies had gone. This report was part of the requirements for my scholarship.

Everything was going fine until I spotted a little yellow note on my mailbox. Its message was plain.

Mr. Hawatmeh, please report to Mr. Williams ASAP today.

My heart sank. Mr. Williams was a frightening man. To me he was like the godfather of the university. If he called students to his office, they were usually in trouble. He could expel anyone. He might tell you that you were not doing well in your studies and that you had to change your major. In my mind's eye, I could see him peering at me, his eyes full of suspicion. Mr. Williams had no hair on his head, not a single one. Moreover, whenever I had seen him, he always had an unlit pipe between his lips. Lips that never laughed. Lips that never smiled. One girl from my class once said that she would rather have God see her with all of her sins than have to face Mr. Williams.

"Oh my God," I gasped. "What is happening to me now?" My knees were shaking. My mouth was dry. Somehow I made it across campus and, standing outside his door, I meekly knocked. There was no reply. I knocked again a little louder. Mr. Williams couldn't hear all that well. I hoped he wouldn't hear me knock, but he did.

He shouted at me and I almost tumbled into his room. I stood up and faced him as an accused man faces a judge.

"Mr. Hawatmeh," he shouted. "Come closer."

I came closer. It wasn't easy as a huge table separated us.

"Mr. Hawatmeh," he said, "do you want to go back to your family?"

"Yes," I said.

"What?" he said. "Is that a yes?"

"Yes!" I shouted.

There was silence as he wrote something.

"Did you like the university here?"

"Yes!" I shouted.

There was silence as he wrote something.

"Is your family expecting you on a certain date?"

"Of course, Mr. Williams, I already have my tickets."

"What?"

"I already have my tickets!" I shouted.

"You have what?"

"My plane tickets."

"Oh, your tickets. You have them?"

"Yes." I answered. I wondered what in the world was going on. Mr. Williams' face looked pleasant enough. He wasn't obviously upset about anything.

"Mr. Hawatmeh," he said, "I understand that you will be graduating this week."

"Yes!" I shouted, getting somewhat frustrated at his simple questions.

"Mr. Williams," I shouted back to him "Why are you asking me these questions?"

He looked up at me. "This morning we received a telex from the Jordanian Military Attaché in Virginia. The Government of Jordan wants you to study the AWACs airborne radar system at Maxwell University. Before you study at Maxwell, you have to take an orientation course and you have to fly from the air force base here in Mississippi. That will take about six months."

"Oh no!" I groaned, suddenly grasping the situation. It was that prayer of Mrs. Dye's last night. I was devastated. I wasn't going to get to go home. God was going to keep me in America. "Oh God!" I gasped, "I can't resist you anymore." So while Mr. Williams was writing in his papers, I cried out to God. "Oh God, I want to accept you as Lord right now."

"What?" Mr. Williams shouted.

"Sir," I shouted back, "I want to accept Christ right now!"

Mr. Williams shook his head, trying to figure out what I was talking about. I just ignored him and knelt down behind the big table and poured out my heart to God.

After a couple of moments, Mr. Williams began to wonder what I was doing.

"Where are you, Mr. Hawatmeh?" I was on my knees praying.

"What are you doing, Mr. Hawatmeh?" I was asking God to forgive me.

"Mr. Hawatmeh, are you OK?" I was better than I had ever been in my whole life.

"What are you doing down there on the floor?" I really didn't think he would understand, so I stood up. "You don't know the story sir," I answered as politely as I could.

He looked at me rather strangely. "Do you agree to this arrangement? Do you want to do the AWACs courses?"

"I guess I have to."

"There is a problem," Mr. Williams went on, "Mr. Hawatmeh, if you want to do this, then you can't go home now. The training starts in seven days."

"Sir," I said, "Am I going to graduate?"

"Yes," he said "When the graduation ceremony happens, we will call you from the air base and you can fly back here."

"That's neat," I thought. So I agreed.

After I left Mr. Williams' office, I called my brother, Abdul Karim. When I told him that I had extended my stay, he became very angry. He insisted that I fly to Jordan to see my family.

So I returned to Mr. William's office.

"Sir," I said "I don't care if you expel me; I want to go see my family." Mr. Williams wasn't very happy, but in the end he managed to get an agreement worked out so that after my graduation I could fly back to Jordan for eight days.

Back in my dorm room I collapsed on my bed. What a day it had been. It was a day that I would never forget. It was a day when relief flooded into my soul. I had done it. I had really given my life to Jesus. Along with my heart, I gave him all of my doubts. "Here they are, Lord," I had prayed, "here are my doubts. I am asking you to fix them."

The next day I ran into Mr. Williams again as I was crossing campus. "You know, Abdalla," he said to me, "your name really is Abdalla, isn't it?"

"Yes," I responded.

"Why do you people choose such long names?"

"It is not that long," I protested gently. "Williams is a long name too."

"Could you answer me a question if I ask you one?" he started again.

"OK," I agreed.

"When you came to my office I had some questions to ask you. But I saw something, something like goodness come over you."

"You are right." I answered. We walked along in silence.

"Can I ask you one question, sir?"

"OK," he said.

A smile played on my lips. "Why don't you put tobacco in your pipe?"

"Get out of here, Mr. Hawatmeh." He scowled. "I don't want to die in a couple of years. I want to see lots of jerks like you in the air, flying and spying."

THE NEXT SUNDAY MORNING I could barely wait to get to church. "Be careful of Mrs. Dye." I told them all. "You people have to make sure you please her all the time." Some of them looked puzzled. "If Mrs. Dye prays anything against you, you've had it," I insisted. I then went on to tell them about Mrs. Dye's prayer and the strange way that God had answered it. That morning, a lot of tears were shed; tears of joy. Everyone was so happy.

After the service, people crowded around to hug me and wished me well. When Mrs. Dye came up to me, I hugged her.

"You old lady," I scolded. "You almost killed me."

"Abdalla," she replied, "you almost killed us by resisting so long." I didn't stay long at the church. I had changed my flight; so after greeting everyone, I rushed to the airport and caught my plane to Jordan.

IT HAD BEEN THREE long years since I had been in my village. Many people gathered at the airport to meet me. Once again we traveled in a convoy back to the village. I felt like a hero returning after battle. Many old friends and neighbors came to greet me. Some of the children stared at me in awe. I had been to America!

Father was true to his word. He slaughtered three rams, and my mother and sisters prepared a great feast. My brother, Abdul Karim, had been in Saudi Arabia and had come home so we could all be together. We talked and we laughed and everyone enjoyed the occasion. I unpacked my gifts and everyone seemed pleased that I was home.

"Abdalla," Abdul Karim said to me, "I swear to God that you must have a very pretty girl friend there in America."

"Why do you think that?" I asked him.

"I can't believe you are going back just for your studies," he chided. "It's got to be a girl friend."

"Look," I told him, "you just don't know."

Everyone wanted to know what America was like. I told them many stories, but I never told them about my new faith. My family knew I was going to church, but they kept saying to me, "When you grow up you may benefit from these things, but it will all be washed away." They never took it seriously.

All too soon my eight days were over, and I was back in America. I stayed in the same area for four and a half more months and then I went on to Maxwell University. I accepted the Lord in 1980, and I was baptized afterward in the little Pentecostal Church in Ocean Springs, Mississippi. I was excited about my new Christian faith, and perhaps I was a little naive. Never in my whole life had I heard of a Muslim leaving Islam and becoming a Christian. I never stopped to think about it, and I never stopped to ask myself why. I knew I had found God and I had found peace. It didn't matter to me what the future held because I had found the one who held the future.

CHAPTER EIGHT

Grow in grace and knowledge. II Peter 3:18

WHEN I RETURNED TO AMERICA, MY STUDIES
CHANGED. I was now more involved in training than academic
studies. I was attending Maxwell University in Alabama, which
was nearly a three-hour drive from Mr. Love's. Although I was
far away, I still found myself driving back to Ocean Springs for
Sunday morning services. Sometimes I could arrange it so that
my training flights would leave me in Mississippi. I could then
attend the Tuesday night prayer meeting and the Thursday night
Bible Study. The people at church were amazed that I traveled all
the way from Alabama to Mississippi to go to church. "It's because
I like your coffee," I always told them.

In time, however, I started to attend an evangelical chapel
on the university campus, but I really didn't fit there. My heart
was more with the families that I had become close to. However,
since I couldn't always get back to Ocean Springs, I occasionally
went to the university chapel. On a couple of occasions, I visited
a large church in the city of Mobil. It was a huge church but I
never enjoyed being lost in the crowd. I found it hard to get to
know people. I liked small churches where people knew each
other.

The Man From Gadara

Life in Alabama was easier for me. I was doing well in my studies and I had no other agenda. I was studying for a Masters in Science (Early Warning and Aircraft Controls System Engineering). I flew in planes, attended lectures, and worked on my thesis. It was easier than my bachelor studies so I had time to look around at what was happening on campus.

I soon noticed one young man from Minnesota who seemed to be ministering to the students. I was curious about him. "Richard," I said one day, "why are you doing this? Is someone paying you to do this?"

"No," he replied, "this is my ministry." Having a ministry was a new concept to me.

As we got to know one another, Richard started to ask me more about my relationship with God. He was very happy to discover that I was a believer, and he asked me about my Muslim background. He knew more about missions than Mr. Love and was really excited about my coming to Christ. In my heart I knew that my receiving Christ was offensive to Muslims, but most Americans didn't seem aware of this.

Richard invited me to join some of the students for a Bible Study. During my time there, I discovered that there were people who were trying to help others become Christians. What was exciting to me was that they were not only targeting non-Americans like me, but they were targeting everyone. God accepted everyone. Everyone had the same value. Everyone had the right to accept or deny. Everyone! That somehow made me feel safe. I realized that they were not interested in me because I was a foreigner. It wasn't that I was a Jordanian or an Arab or a Muslim. They were targeting everyone. When they talked about sin, they were talking about their sins and my sins. I was one of them now. Others were now accepting me as a Christian and that was important to me.

One day they asked me to pray for Bonn, one of the students who was a genius in engineering. Bonn would sometimes get into trouble because he would smoke marijuana. Although he was a Christian, he still struggled with this weakness. The students didn't hide from me the fact that he smoked marijuana. They trusted me. They trusted whoever was a believer.

So one day they said, "Abdalla, can you pray with Bonn?"

"Bonn," I said when we were alone, "how can you trust me?"

"Well," he said, "you are a believer." That was it. It was plain and simple. I was a believer and that was good enough for him.

I was thrilled. I suddenly realized that we had a common ground. I belonged. I was one of them. These students linked me to the body of Christ, not just to a small church in Mississippi with nice pies and coffee. No, it was more than that. I was linked to the wider body of Christ. People everywhere were part of this body. I felt like I had come home.

Soon after this, I began to think about what was next. Now that I was a believer, was there a role that I was to play as a Christian? Mr. Love had often encouraged me. "Abdalla, take what you have heard; go tell people, but in time. Be wise, especially in your culture. I don't know, is it prohibited for you to do that?"

I nodded.

"Then," he said, "you need to be extra wise. I don't know how you should do it, but be wise."

I never led anyone to Christ while I was at university but I shared my testimony and I watched as others were led to Christ. One student jumped to his feet after kneeling and asking Christ into his heart. He was crying and smiling, and he hugged me. I didn't hug him back, but I saw his tears and I started to realize what he was going through. It had happened to me, and now I saw it happening in others.

During my time at Maxwell, I saw over ten people accept Christ. One time I went witnessing with Samuel, one of the students. He wanted to witness to a particular friend of his. He thought he would need to make at least five visits before he could share fully about Christ. However, when we talked for a little more than an hour, his friend accepted the Lord.

"Well," I said afterward, "does that mean he was smart, or was he just ready?

Samuel looked at me. "It was the Lord's timing," he said.

We were walking back to our car and suddenly we started jumping and skipping as we were running. The experience of leading someone to Christ had left us giddy and happy. As we jumped around, I mistakenly jumped from the sidewalk into the street. Suddenly I heard car tires squeal and a car zoomed passed me. The driver was a young student and he raised his finger to me and shouted obscenities. Samuel and I just started laughing harder.

It was a real joy to see people finding the truth. It didn't matter to me who they were. They were just people, and God was opening their eyes to the truth. Serving God this way was more exciting than I could have ever imagined.

GRADUATION DAY WAS FUN, but in many ways it was a sad day. I had come to know these students and now we were saying goodbye. Most of the students were looking forward to their first jobs and talking about what the future held, but I knew I had a contract to fulfill. The Jordanian government had paid for me and now I needed to pay the Jordanian government. In exchange for all of my free education, I had agreed to serve the government for fourteen years. While I knew that I would have a job, I knew that the job would not be one of my own choosing.

So I returned to Jordan and enjoyed the warm reception of my family. Everyone was proud of my academic achievement. I had done well, and now I would be offered a nice government job with good pay.

When I arrived to take my job, the government had some thinking to do. The Jordanian Air Force did not have an AWAC program so they loaned me to the country of Greece for nine months to teach AWAC engineering near Athens. I met a couple of Christians in Greece who told me that there was an evangelical church in Athens, but I never attended. I was busy with my work and I was enjoying the good food and nice music. I was a Christian but I didn't exert myself spiritually.

After Greece, the Jordanian government sent me to Saudi Arabia for two months to train several engineers in AWAC technology. I lived on a compound full of Americans and other foreigners. I was only teaching a course and was there for a short time so I didn't bother to witness.

After Saudi Arabia, the Jordanian government sent me to Egypt to teach a course there. Following this, I was sent on a secret mission to the country of Iraq. At that time, the Iraq - Iran war was taking place. My Jordanian helicopter pilot took me to some secret place in Iraq where I was transferred to an Iraqi helicopter.

During my time in Iraq, I saw many things. Most of my time was spent in the air, as planes constantly refueled us. During this time, I saw missiles flying and bombs exploding. I saw floods of people from Iran kissing the Qur'an and rushing forward, many of them to their death. My job was to be a 'second Arab opinion.' I had to fill out reports for both the Jordanian and the Iraqi government. In the end, I received a letter from Saddam Hussein thanking me for the part I had played.

During my time in Iraq, I grew concerned about what I was doing. I began to see that my AWAC training could be used for both good and evil. I decided to ask the Jordanian government for another role.

Since I was not directly serving the Jordanian Government using AWAC, they suggested that I become a teacher at the Jordanian Air Academy. I agreed, and soon I became a teacher of Electronics.

During all this time, I had told no one that I was a Christian. In America, Christians had surrounded me, but here in Jordan, I was surrounded by Muslims. On top of this, I was part of the government body, and I had to represent the government. It didn't take much rationalizing to convince myself that I could not reveal to anyone that I was a Christian.

"I can't speak about Christ," I would tell myself. "I can't announce my faith and I can't attend church because I have a lecture on Sunday mornings. I can't do this and I can't do that. I simply can't..." There were too many barriers.

During this time, I met one man that I could talk to. His name was Roy Whitman. He was a very humble Christian worker who had ministered in Jordan for many years. He took it upon himself to encourage me. "Abdalla," he said to me one day, "If you can't come to us, Dora and I will go to you in the spirit. We know exactly where you are and we will pray for you every day."

I met Roy Whitman through the Free Evangelical Church in Amman. Every now and then, I would get a Sunday morning off from the Air Academy and I would try to visit a church. I never told anyone that I was from a Muslim background. This was because the Air Academy was part of the government and I felt that knowledge of my conversion could hurt me. Not only would the government not understand, there were Muslim fanatics around who could make my life miserable as well. As a result, I would arrive at church a couple of minutes late so I could slip in the back and worship unnoticed.

My Hawatmeh name helped cover me. In Jordan, there are two Hawatmeh tribes. One of them is Muslim and the other is nominal Christian. Most people never questioned my background, but Pastor Roy Whitman was curious. Soon after he met me, Roy asked me which Hawatmeh tribe I was from. I told him I was originally from Irbid.

"Oh," he said, "you're originally from Irbid, and then you moved to Salt, so you're from those Hawatmeh?" He started asking me about some relatives, but they were all names from the Christian Hawatmeh tribe.

"Mr. Whitman," I carefully replied, "I was born a Muslim." He smiled as I said that and I could tell that he was pleased. "Please," I begged him, "please keep this between you and me."

So Mr. Whitman knew, but to other people I was just Abdalla who worked in the Air Academy and periodically attended church. Very few Christians got to know me because I would slip in and out of services as quietly as possible.

After meeting Roy Whitman, I started to meet some of the other Christian leaders in Amman. I was interested in learning about the Christian community in my country, so I made it a point to seek out the evangelical pastors and the Orthodox and Catholic Church leaders. I was very cautious, but I wanted to know more about who these people were. I wanted to belong to the Christian community, but I was afraid that knowledge of my conversion to Christianity would bring me trouble. In my country, families are very proud of their religious heritage, and it would be a great dishonor to my family if it was discovered that I had left the family religion to join Christianity.

Through my contact with Christian leaders, my life was challenged. I found myself wanting to choose between my faith and my job. I was in an excellent job. When I worked in other countries, I often received a double salary. In Greece, I was paid three salaries: one from Greece, one from Jordan, and one from Westinghouse Corporation. I took the money I was earning and I built a house near my village. With the high salary came respect. I had everything a man could hope for. But my faith was going downhill and it bothered me.

Instead of thinking about the Lord, I was thinking about what I should buy, what I should do, and where I should travel. I had become a worldly man more concerned about who I was seen with than who was my Savior. My faith was still warm, but it was not hot.

"Lord," I prayed one day, "I'm strangled with this contract to serve the government. I can't get out! I have years left to serve, and this job is killing me. Look at my faith, Lord. How can I explain to people about giving up a job like this? Many young men look up to me. I have free gasoline, free housing in Amman, free airplane tickets to fly everywhere, up to twenty times a year. Lord," I prayed, "show me your way. I don't know anything about Christianity except what I learned in Mississippi and Alabama. How can I live as a Christian in this country?" It didn't take the

Lord long to answer my prayer. He did it in a way that I never expected.

In the Air Academy we trained engineers and pilots. I was teaching one of the hardest subjects, Digital Techniques. Because I had up-to-date training and possessed a Masters Degree, I was put in charge of the electronics section of the Academy. Most of the other teachers only had a Bachelor Degree and some simply had experience.

One of my students was called Issa. One day I looked at his file and saw the terrible marks he was getting. I was amazed that the Academy still let him study, so I called my secretary and asked her to book an appointment with this student.

"Wait," my secretary said, "Mr. Hawatmeh, you need to be careful."

"Why?" I said, "he's simply a student who is not doing well. Just call him into my office."

"Mr. Hawatmeh," she said, "he is from a Christian tribe but he wants to become a Muslim. All the Muslim Brotherhood people are supporting him."

"Oh?" I said, "Then he must come to my office."

A few days later Issa came to see me.

"You seem to be having a lot of trouble with your studies." I told him. "I don't understand why you are still in the program."

"Mr. Hawatmeh," he said, "I have some special circumstances."

"Oh?" I said, "What are they?"

"Well," he replied, "God opened my heart to the truth."

"Good," I said, "I want to hear more." I could feel the tension growing within me.

"I became a Muslim."

"Why? You are a Christian." I was puzzled.

"It is the light, the light...."

He thought I was a Muslim. He thought I would be delighted, but instead I looked puzzled. "Have you ever studied the Bible?" I asked.

"Yeah," he said easily. "I went to church."

"But, did you study the Bible?"

"Yeah, I read the Bible."

"My next question to you is the important one. Have you accepted the Lord as your Savior?"

"Excuse me?"

"Have you ever accepted Christ as your Savior?"

"I'm a child of the church!"

"I know, but have you accepted Christ as your Savior?"

Issa was getting more and more distracted, and I was getting more and more upset. "Look," I told him, "if you had known the truth, you would never have become a Muslim. You have never been close to Jesus. You have never really studied the Bible. You have never been part of the real church. Never! You were always weak, and now you are getting weaker."

It was my first try at evangelism, and I wasn't doing too well. I wasn't like those students back in America. I didn't know how to handle this kind of a situation.

"Look Issa," I said, "you have one week to leave Islam or I will expel you!"

Issa looked stunned. "Aren't you a Muslim, Mr. Hawatmeh?"

"Yes Issa, I was a Muslim, but then I became a Christian. I came to the truth. It is a truth that you don't know about. Now, don't tell anyone about this, OK?"

"OK."

"You can go now."

As Issa left I realized what I had done. Was I crazy? What had I done? In no time the news had spread all over. Everyone was whispering. It didn't take very long before my boss called me in to his office.

"Excuse me, Mr. Hawatmeh, please sit down."

I sat.

"Is what I am hearing true?"

"What are you hearing?"

"You stopped someone from becoming a Muslim?"

"Yes."

"Why?" The man in front of me was a Muslim, so I didn't feel I could discuss any issues of faith with him. "We are paid to teach electronics," I said. Suddenly I felt very patriotic. "We are not paid to discuss religion or propagate faith."

"I'm sorry, Mr. Hawatmeh. Whatever you do, please be wise next time."

There were three engineers in the office at that time, and they were looking at me like I was crazy. They really wanted me knocked down so they could take higher positions. Thank God, no one reacted against me at that time. I continued teaching at the Air Academy for several more years and eventually I discovered a way to appeal my fourteen-year commitment. My commitment was reduced and as soon as I had fulfilled it, I decided to resign. I didn't know what God had for me, but I knew that He would lead me forward.

CHAPTER NINE

Choose you this day whom you will serve. Joshua 24:15

PEOPLE WERE SHOCKED WHEN I RESIGNED from my job at the Air Academy. My mother had a heart attack that very week. I visited her in the hospital and she was quite angry with me.

"This happened because you lost your job," she told me.

"Mother," I said, "I am getting a better job."

"No," she insisted. "All the village women were envious of me because you are my son, and I was so proud of you."

"Mother," I countered, "I'm a man; I can work wherever I want." Nevertheless, my whole family was upset.

"You're crazy to walk away like that!" they protested. "You are in the beginning of something great. You had a good salary, a good position, and you could travel."

It was true. I had everything a young man could want. I had a good education, an excellent government job, and a good salary with free travel allowances on the national airline. Furthermore, I enjoyed my work. To top it all off, there were excellent possibilities that I could move up the ladder to better things. Jordan was a small country, which at that time had a limited number of highly educated people. If I stuck it out, I could be promoted higher and higher. An ambitious man could do much in my position.

Nevertheless, I wanted to quit. I really didn't know why I quit, but I knew that if I stayed, my spiritual life was in jeopardy.

When I realized that I had shamed my family and that I wanted more spiritual freedom, I started to make plans to leave Jordan and return to the United States. If I returned to my studies and pursued a Ph.D. program, then my honor would be restored. If I returned to America, I would also be free to live as a Christian should. On top of that, my Christian girlfriend in America wanted me to come back.

So I started to make plans to leave Jordan. However, I decided that before leaving I would travel to the port city of Aqaba for a holiday. My sister was living in Aqaba and I could stay at her house for a time and enjoy the warm open atmosphere of a resort city. After the tension of quitting my job and facing my family, I wanted to be alone, warm, and relaxed for a while.

While in Aqaba I decided to look for a church. There were very few churches in Aqaba, so I soon found the Evangelical Free Church. The first Sunday I attended, Abu Hani, the pastor, invited me to stay for coffee. The coffee he gave me was awful but the fellowship was wonderful. I told him my story and he seemed very happy.

"Oh my," he said, "You are a Muslim and you have found Christ! Please, be careful and don't tell anyone. This is the port city where there is a lot of security here. Be happy here, and fellowship with us as much as you want." He paused. "Say, what are you doing here anyway?"

"I'm just here as a tourist, and then I'm going out of the country."

"Where are you going?"

"To the States."

"Yeah, that's better. You will be safe there. Stay in the States."

It was as if God was confirming the next steps ahead in my life. I was excited about returning to Maxwell University and studying again.

However, in Aqaba the Lord spoke to me. He was directing me to do something, but I really didn't understand at that point. In those few short weeks the Lord started to work in my heart. The Evangelical Free Church was in the process of constructing a new building and many pastors and church leaders dropped in to see what progress was being made. During my stay in Aqaba, I met many of the leading evangelical pastors from around Jordan. They were all coming to help encourage the church and talk about the building process. As they visited I had opportunity to talk to them all. Their lives and dedication to full time ministry challenged me in a special way.

It wasn't that I could not hear the Lord. I was reading my Bible and listening to tapes in my car. In the north of Jordan I would watch Christian programming on Middle East Television whenever I could. These programs were beamed in from a television station located between the boarders of Lebanon and Israel. I enjoyed many of the teaching and preaching programs and they helped disciple me. But I received a call from the Lord while in Aqaba. I didn't understand it until several years later.

In Aqaba, I met a number of nominal Christians who were communists. When I had opportunity, I witnessed to them. I had great fun doing it as I liked to tease them with the fact that I knew more about their religion than they did. When we got into discussion, I had to teach them what the Bible said.

Without my knowing it, God was slowly showing me a plan. There were opportunities to stay in Jordan and serve the Lord. There were people in Jordan with whom I could share my faith. However, my heart was set on America and, consequently, I never really heard what the Lord was telling me. I wanted to enjoy the freedom that the west offered. I wanted to finish my Ph.D. And I wanted to get married in America.

Ever since arriving back in Jordan I had kept up correspondence with my old American girlfriend. In America, we had discussed marriage but when I told her I needed to serve the Jordanian government for fourteen years, she was unsure. She didn't want to live in Jordan so our plans were put on hold.

The Man From Gadara

Once I obtained my release from the government and started talking about returning to the USA, our relationship flourished. We then started planning our wedding. We set a date and printed invitation cards. Mr. Love was to be my best man. My girlfriend's father was a pastor. He was the one who baptized me and now he would be the one to marry me.

My family wanted my girlfriend to visit Jordan, but circumstances prevented it. Instead, she sent a picture. My mother was very impressed with her picture and kept it for many long years afterward.

I was happy. I had a plan and the future looked bright. I said goodbye to my mother in the north, visited Aqaba and then made final preparations to fly from the capital city. My plan was to first fly to New York, then Atlanta, Georgia, and then on to Gulf Port, Mississippi. I would then get married and then we would move to Maxwell, Alabama. That was it. I had a one way ticket.

While I was in Aqaba, a believer there told me about a conference that was being held in Cyprus. I didn't know what a missions conference was. I didn't even know much about Cyprus. However, people seemed to think it was a good idea, so I changed my plane ticket so I could travel to Cyprus. I still had time. It was a month before I was to get married.

Unknown to me, the Lord had different plans. The missions conference in Cyprus changed my life. I saw something of the missionary movement. All kinds of mission organizations were keenly focused on reaching Muslims for Christ. I talked and prayed with Christians from other countries who wanted nothing else in life than to see Muslims come to Christ. Many of these Christians wept while they prayed. As they prayed for laborers to go into the Middle East, I realized that I was running away.

I also met people who were training to be missionaries. Some had left their families in the west and had come to minister in my part of the world. "This is a shame," I thought to myself. "It is a shame for me to leave all of this and go to America just to be there."

The Man From Gadara

Something was changing in my heart. I knew that if I was to follow God's plan for my life then I could not return to America. God's place of ministry was among my own people. But giving up America meant giving up my girlfriend. It hurt me a lot, but I had to do it. I had no choice. Losing my girlfriend was going to be like losing life itself, but I felt that I must choose between serving God and pursuing what would be nice for me.

I called her in America and we talked on the telephone. I tried to explain it, but there was nothing to explain. She knew about ministry. She had experience working in the church and in Sunday School. We had dreams of ministering together some day. She and I would lead the youth group. She knew a lot about ministry but she didn't know about missions. Now, missions had gripped my heart. When I broke the news to her she was heart-broken. Her father had built us a place to live in America. All I had to do was get on the plane. I still had the ticket. But God had gotten a hold of my heart.

We called each other several times. I didn't want to go to the States, so she told me that she would come to me in Cyprus. "Listen," I said, "if you want to live with me in Jordan I will be the happiest person in the world. But I don't want to go to the USA."

"What happened?" she cried. "People are expecting us to get married!"

"Look," I said, "I can go to the USA to get married, but I won't stay. I have to come back. If you want to do that, then I can leave right now. I still have my ticket."

My girlfriend came to Cyprus and then returned to the United States without me. What should have been a very happy occasion turned out to be a very sad one. I wandered around for few days and then I got drunk. I hated God for two or three weeks. I hated religion. I hated everything. But I couldn't fly to America. I couldn't get on that plane.

Now when I look back at God's plan, I know his plans are better than our plans. I wrote several letters over the following years to explain how the Lord had used me in ministry. I explained how others were changed and how the church had changed. Not because of me, but because of Jesus. I wanted her to feel that we didn't loose, but rather that we had gained. It was a very difficult time in our lives but, with God's help, we faced the pain and moved on.

I FOUND A JOB AS A TRANSLATOR with a mission that worked with children. I translated materials for them, but I found the work unchallenging and I wanted something else.

Unknown to me, the Jordanian Government gave my name to the Cypriot government. The British government was handing over two radar stations to the Cypriots and the Cypriots did not have anyone who could run the radar stations and were looking for someone who could train their technicians.

When I left Jordan, I had given my business card and forwarding address to the director of the Air Academy. Over the years, I have kept him informed of my address and sometimes I get invitations to lecture. There are very few Jordanians with AWAC training, so whenever I go to the States I take upgrading courses from Maxwell University. Along with this, I get magazines and journals to keep current in my field.

One day I received a telephone call from a man in the city of Limassol.

"Mr. Hawatmeh," he said, "we want to talk to you about work. Do you want to work with us?"

"Sure," I said, "but you know my career is kind of strange."

"Aren't you an AWAC Engineer from Jordan?"

"Yes."

"The Jordanian consulate here in Cyprus gave us your phone number."

"Is there a Jordanian consulate here? I thought I was the only Jordanian in the country."

"Oh, no," he laughed.

After a couple of days I met the Cypriot people at the Jordanian consulate. The Cypriots needed to train five or six radar technicians. It was just ground radar and it required no involvement in war, so I agreed to work for them. The first thing we did was to move the radar sites so that they faced Turkey, an old enemy of Cyprus. Then we went about the business of getting them to work and getting the staff trained.

DURING MY TIME IN CYPRUS, GOD BEGAN TO WORK in my heart. In the churches and through a Youth With A Mission training program I met other people who came from a Muslim background. I was surprised to meet others who had left Islam. Two or three of them were from Egypt. They had left their homes and fled from their fathers and mothers. To me it was a shock. I really loved my family. I was a villager at heart. I grew up with my family around me and I loved everything they cooked and everything they joked about. I was a family man. I was sorry to see these people in this state. "How could you leave your mothers?" I asked.

"The Bible told us to leave her," they insisted.

"No it doesn't," I said. "But if you left, then the Lord will work it out."

Those two years in Cyprus were very unique for me. I learned how to witness to people and how to share the gospel. The Lord was working in my heart and He used the students as well as the classes. If the classes were like water to my soul, then the students were like a stick that stirred everything up. The Egyptian believers especially touched me. I couldn't believe how simple they were, and yet how joyful they were. It was easy to deal with them. I, however, was proud and hard while they were wonderfully receptive and warm. I was from a better situation. I had attended university. I had money saved up from the excellent jobs I had held. Yet, I saw someone who only owned a T-shirt and shorts, and he was content. I had two full suitcases of suits, complete with ties. I had new jeans and fashionable clothes. I had a car and could go up to the mountains when it was hot. But I was not always content. However, by the time I had finished the training course, I had started looking up to the Egyptians rather than down on them.

The Man From Gadara

In my country, we look down on Egyptians and employ them to clean and serve. Serving others was not even in my thinking. It was out of the question to serve someone who had lower social or financial status than you. I even refused and balked at taking my turn at washing dishes, but slowly God changed me to understand the need to serve my brothers and to serve others. I discovered that if I serve someone else, I am honored more than if he serves me.

I also attended a church in Cyprus and the Lord used the pastor and others to teach me many things. After church on Sunday mornings we would often go to the beaches or parks or even the red light district to witness to people. Little did I realize how much God was using this time to prepare me for the ministry He had waiting for me.

CHAPTER TEN

The believers rapidly multiplied. Acts 6:1

WHEN MY JOB ENDED IN CYPRUS, the Cypriot government offered me a raise and asked me to stay. I appreciated the time that I had spent in Cyprus but I was ready to move on. I knew that in some way the Lord was directing me to minister to Muslims.

As I pondered the path ahead of me, I had many questions. How could I function in Jordan? How could I reach Muslims? People would know me. They would know who I was. In Cyprus, I was just an Arab from the Middle East. Back in Jordan, I would be known. People would soon know who my father and mother were. Although doubts plagued me, I knew I needed to go back.

Then my brother, Abdul Karim, called me. My father was getting older. On his papers it said that he was 105 years old. My brother insisted that I return. So, in 1988, I flew back to Jordan. Later I was thankful that I did because one year later my father died.

Bob and Margie Prather were an American Christian couple living and working in Amman. They opened their home to me, so I had a place to stay. Bob and Marge were like parents to me and I enjoyed their company very much. During my first weeks back in Amman I used their home as my base. I also met a young man by the name Bob Clark

He arrived at the Prather's home one night to collect a suitcase that I had carried from Cyprus. Little did I realize at the time that our lives would soon be intimately woven together.

As I visited people in Jordan, I thought that I could not stay in Jordan long. I was aware of several ministry opportunities, but all of them were in places other than Jordan. Some people had invited me to live and work as a radar engineer on the OM ships as they traveled around the world. I almost took this job, but a good friend told me I would not be happy with this kind of work. I liked to be with people but, on the ship, I would be dealing with the same Christian people all the time.

An airline in Berlin was looking for an AWAC consultant and teacher. This appealed to me because I thought I might be able to develop a ministry to Turkish Muslims living in Germany. Then a church in London invited me to work with them in reaching Muslims in that city.

On the other hand, my brother, Abdul Karim, was insistent that I join him in Saudi Arabia so that I would be closer to the family; and to top it off, my family had all kinds of ideas of where I could work so I could be closer to them.

In my heart I really wanted to minister to Muslims but I realized that I needed a job just so I could live. I told my brother that I needed several days to think about it. Really, I wanted to pray about it.

The funny thing was that I felt that my time in Jordan was just a vacation. I wasn't planning to stay for more than a month. So I left my suitcase with the Prather's and traveled to the north to visit my family for a short while. I planned to return in a couple of weeks and get a visa for Germany.

However, while in Jordan I found myself. I knew where I was and I was familiar with my surroundings. I felt close to the people. The moment my foot touched the airport, I knew I was home. I wanted to be there. I knew I really wanted to reach Muslims and it felt right to be in Jordan.

I knew in my heart that it was the Lord's will for me to be back in my home country. While I knew it, it still wasn't completely my will. So I prayed and asked God to guide me and show me what His will was, and to give me peace about settling back into Jordan. My family reacted very positively about me coming back, but they were still suspicious over my leaving the Air Academy. My father started talking to me about going back to the Air Academy so I could get my old job back. But I didn't want to go back to the Academy.

My family knew I had gone to church and that I had had a Christian girl friend, but to them it wasn't a big deal. My family also knew I regularly went to church in the States and that my girlfriend's father had been the pastor. They even knew I had been baptized there. But they really didn't understand what it all meant. They thought it was all in the past and part of my rebellion as a teenager. They thought I would eventually settle down, get married, have a family and it would all be over. Now that I was in need of employment, they started coming up will all sorts of options.

Knowing that I needed to make a decision, I prayed to God and asked him for a sign. "Lord, if you really want me to stay here in Jordan, then I want to see three Muslims accept Christ this week." I was very naive. I prayed hard, and I really believed. If God didn't bring three Muslims to Christ that week through my ministry, then I would leave Jordan.

I traveled back to Amman and stayed again with the Prather family. Bob Clark had phoned and left several messages for me to call him. I did so, and we started to build a good friendship.

A Canadian Christian businessman then invited me to help him in his computer company. He was based in a trading and engineering company in Amman selling computer programs. He and his family encouraged me a lot and soon we were good friends. Through my work with his company I started to meet people.

I was single, so I could visit people at lunch breaks and after work in the evenings. During this time, I did not tell anyone about my prayer request for three converts. I knew God was not going to put three Muslims in a basket and place them in front of me, so I started to pray for these three and to ask God to show me where I was going to find them.

Each day I visited a small corner cafe where I had lunch. Each time I was there I had an opportunity to talk briefly with Muhammad, the waiter. We talked about his family and his job. One evening, I returned to the cafe for a cup of coffee and Muhammad and I got talking again.

This time he started asking me questions about my family and what I was doing in Amman. Eventually I steered the conversation to the place where I could ask him if he knew anything about the Bible. He asked me if I was a Christian and I told him a bit of my testimony. Then we arranged to visit together after his work.

When we met, I didn't have a plan or course of action to follow. I was very afraid, because I knew I was doing something risky and against the logic of these people. Nevertheless, I shared the gospel with him that night and the next day I prayed with him to accept Christ. I didn't have a lot of theology to share, but I poured out what I had and God blessed it. I read a little from the Bible and shared my testimony. I had nothing to give Mohammed other than my simple faith in Jesus. Before I knew it, I had my first convert.

The next convert was Hani. I met Hani through my work. It took less than six hours and he accepted Christ. He is still a believer today, living in Amman with a believing wife and kids. Hani is very dear to my heart and like a son to me.

The third one to come to Christ was an Egyptian parking place worker in the building where I had found an apartment. His name was Jamal, and I visited him several times in the parking garage and shared with him. He always had Quranic chanting blaring out of big speakers. Several people had talked to his boss about it. His boss was a nominal Christian but had to put up with it because Jamal was a Muslim in a Muslim country. Who could deny a person the right to listen to the Qur'an? Seven days later, he started to play hymns.

When this happened, a neighbor came and asked his boss, "What did you do to him so that he stopped the Qur'an and started playing hymns?" His boss was as puzzled as everyone else.

That was the very first time I had prayed with people to accept salvation. I felt that this was proof from the Lord that I was to stay in Jordan and do what the Lord wanted me to do.

A short time after this, Bob Clark took me out for lunch and he shared with me how discouraged he was. "Abdalla, I've been in Jordan for the last two years and it's not working. I just want to reach Muslims. Can we work together?" "Sure" I told him "we have a meeting on Wednesday. Can you come?"

"What?" he stuttered, "Who is 'we'?"

"A group of new believers." I said.

"New believers? Already?" he gasped. I just smiled. Wednesday would be our first meeting.

I knew in my heart that these three did not believe because of something that I had done. They were a gift from the Lord, a confirmation that I was to stay in Jordan. I knew in my heart that it was the voice of the Lord answering my prayer and saving these three people just to prove to me that He wanted me in Jordan. From this small beginning I started to reach out to people whom God brought across my path.

For example, one Sunday, something strange happened to me. Usually I did not work on Sundays. Sundays were a day for going to church, so I was surprised when the Lord spoke to me and told me to go to the office. I resisted. "Lord," I said, "its Sunday, why would I go to the office? It's closed."

But the voice continued, so I traveled across town and came to the building where the office was located. As I entered the building I discovered that the elevators were not working. "Oh Lord," I protested. "I'm not going to climb up all those steps to the seventh floor! Not on a Sunday! Especially when I don't even work on Sundays!

However, the Lord kept saying, "Go to the office." So I started climbing up the stairs to the seventh floor. I never reached the seventh floor. Between the fourth and fifth floor I found a man in his fifties sitting on the stairs. At first I thought he had had a heart attack. He seemed very tired and he was sweating hard. It was a warm September day, but he was really sweating.

"Is there anything I can do for you?" I asked him, at the same time thinking, "Maybe the Lord wanted me here for this man. If I had taken the elevator I would have missed him"

"Can I help you with anything?" I said again.

"No thank you," he said. "I was just coming here to see somebody."

"Oh?" I said. "Who were you coming to see?"

"I'm coming to see someone named Abdalla Hawatmeh."

"I'm Abdalla Hawatmeh," I told him. "I don't go to the office on Sundays so it must have been the Lord who sent me here."

He told me that he had been advised to see me. He was a believer of sorts. From that day, I started discipleship lessons with him.

Slowly but surely a small fellowship started. For the most part, I worked alone. When I was in Cyprus, I had worked in a team and there were others to help in making decisions. Now I worked alone. Yes, I had friends like Bob Clark and Bob and Margie Prather. They all encouraged me as best they could but the only person from the foreign community, however, who spoke Arabic well and was able to come along side of me was the Canadian Christian businessman. So at this stage, I did most of my ministry alone.

Our first fellowship meetings were quite difficult. How can three single men and myself sing? They didn't know any hymns so I had to sing alone. I would make the tea, welcome them at the door, pray for them, teach them, sing a hymn, pray, and shake their hands at the door, and say goodbye. The new believers were like statues just sitting there. They were very new at being believers and I was very new at being a leader.

The Man From Gadara

NOT LONG AFTER THIS, a Jordanian church worker called me at the office and wanted to talk to me. "Abdalla, I need to talk to you about something that is happening."

"Go ahead," I said.

"There is this sister, a girl who has escaped from her parents."

"Um," I replied, "Why are you telling me this? Call the police."

"We sent her to you."

"What?" I started to get alarmed. "Where did you send her?"

"To your apartment."

Suddenly I was angry. "I thought you people were naïve!" I burst out. "What will people think? What will my neighbors think? I'm a single man living in an apartment building. My neighbors know me. How can you send a girl to my house?"

"I'm sorry, but she's already on her way."

"Oh my," I thought. "This is a very conservative country. If I act quickly I can save my reputation." I hung up the telephone and thought fast. I needed to call someone for help. I needed a female. I immediately thought of Amal, the secretary. She was a very new believer, but I needed a woman to meet with this girl. Perhaps she could help.

I first met Amal through my work. She was from a Greek Orthodox family and had five sisters and two brothers. She was just getting to know some evangelicals when I met her. She thought she was a believer, but she really wasn't. A short time later, I met Amal by surprise in my own neighborhood. She and her family were out walking one evening when we bumped into each other. I discover that they lived in a neighboring apartment building. Maybe I could call Amal now and ask her to help me.

While I was thinking of this the telephone rang again. This time it was my neighbors. "Abdalla, there is a girl sitting on the steps outside of your apartment."

"Good night," I thought, "this is the end of my career as a missionary."

Aloud I said, "Yeah, I know about her. Someone is coming over right away." Thankfully my neighbors offered to let her into their apartment until someone arrived for her.

Amal would be the natural one to help me. I needed a woman to help me out so in desperation, I called Amal. After all, she was a neighbor and quite close to my apartment. When I explained my problem to Amal, she was alarmed.

"No Abdalla," she said. "I'm scared to death. My family might beat me."

"Please do it," I begged. "Please go to my house and see her."

Finally she agreed and went to my apartment. I came as soon as I could from the office. When I arrived at my neighbor's house, I asked Amal to stay for a while. Then I asked my neighbor to stay close by and make tea or something in the other room. I needed to have someone around while I spoke with these women. In our culture it would be a great shame and embarrassment if I were alone in an apartment with a woman.

As soon as I was alone with Amal and the girl, I told the girl, "Please, don't you ever come to my house again like this. Go to a church and have them call me. I'm a single man and people will talk."

Then, with Amal beside me, and the neighbors in the other room, I heard her story. She had run away from her home. Someone had abused her. It took a while, but slowly we got her story from her. She had been abused sexually. I was shocked by her story. Her brother had abused her when she was young.

"What?" I gasped. "Why have you come to me?" I quickly found an excuse to leave the room and I called the Christian workers who sent her to me. "Why in the world did you send her to me?" I asked.

"Well," they said. "She is a believer from a Muslim background and we know you care for Muslims."

"Oh," I said. "You might be right." That day we started a ministry for women.

I prayed hard as I returned to Amal and the girl. "Look," I said, "As a Jordanian, I advise you to call your family right now and let them know you are alive and OK." She did that. "And now," I told her, "you also need to leave here and go straight back to your family. There is no place here or anywhere else for you except with your family."

She was very upset. She got up to go and then she ran down the stairs, out of the building and down the street. I didn't want to run after her. I was afraid that a police officer might shoot me if he saw me chasing a woman down the street. I just let her go. Then I called Jamal in the garage.

"Jamal," I said, "can you come with me and look for a girl who ran away?"

"Sure," he replied, and in a few moments he arrived with a car. We drove around for several hours until we found her in a park. She was sitting alone on a park bench. We brought her back with us, and then I called her family. It was my first time ever calling a family on behalf of another believer. Little did I realize that it would be far from the last time.

"You Christians," her father roared over the telephone. "You Christians have ruined our daughter. She has stayed several days with you. We are going to go to the police, and have our daughter checked to see if she is still a virgin!"

"What?" I gasped. They were trying to trick me. I was going to hang up, but I listened until they were finished. The father and mother were both on the telephone on different lines.

"Now you listen to me," I said to them. "If you go to the police, I will go to the police. I know what happened. She has been abused in your home. Your son abused her when she was 12 years old."

They were immediately quiet and then they agreed to take her back home.

"Where is the girl now?" they asked, much more subdued.

"We found her on the street," I replied, "It is almost evening and anyone could do anything with her." They agreed to come and get her.

The Man From Gadara

This was a turning point in my ministry. We were now getting into some serious issues: crimes, family related issues, males, and females. Families in Jordan are very close. They are very different in the way they live from people in other parts of the world. Families think and act together. It is not wrong and it is not right. It is our culture.

From this point on, in one way or another, our ministry started to get known. It was in some ways unfortunate because we did not want to be known but, through this, God brought seekers and new believers to us.

Almost a year after I had arrived back in Jordan, we had a conference of twenty-three adult believers from Muslim backgrounds. It was a good conference with invited musicians and speakers from the local churches. At that conference I began to see a church emerging from these believers. We had grown from a handful of single men to a group that included men, women, and children.

Unfortunately, the eyes of the Intelligence Department of the Government of Jordan also focused on us and they started calling people in for interviews.

After the conference, regular meetings continued in my home. My working relationship with Amal was also starting to grow. Whenever I needed to minister to women, I would find some way to arrange it so that Amal could be present. Amal even managed to attend some of our meetings. She also started attending some of the services at a local evangelical church. She usually went in secret because her family were staunch Orthodox and they did not approve of anything evangelical. If her family disapproved of her attending an evangelical church service, what would they think of her mixing with a group of Muslims? Time would tell.

CHAPTER ELEVEN
The Good News was spreading. Acts 12:25

IN 1989, WE STARTED THINKING ABOUT LEADERS. Our
church was no longer a small weak group. We had grown and
now we were starting to wrestle with new issues. Sometimes, I
had to rebuke other believers. I even started to encourage the
young men to marry Christian girls if they could.

In our conservative culture, single men and women seldom,
if ever, mix. In the meetings in my home, however, men and
women mixed with each other. I had to watch this situation closely
because the young men from a Muslim background really didn't
know how to act appropriately around young women. Fortunately
for me, my time in America had helped prepare me for this.

One time I grabbed one young man by his collar and pulled
him away from the group.

"Come with me." I insisted. "Stop messing with that girl!
If you want to marry her then talk with me, but don't you ever
mess around with her like that again." I was a young single man,
but I needed to take charge. This young man was always talking
with the girl who was sent to my home the first time I worked
with Amal. Sometimes he would arrange secret dates with her.
He would tell her to wait somewhere in the city and then, often,
he wouldn't show up. It became so bad that she would call me at

night and be angry with me, as though I was the one who was doing it.

When I realized that the young man was serious, I started to meet with them and counsel them. I gave them books to read and we would talk about what marriage meant in the Word of God.

"Look," I told the man one day. "Don't rush into an engagement. Get to know her in a proper way. Don't just look at the outside. Think of her spiritual life. Make sure she is the right person for you. Behind that lady is a story."

He looked at me waiting for me to continue. Then, as carefully as I could, I told him about how she was abused as a young teenager. I told him about how she came to the Lord and how her family tried to kill her. They had placed some bottles of butane in her room while she was sleeping and had opened them up. They sealed the windows and doors and left. A short while later the neighbors smelled gas and called the fire department. They came and broke down the door and discovered the attempted murder. The authorities almost jailed the father. I was rather blunt as I told him the story. I guess I wanted him to understand the kind of situation he was getting himself into.

Unknown to me, that night, the young man took his mother, his sister, and his brother and went to the girl's house to arrange an official engagement. I was peacefully unaware of all of this until one o'clock in the morning, when I heard someone knocking at my door. I opened the door and there stood the young man.

"What is it?" I said sleepily.

"Let me in. Do you have some water? I'm thirsty."

"It's one in the morning," I protested.

He started crying.

"What's going on?" I asked again, suddenly a bit softer.

"I took my mother and sister and brother and went to ask for the girl."

"You what? Are you crazy? Why did you do that? Things still need to be arranged!"

"I know."

The Man From Gadara

"OK, what happened?"

"My mother clashed with her family over the price of the dowry. My mother told the girl's family that their daughter was not educated and not very pretty, so she didn't deserve that much money." He was crying now, and I was laughing at how ridiculous this all was. "They said that if we come back again they will beat us up. We left. Now my chance is ruined."

I let him into my apartment.

"OK," I said, trying to encourage him. "Let's give this time. We need to pray about it and see what we should do."

ABOUT FOUR WEEKS LATER, I took my brother-in-law with me and we went to visit the girl's family. My brother-in-law was now a believer and it was good to have someone I could work with. Before we left, we arranged to have ten people praying for us. I picked up the young man and we went back to the girl's family. This time we were three men and we acted as an official party to request a bride. When we arrived at the house, we announced who we were. Again my Hawatmeh name served me well.

"Oh," they said, "we have some relatives who have married Hawatmehs, come on in."

"Lord," I prayed, "please let them forget my name and my voice." The girl's mother and father had spoken to me over the telephone the night we had found their daughter in the park. I was sure that they still had my telephone number and name. Now, a few months later, I was in their home on an official bridal request. I spoke carefully.

"We know that a few weeks ago you had trouble with this man's family," I started, "but this man's family is now acting correctly and from the door he wants to announce that he would like to marry your daughter. We are here to represent his family to you."

We talked for a few minutes, and then they gave us a price. "For you, you are good Hawatmehs, we agree that we don't want money. His family thinks we are after money, but we don't want money, and we don't want gold, we just want 500 JD." (This is about $700.00). "Wow," I thought to myself, "at that price, give us two girls." My brother-in-law was horrified and he quietly whispered to me "This is cheap. It's not good. Something's wrong with her." Of course, he did not know her background as only Amal, the bridegroom and I knew.

Her family said "Does he have a house and furniture ready?"

I replied that he was a handyman and he could work and fix things up. It was true; he was very good but he didn't have a place ready for them to live in. However, despite this, it was all over in ten minutes and we had agreed to the terms and conditions of their marriage.

"Let's read the Fatiha from the Qur'an," they said. This was the Muslim way of confirming our agreement. So I lifted my hands and while they read, I thanked God for His goodness that night. They were reading something but I didn't even hear them; I was worshipping God. When we finished praying, we moved our hands over our faces in a washing movement like all good Muslims do. Then I looked at the bridegroom and whispered, "What did you do while they read?"

He smiled, "I did the Quranic thing." I grabbed him by the neck in mock punishment, but I was very happy. I was marrying my children. I was young and single, only 30 years old, and already I was marrying off my children.

A month later, they got married. By this time the bridegroom's family had decided not to agree with it, so none of them came with him.

"OK," I said, "we will be your family." We gathered twenty cars full of people to attend the wedding. None of us were Muslims anymore. We were all evangelical Christians. We joked a bit as we headed off to attend this Muslim wedding.

First we arrived at the bride's house to get the bride. All the people who received us were Muslim leaders. It was fun. They never imagined that we were all evangelicals and that we were coming to get their daughter. When they stood up to pray the evening prayers, we just stayed waiting for them. It was a bit embarrassing, so one of the men with us said, "Abdalla, why don't we at least go stand with them. Just to let them know we are here."

"OK," I said, "You go and do that if you want, but not me." No one moved. After getting the bride, we visited the court to have a civil wedding. After they signed the official papers, we all trooped over to my house and I conducted my first marriage. Truly our little fellowship was maturing. As I gazed at the happy faces of those attending the Christian wedding, I realized that we had come a very long way from being a group of four single men.

ONE WEEK LATER I STARTED RECEIVING THREATS from the bride's family. They felt that we had deceived them. I insisted we hadn't. They discovered that their daughter's new husband was a Christian and they were infuriated. They had known that their daughter was seeing Christians and going to church, but they thought that through this wedding they were marrying her off to a Muslim man who would straighten out her funny ideas.

The young man's family also knew he was interested in Christianity, but they didn't know that his bride was also a Christian. They too thought that marriage and family life would help their son forget about his Christian ideas. Once they discovered she also was a Christian, they too started telephoning me.

"It's you, the Christians...!"

"Thank God" I thought, "they have forgotten they originally accepted me as a Muslim and now they are thinking that I am a Christian." It was a miracle to me that the Lord could put together a Christian family from two Muslim converts. I was so happy at what was happening that I really didn't care about the threats. I knew the Lord could take care of the threats.

In time, we would become more concerned. This was not a game. It wasn't just a couple of single guys messing around with religion anymore. We were dealing with serious matters. As a fellowship, we started putting together some guidelines for us to follow. What do we teach? How do we go about evangelism? How does one explain the Gospel to a Muslim? What should be included in discipleship lessons? People like Bob Clark helped a lot in organizing our thoughts. Then new questions came. What do we do about baptisms? How do we approach marriages? People can get married in a court, but what about a Christian blessing on their lives? How should we do that?

It was 1989. That year, I called five or six evangelical churches to see if they would baptize our new Christians. It made me sad to discover that not one of them would dare baptize the three single men I had initially led to the Lord. I called all of the evangelical churches and they all said no. I found this quite frustrating. Whenever I called, I had spoken to Jordanian nationals. I realized that if I had called the foreign missionaries with these churches, we could have baptized them. However, I wanted these new believers to be baptized by the Jordanian churches and not by a group of foreigners. I also realized that there was some sensitivity between the local churches and the missionaries. I didn't want our little fellowship to be in the middle. I wanted peace with the Jordanian churches. With missionaries it was easy; I could deal with them. They understood the situation and they simply wanted to see people coming to Christ. The local churches were different. At that time they were very reluctant to do anything with Muslims.

When I realized that the churches wouldn't help us, I took Bob Clark and the three brothers down to the Dead Sea to a spot where warm water comes down a stream and flows into the sea. In that spot we made a little dam so the water would be deeper. There, beside the bubbling stream, we held our first baptism service. One by one, the three men gave their testimonies and I baptized them. As they were lifted from the water, I began to sing "I have decided to follow Jesus, no turning back, no turning back... "It was a special moment for all of us, until I lifted one of them and he gasped, "Oh no, my teeth!" Sure enough, part of his false teeth had fallen into the water. We soon forgot about singing and started groping around in the water looking for his teeth. We never found them.

SEVERAL MONTHS LATER JAMAL, THE MECHANIC, faced some major family trouble. His brother had gotten into trouble passing bad checks. He was arrested, tried, and placed in the local jail. Jamal felt it was important to make things right, so he visited his brother and together they came up with a plan. Since Jamal's brother had passed the bad checks, Jamal felt that his brother should leave the jail and approach family members about helping him pay back the debts. We went to the jail warden and then to the police with the idea. In the end, it was agreed and Jamal's brother was free to leave the jail if Jamal would sign a statement saying that if his brother did not return with the money within one week, then Jamal could be sued for his brother's crime. Jamal agreed and his brother went free.

Sadly, Jamal's brother decided not to try and get the money. When he did not return after a week, Jamal was hauled into court, sued, and thrown into jail. Christ replaced us on the cross and Jamal replaced his brother in the jail in Amman. While in jail, Jamal's brother, who was now free, visited him. "You brought this on yourself because you deserve it," his brother told him. "It is all because you are now a Christian."

After a few days, I realized I must do something to help Jamal. I decided to find his brother. Jamal's brother was a driver for a transport company taking goods and people to and from Iraq. It took several days to locate him. When I did, he simply jumped in his car and took off. I chased him in my car and tried to catch him, but he got away.

Next, I decided to try and find him through his place of residence. I understood through his friends that he was staying at a cheap hotel in town. So I obtained a picture of Jamal's brother and I started to make my rounds to the hotels.

"Have you seen this man anywhere?" I asked.

People looked at me carefully. No one asked me what my business was. I usually wore my business clothes and, later, I learned several people had mistaken me for an undercover officer from the Intelligence Department. Slowly I made my way down a long list of cheap hotels until finally one hotel clerk said to me, "He is here; please have a seat."

I sat in the lobby and the staff served me coffee. Then I had another coffee, and finally a third. I waited a little longer and then they served me a Pepsi. They kept calling me sir and offering me free coffee and drinks. Eventually it dawned on me that they must have thought that I was a police officer or with the Intelligence Department. Finally, the clerk motioned for me to follow him. Sure enough, there was Jamal's brother.

Striding over to him, I pulled him aside. "Listen," I hissed. "Come with me right now." He didn't move. "If you don't come right now, I will force you to come. I have two guys outside, waiting in a car. All I have to do is stick my head outside and they will come in."

"OK, I'll walk with you," he agreed. He walked to the car as I tried to convince him to act responsibly in this situation.

He agreed and got into my car. I took him straight to the police. In the end, the police put Jamal's brother back in jail and Jamal was released. A short time later, Jamal left for Iraq to try to find work. I did not hear from him for some time.

Then one day a message came from Iraq. Jamal wanted to get married. However, before he got married he wanted to join a church so that people would trust him. So I wrote a letter of recommendation for Jamal and sent it to him. It seemed to do the trick.

A while later, I got another letter from Jamal. He had found a Christian girl and wanted to marry her, but her family was concerned. They wanted to make sure that he was speaking the truth about being a baptized believer. Jamal wanted to have a baptismal certificate.

We weren't a proper church and we certainly were not registered with the government. In the Middle East, there are Christian churches that have been in existence since Christian history began. These churches have survived through many long years of difficulties and troubles. Now that Middle Eastern countries are under Muslim control, these churches are allowed to continue because they serve the Christian families and tribes in the Middle East. As converts to Christianity, we had no Christian families to identify with. Our families were Muslim and our religion was clearly stated on our identification papers. We were Muslims. Now, however, Jamal wanted an official baptism certificate.

Sitting in my office one day, I made up a certificate on the computer. I found some computer clipart of a dove and placed it at the top. It looked quite pretty. I then signed the certificate and took it to a local evangelical church. I had only recently become a member there, but I asked the pastor to stamp the certificate with the church stamp. To my amazement, he not only stamped it but certified it with the church seal. He then wrote:

The minister who performed this baptism is well known to us and is part of our congregation. He also acts as a minister in our church.

I sent the certificate to Iraq and some time later we heard that Jamal had gotten married.

About this time, we started to discuss what sort of materials we should develop for evangelism and discipleship. Barry and I sat down and started to draw up lists of materials that we needed. The list grew quite long. We needed materials to teach Muslims about marriage. We also needed materials to teach the new converts about Christian leadership. Our goal was not simply to make materials. We needed to have something in hand to use with those who were coming to Christ. We started with evangelism and after trying a number of things, we came up with a series of lessons that we could teach to those who were seeking truth. Little did we realize the impact these simple lessons would have on Muslims around the world.

CHAPTER TWELVE
We must obey God rather than man. Acts 5:29

THE CRUNCH CAME IN 1990. God had given me the opportunity to visit the country of Syria and to minister to people there. I made a short trip and found that God was also at work in the lives of Muslims in Syria. Everything went fine until I arrived at the Jordanian boarder. At the border, travelers pass through several checks. Vehicles are checked by Customs. Passports are checked by Immigration. The Intelligence Department checks for criminals and those trying to escape military service. I wasn't expecting any trouble and, therefore, was quite surprised when the border police had my name. They simply told me that I needed to go to the Intelligence Department in Amman for an interview.

I was a bit shaken. I hadn't realized that the government would be taking much interest in me. In our country, most families and tribes police themselves. Families usually settled things between themselves before involving the police. In the case of someone changing their religion, families sometimes ostracized the person. In rare cases where someone spoke out against Islam or Christianity, the families would attempt to kill them. Honor killings in families were not strange. If someone severely dishonored his or her family, the possibility of revenge was there. If a young girl became pregnant out of wedlock, there was a good possibility the family would feel she had dishonored the family name and they might respond negatively. In some severe cases, she might even be killed. I was aware of all of this and realized that most Muslim countries have special laws that cover honor killings.

At this point, my own family was not acting upset or concerned. My immediate family knew of my interest in church, and they knew that my American girlfriend had been a Christian. They thought my attraction to Christianity was simply a youthful whim and that in time, it would pass by, especially if I married a good Muslim girl and started to have a family.

So, when the Intelligence Department requested an interview, I was quite puzzled. In my working career, I had been a government man. I had a good record with the government. I was a Jordanian citizen from a good ethnic background. I was not a Palestinian or Armenian refugee. Like the apostle Paul, I had all the right credentials. I had respect because I had attended an American university. I had been a military man and had obtained officer rank. I had security clearance to both the royal palaces and to the Defense Department's Operation Room. On top of all this, I had not committed any criminal acts.

Now, the Intelligence Department wanted to see me. It was a sobering thought. The Jordanian Intelligence Department is considered by many to be the secret police of Jordan. Officers generally do not wear uniforms. They act independently of the regular police or the army. Their function is to deal with any internal threats to Jordanian security. They were busy keeping their eyes on the local branches of the Palestinian Liberation Organizations and the fanatical Muslim organizations.

So, I prayed for several days and then I braced myself and went for my interview. Their office was only two or three minutes from where I worked, so I took time off during office hours to walk over to the Intelligence Department's big gray building.

The people at the front had my name, and they took me down a number of long corridors until I arrived at a small office. I was asked to sit inside.

A few minutes later a nice looking young man came in. He was slightly older than I was, and he asked if I wanted tea or coffee.

"OK," I agreed, "coffee would be nice." Coffee is also the Jordanian sign of friendship, and this seemed reassuring.

The young man started by asking very simple questions.

"What's your name?"

"What is your father's name?"

"What is your mother's name? Your brothers'? Your sister's?"

"Where did you graduate from?"

"Where did you work?"

These were all very simple questions, but there were tons of them. I had arrived at their office at eight in the morning, and I didn't leave until four in the afternoon. I sat in the same room with the same person the whole time. He never left the room except to take half hour lunch break and, during this time, he placed two soldiers outside the office door.

By four o'clock, I was exhausted. "Thank you," he said, standing up. "Don't tell anyone about this and come back tomorrow morning."

I was free to go. It had been my first contact with the Intelligence Department. Little did I realize that the young man sitting across the table from me asking me all sorts of questions was an officer who had been assigned to my case. The first time we met, everything was very friendly. That was soon to change. In the years that followed, this one man, Abu Sayed, would come to know more about me than perhaps I knew about myself. In time, I would view him as my enemy; when we would talk, he would hide his agenda and I would hide mine. However, during my first interview, we were simply two young men sitting across the table from each other. Now, years later, he has been promoted to become a high-ranking officer while I'm still a simple minister of the gospel.

THE NEXT MORNING THINGS WERE TOTALLY DIFFERENT. I was escorted back to the same room and sat in the same chair. This time, however the officer across the table from me was totally different. This man had a sour face and an angry personality. The first man had been pleasant. This man was mean. The officer I talked to the first day would use words like, "Mr. Hawatmeh," and, "my friend." He would never repeat a question. Whatever answer I gave he would simply take his pen and write it down. His voice was gentle and every now and then he would ask me if I would like tea or coffee.

This new man was different. He never asked me if I wanted tea or coffee. He shouted questions at me and he almost never believed my answers. He always wanted more.

"Who did you meet yesterday?"

If I simply said, "A few people," he would start shouting, "Who are they? What are their names? Where do they live?"

When I told him, he continued his questions. "Where did you meet them? Who else did you meet?"

This questioning went on most of the day. I was thankful when at four o'clock he told me it was over. I was finished for that day, but I was to come back again the next morning. I left completely devastated.

THAT NIGHT I PRAYED A LOT. I had agreed not to tell anyone about the interviews. This was a cross I had to bear alone. I was also concerned about my job. I had now missed two days at the office and it looked like I would be missing several more. As I prayed that night I felt a renewed sense of peace. I decided that the next day I would take a slightly different track. I would not tell them everything. I would answer their questions as carefully as they asked them.

The next morning we started again.

"What are you doing here?"

"I'm working with a company."

"What are you doing there?"

"I'm the technical manager doing some engineering."

"Why were you in Cyprus?"

"Working as a technician for the Cyprus Telecommunications Authority."

The questions went on and on until suddenly they took on a new slant.

"What is your relationship with the churches?"

"Just friendship." I thought I had fooled them. I wasn't sure if it was considered lying, but I didn't give him all the truth. They asked more questions, but my answers were evasive. A second officer joined us. After a few minutes, he spoke to me.

"If you don't give us the truth easily, I will call a couple of men to take you down stairs to be tortured for a couple of hours. Then I will bring you back." His eyes were icy cold and his face was somber. I wasn't sure if it was a real threat or not. I needed to find out.

"Look," I said. "You don't need two guys. I'm a skinny man. If you want, I could go down stairs by myself. I'll torture myself and then come back."

He laughed. "Don't mess around with me," he said, trying to be serious.

I thought I had managed to break his meanness when suddenly his questions became rude.

"What did you do with these women in your home?"

"I, hum … I…"

"Did you sleep with them?"

Suddenly I was angry. I reacted before he could repeat his question.

"If you repeat this question again," I said, my finger suddenly waving in his face. "I will sue you. My morals are better than yours. You are doing this because you receive money. I am a loyal citizen. You are just an employee of the government. If you repeat this 'women thing' again, I will sue you in the civil courts for slander. Remember, I am from the Hawatmeh tribe!"

My anger was slowly warming up and for the first time, I saw uncertainty in his eyes.

"No, no," he protested, "it's OK. I'm sorry. I didn't mean that."

The questions continued, only now the atmosphere was a bit more charged and the questions a bit more subdued.

When four o'clock came, we finished, but they wanted to see me back the next day. On and on it went, day after day, for almost three weeks. My job was in trouble and my nerves were getting frayed.

Through all of these questions, I discovered that they knew an awful lot about me. They knew pieces of information that I had said on the telephone. Someone had asked me to do something, and they knew about it. It meant that my telephones were bugged. I was slowly becoming alert to their plans.

A couple of days later, I realized I was being followed. It wasn't obvious at first, but once you are conscious of it, it becomes obvious. Without realizing it, I was carefully studying the faces of those around me, remembering where I had seen them last. I started noticing the kinds of vehicles that were parked around me, especially those with people sitting in them. I never purposely decided to notice these things, but I did as the days of interviews went on. I began to realize the extent of their knowledge about me. I started to try to learn how they had obtained this information. As I learned their tricks and techniques, I slowly found ways of counteracting them. It was the beginning of a cat and mouse game, in which I was the mouse, darting from shadow to shadow. It would take several years before I discovered a more practical and biblical way of dealing with this form of harassment.

DURING THIS TIME, I CONTINUED MY MINISTRY. Even though the eyes of the Intelligence Department were on me, I knew that ministry had to continue. The new converts needed discipleship and teaching and there were always new people wanting to know about the gospel. Most of these contacts came through letters that people had written to the Christian Broadcasting Network. CBN had set up a television broadcast tower in the Middle East and their broadcasts could be seen by people in the north of Jordan, Syria and in Lebanon. As people watched these programs, they were invited to respond by writing in to the broadcasters. The letters from Jordan were collected and regularly carried in someone's suitcase into Jordan and passed to me.

While I lived in Cyprus, I met a man from CBN. Since that time we had kept up contact. After I began my ministry in Jordan, this same man passed by for a visit. During our visit I asked him, "Don't you have Jordanians writing to your Christian TV station?"

"Yeah," he said looking at me, "we have lots of Jordanians who write to us."

"Does anyone follow up with these people here in Jordan?"

"No, I don't think so."

"Can I take some of those letters?"

"Well, we can give you all of them if you like." I liked the idea. And so, since 1990, CBN started sending me lots of letters. In the years that followed, the number of letters slowed down, but initially there were lots of letters. At that time, there were fewer TV stations, less media, and fewer satellite dishes in Jordan. People were content to watch whatever came over local television. CBN was new, it's programs were all new, and thousands of people tuned in to watch it each day.

Following up the letters from CBN became a major task. It soon became obvious I could not handle this task alone. I asked several others to join me. The Canadian businessman who originally hired me decided to move his business into an area of Jordan that was more responsive to the television broadcasts. Then another foreign couple joined them. I stayed in Amman and did the follow up in the capital city and in the south of Jordan.

Together we formed a ministry team. We shared together and formed prayer teams. Sometimes we would walk around neighborhoods praying for those who lived there, that the Lord would open doors into that part of the city.

Our ministry team was not based around any mission organization or person. It was a team that God brought together to minister to those who were seeking. Different ones related to different organizations, but our goals were all similar. We wanted to reach others for Christ and to see people discipled into mature believers. God gave us grace and we worked together very smoothly.

While the Intelligence Department started their opposition, God pushed us forward. On the one hand, we felt pressure and harassment. On the other hand, we found open doors for ministry and discovered people waiting and ready for us. The harvest was ripe. The laborers were few, and there were those who opposed what we were doing.

CHAPTER THIRTEEN
He who finds a wife finds a good thing. Proverbs 18:22

AS THE MONTHS WENT BY, MY RELATIONSHIP WITH AMAL grew deeper. We lived in the same neighborhood and we both felt God's call on our lives to minister. On many occasions Amal had been used by God to minister into the lives of women seekers, and I found myself increasingly relying on Amal.

I knew that a relationship was starting but at the same time I had my doubts about us. I had been very close to marrying before, and it was hard to enter another relationship. Deep in my heart, I resisted any relationship with Amal, even though I enjoyed being around her and working with her.

There was another problem as well. She was from a Christian family and I was from a Muslim family. Since Jordanians operate in a family setting, family members are always involved in the various steps in arranging a marriage. Amal's family would resist any relationship with a Muslim family. My Muslim family would resist any relationship with a Christian family, although they would not be as much against it. Under Jordanian law, when a Christian woman marries a Muslim man, she usually becomes a Muslim and the children are always

114

Muslims. I knew that if I were to marry Amal, we would need to have a Christian marriage. I was not hiding behind Islam. I boldly told people I was a Christian, and I identified more with the Christians than with Muslims. However, officially, on paper, and before the eyes of the government, I was a Muslim. If I was to marry, I needed to marry a Muslim. It was an insurmountable problem only God could overcome.

Our little ministry team liked Amal. I had introduced her to the team and they enjoyed working with her. She was a nice girl, new in the faith, but serving the Lord.

Then one day in 1990, in the middle of all our troubles, I came out with it and asked Amal if she was at all interested in having me as a husband. She responded positively and this worried me. "Look" I said. "I've thought about this but I need more time to make a decision. I am going to Finland on a trip; let me pray about it and see what God has in it."

It was true; I did have a business trip to Finland. However, I also had a second agenda. Bob and Margie Prather were convinced that I should marry a certain Finnish girl. They had met her in Jordan a year earlier when she was studying Arabic and thought that she was perfect for me.

"Lord," I prayed, "if it is your will for me to go back to Amal and marry her then please help me not to like the girl in Finland." It may have been a strange prayer, but Bob and Margie were like family to me. They loved and cared for me as well as for others. Even after Bob died, Margie still cared about me and visited me from time to time. Since Bob and Margie were now my adopted Christian family I felt I needed to listen to them as my elders and respect their wishes. If they felt that a certain Finnish girl was perfect for me, then I felt I should check it out. The company had some business in Finland, so it worked out perfectly for me to fly there.

I planned to visit Finland for 41 days. I could have finished my work sooner but I needed to check out my heart. Life with a western wife would be so much easier. The paperwork would be simple. My culture would accept a western wife as different. None of this would have mattered if I left Jordan and lived in the freedom of the west. I realized that if I had a western wife I would always be faced with the temptation to flee the pressure of Muslim culture and settle in the west. A Jordanian Christian wife would be much more difficult. Our families would clash. After all, one family would be Muslim and the other nominal Christian. Clashes were inevitable.

Finland is a beautiful country and the people were wonderful. I enjoyed my time there, but my heart was in Jordan. By the thirty-fifth day I called Amal and told her I loved her and wanted to marry her.

Once I said it, I knew it was something I had wanted for a long time. Peace flooded my soul and I knew I had made the right decision. Making up my mind had been hard enough, but getting the families to agree was going to be much harder. On top of this, the Intelligence Department was still giving me a difficult time.

SALEEM SALAH WAS THE BISHOP OF THE ROMAN CATHOLIC CHURCH. Several years before, when I had returned from Cyprus, I made an effort to meet the various leaders of the Christian community. Saleem had taken an immediate interest in me, and this resulted in a good friendship developing between us. Through the following years we had many good discussions, sitting and talking about ministry to Muslims. Whenever I came to visit him, he would always get up and close the door and sometimes even close the windows. We would talk and I would share stories of what God was doing and he would laugh. Many times, as I told my stories, I could see tears in his eyes, especially when we got to the part about Muslims accepting the Lord.

The next time I visited Saleem, I told him that I was in love with a girl.

"Congratulations," he beamed, "who is she?"

"You are going to meet her," I smiled, "but I need your help."

"Of course," he smiled back. He and I both knew that in our culture young men and women don't meet and mix. Young people can only meet together in groups. If we were to get to know each other better, we would need a chaperon.

Saleem, however, did better than that. He arranged for us to start six months of pre-marriage counseling with him. I would go one week and Amal would go the next. The last two or three weeks, Saleem arranged to meet with both of us. He had carefully counseled us and considered our personalities, our histories and our wishes and desires in life. When he was done, he was sure we would fit together.

During the counseling time, he would talk to me about marriage in general. He spent time sharing with me how people with a Christian background behave. He told me what to expect from Christian girls. He instructed me how to behave as a Christian man around Christian women. We talked at length about the difficulties we might face in our marriage. Saleem would then meet with Amal and discuss much the same with her about my background and me.

Then the day came when he arranged to meet with both of us at the same time. We sat in his office, our eyes meeting occasionally. We were nervous, but Saleem soon put us at ease.

"I think you two are perfect for each other. Not only that; I think you two should get married."

"Great!" we agreed with him, "we think we should too."

He smiled at us. "So, what can I do for you to help you from here?"

"Saleem," I said, "can you approach Amal's family?"

In our culture, a young man always gets someone to represent him when he asks for a bride. Usually it is his father or an uncle or some respectable person; not many Christian families would send a bishop. Most might ask a minister to go with them when they ask for a bride, but I took the bishop with me. At that time, the bishop was the highest church official in Jordan and he was a very well known man.

117

On the day when we approached Amal's family, Saleem came dressed in his robes, representing the Catholic Church. I came in my best suit. We sat and talked and Amal's family rejected the offer.

"Don't you even think about it!" they almost shouted. "He has a Muslim background and in our eyes he stays a Muslim."

Saleem tried to interject but couldn't.

"We would never agree to this. He can be our friend and our brother but never our brother-in-law or son-in-law."

The family was adamant, so we left. I felt dejected, but Saleem insisted that we should try again after the smoke settled a bit. After all, the family had been surprised by this turn of events. Perhaps they would feel differently as time passed.

Over the next two years Saleem went to Amal's family seven times. Every time they refused. Those were difficult years. During that time, my father died and some time later Amal's mother also passed away. The Intelligence Department continued to put pressure on me, and Amal's family continued to resist. In fact, they stopped Amal from working and insisted that she stay at home and not be allowed to leave the house.

I continued with my ministry. The converts were now meeting at my house three times a week. During those days, we used to have a prayer bulletin board. Many needs would be written on the board and as they were answered we would rejoice and remove the requests. However, Abdalla and Amal's marriage stayed at the top of the list.

Finally we came to a decision in October 1991. Saleem, the bishop, met with us again.

"I think you should get married," he said bluntly. "If you don't, then you should cancel everything and forget it." He paused. "You need to do something; we can't go on and on with this forever."

We both agreed and started putting plans into motion.

The first thing Saleem did was to call Amal's sisters. He bluntly told them that he wanted to marry me to their sister. The sisters agreed, just as Saleem thought they would. Some of them liked me and, when faced with the issue, did not object. Their brothers were the ones who were objecting.

"Well," Saleem said to us later, "I can't marry you here in Jordan, but perhaps I could bless you here. We could have a special ceremony for you. It won't be a regular wedding."

In Jordan, Christian weddings need to be done in a civil court and then churches add their blessing to the marriage. The wedding service is often called a crowning service as the husband and wife wear crowns, and the church pronounces the blessings. Well, since we couldn't be married legally in Jordan, the bishop said that there was nothing against him blessing us, even without the certificate and the crowns. So we were blessed. Then we started to make plans to fly to Cyprus, which is a Christian based nation, so we could be married. A friend in Cyprus checked out the situation for us.

"Sure you can come to Cyprus and go to any church here and get married easily." He insisted. "We have church weddings all the time here."

"Great," we thought, "this is going to be easy."

But nothing was going to be easy. The Intelligence Department called me in the following day for questioning. After a lot of initial questions they finally got around to the reason for the interview.

"Where are you going to get married?"

"In Cyprus."

"You are not allowed to leave the country."

"But I simply want to get married."

"We will not allow you to go."

"What if I go anyway?"

"We will take you and Amal off of the plane by force if necessary."

I was stunned. How was I ever going to get married? I then asked everyone to pray. Within a few days I had made up my mind. We would fly to Cyprus. We would call the Intelligence Department's bluff. If they took us off the plane, then we were back to where we started. If they didn't, then we could get married.

119

In October 1991 we boarded a plane for Cyprus. The Intelligence Department didn't stop us. They had threatened, but they had not followed up on their threats. I wasn't sure if they chose not to or if they were not legally able to do it. Whatever the reason, we were free to fly to Cyprus.

When we arrived in Cyprus, we discovered that we had been given completely wrong information. As in Jordan, the church could only offer us a blessing after a civil wedding. They could not perform the real wedding nor could they provide us with a certificate. We already had a blessing service, but we had no marriage certificate.

I wanted a church wedding, with a certificate, not a civil marriage. I considered all this to be like an Islamic wedding. Besides, having a real Christian wedding was very important to me. It was part of my identity as a Christian.

But not one church agreed to marry us.

It was a very hard time for us. I felt a lot of bitterness. We had to live in separate homes. Amal's family was very upset. I had taken their daughter and run off with her but I hadn't married her!

"Bring her back to Jordan and get married here," they insisted. "Having you two married is better than this!"

"No," I said, "we want to find a solution here."

Even Saleem called me and said, "Look if you cannot get married in Cyprus then get back to Jordan or leave one another. Don't keep on like this. It looks bad to everyone."

The pressure was on and so I did what I had always done when the pressure was on. I prayed. The following day we heard about another minister that we had not approached. He was the vicar of the Anglican Church in Nicosia and he was known to some of the believers in Cyprus. We went to visit him.

He listened to our story and was very sympathetic.

"Look," the vicar said, "I am very new on the island, but I don't see why I couldn't marry you here. First, however, let me call the Ministry of the Interior and see what they have to say."

We waited while he called. He talked to a woman on the telephone who said that she didn't see why we couldn't be married.

When he hung up the phone he was beaming. "We can do it!" he almost shouted. We were amazed!

"OK." he said with a smile, "when do we do it?"

We looked at each other. "How about tomorrow night?"

"Fine with me."

The rest of the morning was a blur. We immediately called Bob Clark in Jordan, and he rushed to a rental shop and rented a wedding dress. We gave him the measurements and he grabbed the dress and jumped on the next plane to Cyprus. He made it by evening.

We phoned people on the island and invited them. By the next evening a small crowd gathered to witness the marriage. Bob Clark was the best man and the Vicar was the officiating minister. It was a wonderful evening. We signed the documents, had a wonderful time with our guests, and then went to the hotel.

EARLY THE NEXT MORNING THE PHONE RANG. Someone on the line said that we needed to talk to the government Minister of the Interior of Cyprus.

"Good night!" I thought, "what has happened now?"

I called the number that they gave me, and a few moments later I was talking with the Minister of the Interior. And he was angry.

"Who do you think you are?" he shouted. "You came here to our country and you broke the law!" He was screaming over the phone. He was really mad. He didn't slander me but he shouted and went on and on.

"No comments," I thought. I didn't say a word.

Then after five minutes of shouting at me, he said, "You bring that certificate to my office right now! I want to tear it up because it is not legal."

As soon as the Minister of the Interior hung up the telephone I called a courier service and told them that I had a letter for Jordan. Could they bring an envelope to the hotel?

While we were waiting for the courier, I had a photocopy of the certificate made for my own use. When the courier arrived, I put my marriage certificate, our wedding pictures, and the video of our wedding into the envelope and sent them to my apartment in Jordan.

Then I called the vicar and we arranged to visit the Ministry of the Interior. When we arrived at his office, the Minister of the Interior was still very upset and he almost deported the vicar from the island. Then he spent fifteen minutes shouting at me.

"You are an Arab. If you come here, you should respect yourself. You should respect this country. We have laws here...."

When he finally showed signs of slowing down, I interrupted him. "Are you finished? Can I say something?"

"OK, what is it?"

"I was in your country for two years working for this government and I respected your country fully. I never broke the law then." I paused. "But isn't it a shame for you to encourage Islam and not Christianity? The Muslims occupy half of your island. Look, I am fleeing the bondage of Islam and I came here for help."

The Minister of the Interior looked at me. Slowly his face changed.

"Tell me again about this marriage. Why are you here?"

"I came here for a church wedding, not a simple civil wedding. I was born a Muslim but I became a Christian. They won't let me marry in my country and remain a Christian. I came here for help. Besides, we called your office first to make sure it was legal."

Then the vicar spoke very politely. "I didn't know if it was possible or not for me to marry them, so I called the Ministry office to check."

The Minister of the Interior nodded and then checked to discover who had been on the telephone that day. In a few minutes he discovered it had been a new secretary and it was her first day at work.

"You know, Abdalla," he said to me. "For 35 years no one has broken this law. You are the first person to do that. But I'm very happy you did. I will certify your certificate as legal."

"Mr. Minister," I replied softly, "it's not me who did this; it is Christ. He has performed a miracle."

As he signed and stamped my copy of the certificate, the government minister smiled. "Please promise me one thing. When you divorce, do not divorce through the church."

"That's easy," I said to him, "We are not going to divorce."

A few minutes later we shook hands and we left. In those last minutes, the government minister was quiet and shy. He had started out being angry and upset but, in the end, the Lord had changed his heart and we left on good terms.

WHEN WE ARRIVED BACK IN JORDAN we took a one month honeymoon. Instead of moving back to my apartment, we moved into the home of the Canadian businessman. He and his family were in Canada and since their home was in another city, we were distant from Amal's family. During this time we tried to approach Amal's family and build bridges of love and friendship. Her family was not happy, especially her brothers. Several times they threatened to kill me.

After four weeks we moved back into my apartment in Amman, which was only 100 meters from Amal's family. Their anger continued for many weeks. Often, in the evenings, we would sit at home alone, with the lights off, so that no one would know we were there. During that time we began to learn that the Lord was protecting us. He had saved us, and now he had also married us, and we would continue our lives together trusting him.

Marriage was a life changing experience for me. I started eating some real food. What a wonderful thing to come home and smell food cooking, not just stale popcorn.

But more than this, I started to have a partner. Amal became an integral part of my ministry. My crazy ideas sometimes became less crazy because I had another person to talk them over with. God brought Amal into my life to be a blessing to me. Through the early stages of my ministry Amal became like a glass of water to me. When I was thirsty, Amal was there to drink from.

With Amal, we started to reach families. Suddenly we started to have women's meetings in our home. Wives began coming to Amal to talk about marriage problems or other issues. We started to think about a children's ministry. Who would care for the children? Before this, I had thought, "Yeah, it's nice to have children around, but we need to have them in another room."

But when Amal came along she said, "Don't you think we should teach the children something?" She opened my eyes to the needs of the children, so we started a children's ministry.

Time and time again, it amazed me how much patience Amal had with me. During that first year of marriage, the Intelligence Department interviewed me over fifty times. Every time, Amal was always there at home waiting with food and a smile and saying how good it was to have me back. Many times she was afraid, but she never discouraged me from the ministry. Even when things really got rough later, she stood with me.

As time went on, Amal's family began to notice our lives. We spent our time serving the Lord, not doing things for ourselves. When Islamic feasts came, we didn't celebrate the way Islam celebrates. When Christian holidays came, we didn't celebrate the way Orthodox Christians celebrate. We didn't drink or smoke. We didn't hold parties or go to dances. Our home was always open for people, and people were always in our home. Before Amal came, I was a single man living alone. Now, with Amal, we were a couple and a family. Our home became a pleasant place where people were welcome and where people could come to talk and pray with us. Amal made the difference.

In the days ahead, people would start to reject me and troubles would come, but Amal was always there with me. When my family rejected me, Amal was there. Even when the Intelligence Department started to move against us, Amal stood with me.

CHAPTER FOURTEEN
And they threatened them. Acts 4:21

ONE MONTH AFTER WE RETURNED from Cyprus, I approached the government to get my marriage certificate recognized and to obtain a Jordanian Family Book. This family book is an important document in Jordan and is used when dealing with government bodies and when putting children in school.

I prepared my documents and at the end of 1991 I started the application process. I had with me the official Cypriot marriage certificate that was sealed and stamped by the Cypriot church and the Cypriot government. I knew I might have some problems, as I had heard that in Jordan the government only accepts court marriage certificates or Islamic marriage certificates.

The clerks at the front desk were very nice. I presented them with my marriage certificate and my wife's and my own birth certificates. Then I politely told them that I wanted to apply for a Jordanian Family Book.

"That is fine," one of the clerks said looking at our birth certificates, "but what is this?"

"This is a marriage certificate from a church."

The clerk looked puzzled. "But you are a Muslim. How could you marry in a church?"

"I am not a Muslim."

"What do you mean you are not a Muslim? You were born a Muslim."

"I am a Christian. See here is my baptism certificate."

The clerk looked even more puzzled. "Excuse me sir; I think you should go and see my supervisor."

"OK." I went up to the supervisor and I told him what I wanted.

He heard me out and then he said, "Close the door."

I closed the door.

"Now tell me again what this is all about."

I smiled and began again. "I was born a Muslim but I accepted the Lord as my Savior. I became a Christian in 1980 and I have been living as a Christian since then. Now it is time to apply for a family book, so I am providing you with enough information about my Christianity to complete the paperwork."

The man looked doubtful.

"Look, here is my baptismal certificate. Here are recommendations from several churches. Here is my marriage certificate, also from the church. My wife is a Christian. She was born a Christian. Here is her birth certificate and her baptismal certificate. Look, there are church stamps on all these papers. We were married by a church in Cyprus and the papers are certified by the Cypriot government." I smiled at him.

He made me repeat it four times.

"This is impossible," he said in the end. "You can't be a Christian. I don't think this is legal."

"No," I smiled, "I think it is legal. King Hussein has introduced democracy and freedom of religion. It is all in Article 13 that King Hussein signed. And," I smiled again, "I have a copy of it. Here it is."

"You know," he said, "if the government knew that I was even allowing you to say all this in my office, they would jail me!"

"That's fine with me," I said still smiling. "All I want is to be registered."

"We can't." the man protested. "You're a Muslim and you will stay a Muslim forever."

"OK, then I will have to go to court."

"I would advise you not to do that."

"If you are saying you cannot register me as a Christian, I think I will have to." I was no longer smiling.

"Give me your telephone number and I will call you in a couple of days."

I left his office, but I never got the telephone call. The Jordanian Intelligence Department must have gotten one instead, because since that day they started working harder on my case.

Soon after this, I decided to open a legal case against the government in order to get my marriage registered. The first thing I did was to get in touch with a number of human rights organizations. Through these organizations, I met Asma Khuder. She was a lawyer and she was the head of a union for women and a local human rights organization. People told me not to bother with her. She was crude and would talk to anyone about anything. I was immediately interested. I needed someone who wouldn't be afraid of tackling a new and different case. I meet with Asma and told her that we needed to be registered as Christians. She agreed to take the case.

People who didn't like Asma told me I should consider a more respectable and established lawyer like Saleem Sweiss. He had years of experience. People felt that he knew the law better and was acquainted with the strange zigzags that are so commonplace with governments and laws. So I visited Saleem and asked him if he would also represent me. I asked him to consider teaming up with Asma on this case, but I think Asma frightened him.

"Look," he said, "I will work by myself and she can work by herself. After that we will see how we can manage."

During the next year we tried many things. With either Asma or Saleem representing me, we tried various government ministries, the Office of the Prime Minister, and even the Royal

Courts. Other lawyers got involved, but we seemed to get no where.

Then Asma decided to approach the king personally. She called me and was optimistic. We started to pray. After the visit, Asma told me that the king had stated that this was a very serious matter. He preached about human rights to her and said that he would get back to her, but he never called her again.

While it seemed that we were getting nowhere, we did make one step forward. The Jordanian Government said they recognized my case as a valid human rights case. They did not deny us the right to raise the point. However, the government never allowed us to go to court. Whenever we tried to move, either the Ministry of the Interior, the Justice Ministry or the Prime Minister's Office blocked it from going to court.

We concluded that they were afraid that this case would set a precedent for future cases. The surrounding Islamic nations might look unfavorably on Jordan if they granted Muslims the right to be registered as Christians.

One day, Saleem Sweiss thought he had a good idea. Jordanian law is based on the Turkish laws of the Ottoman Empire. In Turkey, they have religious freedom. Perhaps if he flew to Turkey to dig out old files about the Ottoman Empire, he could influence our case. The old laws were in place before Jordan became a nation. So he flew off to Turkey and stayed there for three or four days to study their laws. However, it all came to nothing. They were wasting their time and my money. In the end, the lawyers took a lot of money from me. I ended up selling some of my property in the north to help finance their efforts.

After a year of trying to persuade the government, we finally made some progress. In the end, I didn't get a family book, but my marriage certificate was recognized. They exchanged the church certificate from Cyprus with a civil certificate from Jordan. However, in the process, they put my religion down as Muslim just as it is stated in my birth certificate.

I didn't have a family book, I was still classified as a Muslim, but my marriage was legal.

The Man From Gadara

IT STARTED SLOWLY AT FIRST. It was so slow that we didn't notice it immediately. Amal and I were busy with our work and our ministry. Every day there were people to minister to. Some wanted help. Some wanted to know about Christ. Others needed teaching and encouragement. Each day was filled with ministering to people. We didn't notice when some stopped coming to our meetings. People are busy and not everyone can come all the time to everything. Many of the believers were secretive about their faith, and they needed to participate in their family activities in order to keep relationships open. We understood that, so we never put pressure on people that they had to attend or be involved in all the things that were happening.

After a while, however, we realized that something was wrong. People were leaving. No one was angry and no one had any disagreements with us. They just stopped coming to meetings. Then slowly, they also stopped visiting us at home.

By the time we realized what was going on, the exodus was in full swing. We immediately started to visit those we hadn't seen in some time. They were glad to see us and have us in their homes but, one by one, they had reasons why they could not attend our meetings.

"Look, Abdalla, I'm from a Palestinian background. It isn't as easy for us as it is for you. Our work is in danger if we are too closely identified with Christians. I don't want to lose my job."

"Abdalla, my family isn't happy. It's probably best if I'm not seen with you for a while."

Everyone had an excuse. The Intelligence Department had approached everyone in some way. They had quietly approached all those in our fellowship on an individual basis and somehow frightened them. The Intelligence Department had done their homework, and they discovered some point of weakness in each person or family that could be used for their purposes. When pressure was applied in just the right spot, people backed off.

One by one people left. By the end of the year, over ninety percent of our congregation had vanished. Some left for England, Sweden, America, or Iraq. Some just stopped coming. I still occasionally see those that are left in Jordan. I know them; I still visit with them sometimes and once in a while they may drop in on me for a visit. However, they are afraid to sit and talk to us about the Lord. I think it was the Intelligence Department's first success at dispersing a Christian meeting. In the end, there were only a handful of believers left in our ministry. Amal and I started asking ourselves, "Where do we go from here?"

IMAD SHEHADI WAS BORN INTO A CHRISTIAN FAMILY. As a young man he traveled to America to study theology at Dallas Theological Seminary. When his theological studies were over, he and his wife moved back to Jordan and were seeking the Lord for direction in ministry.

Imad was a part of a local evangelical church, but the church was passing through some difficulties as it changed from being led by missionaries to being led by Jordanian pastors. Imad arrived on the scene, but he had no ministry and was looking for something to do to serve the Lord. His time in America had not only prepared him theologically, but it had challenged him about the social aspects of Middle Eastern Christianity. He was open to mission work, especially work among Muslims. Consequently, when Imad heard about me, he came to meet me and to see if there was anything he could do for us.

After listening to each other, we decided to switch our meetings from my home to a church. This way people were not coming to Abdalla, they were coming to a church. If the Intelligence Department wanted to scare people away, they had to speak against the church, not just an individual. It made sense, so we threw ourselves back into ministry with a fresh vision. We switched the meeting to a downtown church and we started with ten to fifteen people.

As the numbers grew, so did the opposition from the Intelligence Department. It all came to a head one day, as God allowed me to see how far the opposition had gone and to what extent they had been successful.

The room was full that night. I stood up to lead the meeting and Imad Shehadi was to do the teaching. Suddenly a lady stood up and said, "Abdalla, you need to know what is going on in the group."

"What?" I thought. "This is very unusual."

The lady made her way to the front of the meeting. "Abdalla, they are saying all kinds of slanderous things against the church. These people sitting here are saying that you are a hypocrite. They say that you are a liar, but I think that they are liars. They say good things to you now, but when your back is turned, they say bad things."

I was stunned at what I was hearing. I didn't know what was going on. "Abdalla," she said, "listen to me. They think you make money from gathering believers. They think you have a link with Israel. You work for foreign governments and agencies. They even say you built a house out of money you took from this ministry."

I was shocked at what I was hearing. I stood up. I was going to have to defend myself that night. I did not know it then, but the government of Jordan had managed to work through one of the local ministers. He is now no longer part of the ministry in Jordan but at that time he was an active minister. The Intelligence Department had found a way of passing wrong information to this minister, and this minister had passed it on to the church. It was part of the government's effort to demolish our church, and it was doing a good job.

As I stood up, another member of the group stood beside me.

"Shame on all of you," he said. "I visited Abdalla's home in the north ten years ago. It was built by Abdalla when he worked for the government, not from money collected in this ministry."

However, the damage had been done and it took a couple of weeks to settle it. I visited each member of our group, discussing the rumors with them. "Didn't you know me from day one? Didn't you know me over the last four years? Didn't you enter my home, eat my food, and even sleep in my beds when you needed to? You know me inside out! Didn't you visit my office? Do you not know those who work with me? Didn't you visit my home in the north?"

After visiting everyone in the fellowship and seeing the doubts on their faces, I felt tired and discouraged.

"Lord, what can I do? The ministry is not doing well. Should I leave? Should I quit and do something else?"

However, while there were those working hard to discourage us, there were those praying and working hard to encourage us. Imad Shehadi, Bob Clark, and the ministry team in the north always had positive things to say.

"Abdalla, you must stick around."

"Abdalla, this is the work of the enemy and we must resist it."

In the end, I decided to stay but I also decided that we needed to change our policy.

From that point on, as people came to Christ, I would work with them separately until I was convinced that they were on the right track with Christ. At that point, I would introduce them to the fellowship of believers.

Something was still missing, however, and I realized that we needed to think through what we were doing. We needed to develop some strategy. We needed to examine the things that we had learned and to establish some basic standards on how we would work together. With that, we started a new era.

We almost lost the church. It took over a year to discover in detail that each new convert had been completely investigated then threatened against even talking to Abdalla Hawatmeh. With time and threats, the people were gone. In the end, Imad Shehadi, Bob Clark, and I sat waiting for people to come. Only one person came one night, but we had the meeting anyway. We always had the meeting. We would have had meetings even if we were alone.

But the Lord was purifying the ministry and purifying us at that time. We lost many believers but it wasn't through any personal or theological issues. Even today, if I meet them on the street, they will hug me. It was not personal. They were simply afraid.

"Abdalla," one of them told me, "we can't be like you. You are courageous and you don't care. We cannot be that way because we'll lose jobs and family." These people are so dear to me, and I really feel for them and the trouble they are going through.

In the end, we moved the meeting to Imad's house, at the south end of the city. At that time we had only one couple and a single person. Three believers had stood against the pressure. It was better than nothing. We were happy to see them and we picked up again from there.

ONE DAY, THE MINISTRY TEAM DECIDED TO MEET and talk things over at a restaurant. We realized that we were working from a position of weakness. The evangelical church we were meeting in was itself struggling.

During the meeting, I started joking with everyone.

"Why am I partnered with a bunch of losers?"

We were all laughing.

"Imad," I said, "you're a loser; let's look for someone who can really support us."

Imad stopped laughing. He is a very humble man and he said, "I think you are right. Not that I am a loser, but I think you should find another base to launch out from." Imad later founded the Jordanian Evangelical Theological Seminary (JETS) and became one of the spiritual leaders in Jordan.

After some discussion, we decided to use my membership with an evangelical denomination to open a door into that ministry.

Within a few days of our meeting in the restaurant, I approached the pastor. I had a plan. The Sunday evening meeting had been cancelled as there weren't enough people attending to keep it going. I offered to start it again for the church. However, I had a lot of conditions. We Muslim converts would lead the meeting. We would promote it as a regular church meeting, and we would promote ourselves as a church body meeting in this registered church building. It was something I had dreamed about for a long time. The pastor needed time to talk it over with the church elders.

In the end, they agreed we could start the services, but they didn't agree that we could be our own entity. We started anyway, thinking that in time we would be accepted, either as a body of Muslim background converts within the church or as a separate group using the church building. In the end, neither worked out.

Our meetings didn't last more than a couple of years and then we ran into a wall. The local church accepted us as people who were attending the church. We were a part of the congregation, but we were always outsiders and never really sure of what was going on. We did not feel we were accepted as an integral part of the church, nor did we have our own identity as a fellowship of Christians from a Muslim background. I would lead the meetings and gear them towards the needs of those from a Muslim background. However, the Sunday evening service was open to everyone. Soon the local church agenda and our own agenda, as converts from Islam, started to clash. It wasn't working.

Finally, we Muslim background believers held our own business meeting and the majority said, "Let's get out of this place." We had nowhere to go and our numbers were growing. The group consisted of a large number of people I had prayed with personally, but we also had a growing number of people who had come to us through other ministries. In many cases, missionaries working in Jordan would direct their new converts to our fellowship and we would start discipling them. It took time to earn the trust of the church, but we really didn't fit into the main life of the denomination as we were solely interested in people from a Muslim background. The rest of the church was made up of believers from Orthodox and Catholic backgrounds.

I functioned as if I was one of the elders in the church. I would lead and sometimes preach. I even formed Bible Studies and discipled some of the regular congregation. I shared in the Evangelism Explosion program and other evangelism ideas in the church. At the same time, our ministry team shouldered the ministry to believers from a Muslim background.

In my heart, I really wanted to gain the trust of the church. I wanted to partner with a local church and share efforts and vision. I think the Lord gave us much grace at that time to do this. As a result, we came to a place where the evangelical churches in Amman began to trust us.

We could make a phone call for whatever we wanted. If we had some activity and wanted to use a building or to hold a baptism, to marry someone, or to do whatever, the Christians didn't ask any questions.

At least four churches certified the baptism certificates I had created. They never argued with the motivation behind the ministry. They never argued about character. They came to my home; I visited their homes. The local Christian leaders came to accept Amal and I as fellow ministers in the gospel.

That year was a year of growth and of testing. God used that year to help us gain the trust of the churches and to unite us against the pressures of the government. If we had not been committed and united with a church, the Intelligence Department could have crushed us again.

Nevertheless, the Intelligence Department kept up the pressure. By 1993, I was going for an interview with them almost every other day. I had started my own business but, through this pressure, they managed to see my business disintegrate as I wasn't able to work full time.

If I needed to travel to Syria or somewhere, they would tell me, "You can't leave; you must report to the Intelligence Department." I would have to leave the border and travel back to Amman and report in. Then they would ask the same questions they always asked.

Soon after this, I started getting threats on the telephone. Sometimes they would say that they would kill me or that they would put a bomb in my car. I didn't dare talk to Amal about it. One man called me several times at night and threatened Amal. "When you leave tomorrow, I will come and rape your wife."

I didn't want to tell Amal so in the morning I insisted that Amal come with me to work. Then while we were away, someone robbed our home. This happened more than once. They would take whatever they could find. A radio might be missing. Four times they broke in and stole our rent money. We didn't want to scare the fellowship, so we kept it to ourselves.

I had to check my car whenever I wanted to get into it. I had a mirror and I would search under my car before I started it. I kept the mirror in my trunk until someone said I should hide the mirror outside. "Maybe they will put a bomb in your trunk and when you turn the key to open it, it will blow up," they said, trying to be helpful.

Those were difficult days. It was hard to tell who was threatening me. Was it the Muslim fanatics? Was it the Intelligence Department? Then, during the summer of 1993, the Intelligence Department assigned someone to watch our home. They were there for more than three months. During that time, I often saw a man standing across the street watching us. I wondered about him and when I asked the Intelligence Department about him they said he was put there to guard us. What danger were they guarding us from? We may never know.

DESPITE THE TROUBLES, GOD WAS STILL AT WORK. We received many letters from the Christian Broadcasting Network. Through those letters we made many promising contacts. CBN was flooded with letters and they in turn flooded us with letters.

In response to these new opportunities, Bob Clark and I decided to formalize the lessons we were using so that we could train others to use them.

We began by analyzing what I was saying to people, isolating what methods and approaches were working best. We then compiled a series of six lessons which represented the materials I would share with someone who was interested in the Gospel. We simply called these lessons the Discovery Lessons. It wasn't long before others started using these Discovery Lessons and I soon started hearing reports from other countries where

Christian workers had found these lessons useful. A television documentary series based on the Discovery Lessons was eventually developed and released in video form and aired over satellite television in the Middle East.

Those years were the hay-day of ministry. God gave us contacts from all over Jordan. We had contacts with students from universities. People in the north of Jordan saw television broadcasts and responded. God gave us contacts with people in the Jordan Valley and from as far away as the Aqaba port in the south. We would visit Bedouin Arabs in the desert and wealthy people in their huge houses. I would drive everywhere just to meet with people. Most of the contacts were from CBN, Middle East TV, Voice of Hope, and Monte Carlo radio broadcasts. Others were just names given to me by other Christians in Jordan.

During this time, it was impossible to earn much money. Between the ministry trips and the interviews with the Intelligence Department, I had little time for business. My own small company, called Gadara Investments, was going through hard times, but I was free to take whole days to travel around Jordan visiting contacts and encouraging new believers. 1993 and 1994 were years when God poured out his mercy and grace on the country of Jordan.

CHAPTER FIFTEEN

Precious in the eyes of the Lord is the death of one of his saints. Psalm 116:15

ONE DAY I RECEIVED A LETTER FORWARDED TO ME from the Christian Broadcasting Network. The letter was from a young man by the name of Kamal Muhammad Saari. I don't mind mentioning his name because he is dead now, so the Intelligence Department cannot do anything against him. In his letter, Kamal mentioned he was crippled, but he only asked us to pray for him, nothing else. He said he was twenty-one years old and had been watching Christian programs on television from CBN.

In 1990, I started to visit him. I would go every month or two with my car down the steep winding road into the Jordan Valley. The Jordan Valley is one of the deepest places on the earth, and the Jordan River eventually ends in the Dead Sea. Kamal lived in a small village called Wadi Liabis along the valley floor. His house was on the edge of the village, which consisted of a cluster of houses with rough dirt tracks that ran between the dusty walled houses and yards.

Kamal's family were farmers, not rich, but not too poor. He had a mother, father, six brothers, and one sister. Kamal had Cystic Fibrosis and in 1990 he could still write, hear, talk and move his head and his hands. That's all. If he wanted to move from his bed, he needed to be helped.

At first, my visits were quite social and I tried to encourage him in his situation. After that, whenever Kamal was in need of encouragement, he would ask for me. His mother usually called me and would simply say, "Kamal wants to see you, can you come?"

"Sure," I would always answer and I would leave whatever job I was doing to go to him. I enjoyed visiting Kamal and I encouraged him to continue watching the Christian broadcasts that were shown over Middle East TV.

"Look," I said one day to Kamal, "you are a friend of mine; what can I do for you?"

"Pray for me," he answered. "Pray that I could be a Christian like you."

That opened the door for me to share Christ with him.

When he received Christ in 1993, it was the best day of my life up to that time. However, I knew he was dying. He had months or maybe even a year or two to live.

So I explained to him in three or four visits what I knew about Christ, and he confessed faith and accepted Christ as his Savior. The amazing thing was that he told his family about it. I didn't tell them. He told his own family.

"I believe in Christ," he told them. "Christ can heal me."

After that, for many weeks Kamal spoke often and longingly for healing. He really longed for it and soon I was longing for his healing as well.

Nevertheless, from late 1993 he slowly got worse. At that time he started losing his speech and one of his hands became completely useless. He could still hear very well, but he wrote with one hand what he wanted to communicate to me.

"What does Christ mean to you?" I asked him a few months later. "What does Christ mean to you, and what do I mean to you? And what can Christ or I do for you?"

Slowly and carefully, Kamal wrote his answer. "You are my brother, and Christ is my Lord, and what I want you to do for me is to bring me a wheelchair. That way you and I as brothers can go out of this house and have a nice time somewhere on the streets."

I was encouraged by his answers, but the wheelchair idea wasn't very practical. The streets outside his home were not really streets; they were rough rocky paths. It would have been easier for me to carry him.

Nevertheless, I said, "Amen, I will try to do that."

When I got back to Amman, I talked to several people and they and our little fellowship gave the money. A few days later I went to a health supply store, got a wheelchair, and took it to him. When Kamal saw the wheelchair, he just couldn't believe it. He thanked me many times. "It's not from me," I told him. "It's from other people who care and pray for you."

That day Kamal cried. I cried with him, because he couldn't express the feelings he had in his heart. Later that day we decided to try out the wheelchair. I carried his light body from his bed and sat him proudly in his chair. For the first time in months, maybe years, he was going outside.

The sun was shining and the heat shimmered from the rocks and stones on the path. The wheels left marks in the dust and sand as witness to this important day in Kamal's life. He was free of his bed and proud to be outside.

As we moved along the track, people would recognize him and stop to say something.

"Who is this with you, Kamal?

"This is my brother," he answered proudly.

"We know all your brothers," they said, "but this is not one of them."

When Kamal answered that this was his brother in Christ, people would scowl and shake their heads.

Others said, "What? What are you saying, 'Christ'?"

No one we met had a positive response to his talk about Christ. Some thought he was just sick and talking nonsense.

For several years our relationship progressed but, in the end, my visits started to decrease in number because Kamal was getting weaker and communication with him was becoming increasingly hard. In the end, I would go every two months and just pray with him.

I remember on one occasion taking some of the church brothers with me to visit with him. He seemed to be more encouraged. After that I tried to take others with me, and their visits encouraged him. He loved to know that there were Christian brothers caring for him and loving him.

Often on the visits, I would sing hymns for him. I remember Kamal praying for me. In his very weak voice he would whisper, "Father, help Abdalla to always be a brother to me, not just now but also in eternity."

I was relieved when I heard this. "Lord, thank you that he is thinking about eternity." I wasn't thinking that much about it myself, but eternity was drawing closer to Kamal. It humbled me that this young friend who, though he was dying, was praying for me.

During the months that followed, I received phone calls from his family. Kamal was depressed. Kamal missed me. Kamal wanted to see me. Kamal wanted me to come right now!

Sometimes right now meant twelve at night. But Kamal was special to me and I would get in my car and drive to the Jordan Valley in the dead of the night. The trip would often take one and a half hours, but Kamal was worth it. He was one of God's dear children. If it was too late I stayed overnight there, just so I could lie on a bed in the same room and talk to him, pray with him and share with him during the night hours.

To me, Kamal became more than a brother; he was a dear friend, a friend whom I joked with and had fun with. One time I drew pictures of animals on a paper for him; I made the sounds of these animals and he laughed. His hearing was perfect to the end and he enjoyed these games with sounds.

Then the fateful telephone call came in 1995. The Lord allowed me to get the phone call. His family called while I was out visiting. But on that occasion, I left the phone number where I would be with my secretary. I was actually in the city of Irbid when I called her and told her that if there were any urgent calls for me I would be at that number. I had never done that before, and I don't know why I did it on that particular day.

Later that day the call came through from Kamal's mother. Kamal was going downhill and they thought he was dying. I rushed to Kamal's home. I remember finding only three of his brothers, his sister, and his mother and father. Three other brothers didn't even show up. They were busy. So I was there and he died that day while I was with him.

He looked at his family and spoke. We were amazed that he could talk. "I want to embrace all of you," he whispered. I waited until the last because I wanted the family to go first. When it came to me he told them, "Yes, I have three other brothers that are not here, but it is enough for me that my older brother, Abdalla, is here."

It was so meaningful to me and to the family. They all shared how happy they were that I was there and later they let me carry his coffin to the graveyard.

Before Kamal died, I asked them, "Can I have two minutes to talk with him?"

They said go ahead, so I asked him some very straightforward and clear questions. During this time his brothers where there. One of the brothers left after a short while, but the other stayed.

"Kamal," I asked. "What do you see now?"

"Abdalla, I see Christ at the end of a tunnel opening his arms and he is calling me. He is asking me to come."

"Do you want to go?"

"I wish I could. It looks so beautiful there."

I said, "Feel free to go. Help yourself." I really didn't know what to say. It was like saying goodbye to a dear friend.

I was crying, but he was not.

"Abdalla, look around the country for more disabled people like me."

"Kamal, it is you who invited me into your life, without me looking for you. You are the meaningful person; I am just a

142

tool that the Lord is using. You were the one who called, and the Lord directed me to you."

I wanted him to smile so I added, "When you go now and see Christ, greet him for me."

He smiled.

"What do you want now?" I asked him. "What is the last thing I can do for you?"

"Sing a song for me."

I sang him a little hymn in Arabic. It was a song about inviting the Lord into one's life and asking God for forgiveness for what is past and what is coming up. Then I prayed for him.

All this while, his mother and his brother were with me and they cried for him.

Then at the very last, he looked at his mother and told her, "I love you, mother."

Then, suddenly Kamal was thanking everyone and saying goodbye. It was like someone leaving on a bus or plane. I then prayed with him again and he said, "Amen."

Then he prayed, "Thank you, Lord, for being my Father, for salvation that I have through the blood of Christ. In Jesus name, Amen."

He was fully aware and speaking. That in itself was a miracle. Then he left us very peacefully. That was July fifteenth, 1995.

Before he died, he had asked his family if I could help carry his coffin to the graveyard. In the Islamic religion, there is an open coffin. It is a box covered with a blanket and more like a long shallow manger, with four handles.

We did not have to go to the hospital or police. The family reported his death but everyone knew he had been sick. I helped the family wash him after he died. I remember sharing with his brothers while we were washing his body. I explained to them that for believers in Christ this body is just a tent. The real Kamal had already departed to be with Christ.

As we were washing, one brother asked me, "How can you wash with us? You are a Christian!"

"Why not?" I replied, "I will die one day and the same thing will happen to me. Perhaps then there will not be any water left in Jordan to wash me."

When we finished washing him, we wrapped his body in a long white cloth. It was not a linen cloth, but rather a white cotton sheet known as *al kafin*. We also wrapped his head in a separate piece of cloth. Then we wrapped his hands across his chest and, finally, his feet.

His body was so thin and weak it was almost invisible. He was so peaceful in our hands, like playing with a doll. We wrapped him, put him in the coffin, and covered him with another cloth, like a bedspread. Then we carried him into his mother's room and there we left him for the women to see. About thirty or forty people had gathered and the women gathered around him for the last time.

While the women were with his body, I went outside and borrowed a roof rack and placed it on the roof of my car. We then took the coffin from the women's quarters and placed it on the roof rack. The men walked slowly beside the car while I drove, and we started up the dirt road that goes to the graveyard.

At the top of the hill we stopped, took off the coffin, and carried him the last 100 meters through the gate to the grave.

A sheik from the mosque was waiting at the grave and the people crowded around. The sheik waited until the crowd had gathered and then he started chanting some Quranic verses. Finally, he finished and spoke directly to the coffin as if he was speaking to Kamal, as sheiks all down through history have done since the founding of Islam.

"Kamal," he said to him, "you are the son of a servant of God, and you are a servant of God. Now at this very minute two angels will come to you asking you a few questions. They will ask you:

What is your religion?
Who is your prophet?
What is your book?"

The Man From Gadara

He paused. "Don't be afraid. With no reluctance, answer them: Islam is my religion, The prophet Muhammad is my prophet, and the Qur'an is my book." I started thinking to myself, "You should really leave that to Kamal to answer. Leave it to him because he has different answers than you think."

His brother who had been with me in the room came closer to me and whispered, "What do you think about these questions? What is he going to answer?"

"Well," I whispered back, "he is going to answer differently." Then God gave me boldness, and I spoke aloud to the sheik so everyone could hear me. "Can I talk a little about him?"

"No," the sheik said abruptly.

"No, I want to," I insisted, "I want to tell you something about Kamal. I have been his friend for the last five years. And I want to tell you what I know about Kamal."

His brothers all agreed. "Yes," they insisted, "please let him say whatever he wants. He is a guest from Amman."

"Actually," I said carefully, "I'm originally from Um Qais, but I am now living in Amman." I paused, gathering strength. "I knew Kamal because he wrote a very sweet letter to Middle East Television. I am here as a friend. I am not here as Middle East Television or anyone else. I loved Kamal as my brother and my friend. Kamal shared with me before dying that Jesus was waiting for him at the other end of the tunnel."

At this, there was some mumbling from the crowd.

"I just want you to know," I continued, "that we as society should take care of these needy people. We should not treat them as just nothing. Kamal was worth much more than what you think. I think Kamal now is with the Lord and he is happy there."

Very few people came up to me afterwards, but one man came to me and said that he watched Middle East TV.

We buried him that day. Afterward, the family and friends ate food together, and I had opportunity to talk with different people about Kamal and about Christ. Afterward we became linked with a couple of other people who started studying the

Bible with us and some of them gave their lives to the Lord a year and a half later.

I miss Kamal; I miss him a lot. When I think of him, I become sad because I have lost a wonderful friend and brother in Christ. However, I look forward to when I will see Kamal in heaven some day.

CHAPTER SIXTEEN
The Word of God continued to increase. Acts 12:24

MARIA WAS BORN JUNE 8, 1993. What a joy it was to have our own little baby girl. We were now more than a husband and wife; we were now a family. Having a child, however, presented us with a new challenge. Would this child be registered as a Muslim or a Christian? God had presented us with new opportunities to trust him.

I went back to my lawyers, Asma and Saleem, and said to them, "Now I have a daughter and she is a Christian and she needs papers! Here is a baptismal certificate for her. (We had to have her baptized in the Catholic way in order to get a certificate.) We want to apply for her papers as a Christian."

The lawyers were impressed and took the certificate and all the other papers and we started again. They spent a lot of time, and I spent a lot of money, and in the end nothing came out of it. The paper work ended up on hold in the office of the Prime Minister, and it never moved after that. The Prime Minister's office just swallowed it up and it disappeared. Every time the lawyers visited the people at the Prime Minister's office, they gave every excuse in the books to keep the papers from moving forward.

By 1995, the government decided to start putting pressure on me to end my case. One day I was called into the Ministry of the Interior and asked to go to the office of Mr. Hammed, the Minister of the Interior himself.

Mr. Hammed got right to the point. "Abdalla, if you don't stop your case against us, we will open our case against you." It was a clear threat. "And," he continued, "we will throw you in jail for good. We don't care about your human rights case. If it violates Islam, then it doesn't matter."

I left, knowing that the government was becoming upset with me. Later, I discovered that the government was refusing even to talk about my case. They were upset that it was even being raised. However, they had to admit that it was a recognized human rights case. They admitted that it existed on paper. However, I was repeatedly told that now was not the time to discuss it. There were security issues involved. The case was closed indefinitely.

It was a very frustrating time for us. Our child was growing and she had no papers. Then almost a year after we started, we were allowed a short court appearance. The lawyers simply agreed to request a birth certificate for Maria, and so this was all they asked for. The court agreed and they issued a birth certificate. It was simply a birth certificate and said nothing about Islam or Christianity. After that, we requested a family book again and this time they issued one, but there they stated my religion as Islam. As Maria was my daughter and, thus, connected to me, under Jordanian law, she was considered a Muslim. It didn't matter if she was born into a Christian home by Christian parents, baptized as a Christian and if she herself chose to be a Christian. She was a Muslim according to Jordanian Law, regardless of Article 13, which stated that Jordan had religious freedom.

ALL DURING THIS TIME, I continued my work so I could support my wife and family. I also continued to carry on my ministry, receiving letters from radio and TV broadcasts and trying to follow up people and present them with the gospel.

I once had a letter from a Bedouin Arab named Mahmoud. Bedouin Arabs live in black goat hair tents in the desert. Mahmoud lived in an area of northeast Jordan called the Badia. This area is a wild dusty area full of rocky hills and valleys.

Mahmoud was employed with the Badia Desert Police Force and he patrolled the tribes in the desert areas. He wrote to me that he had been watching Christian programs on Middle East Television and was interested in what they were saying. His letter had been sent to Middle East TV, who forwarded it on to me. I then answered it and sent it back to the TV people. They then sent it to Mahmoud. It took almost six months for Mahmoud to get an answer from me. I then made steps to contact Mahmoud and visit with him.

I arranged one day to visit Mahmoud in his desert home near to the Iraqi border. I left Amman at eight in the morning and I reached the area around ten. I only saw three other tents in the whole area. It was a very rocky desert location, but there was Mahmoud waiting for me on the side of the road. I parked my car and we started to walk into the desert. After two kilometers, we reached his tent. I had Lesson One of the Discovery Lessons with me and I wanted to sit and teach him. Mahmoud however was not alone. His family was there also.

I greeted his father, mother, and brothers. His mother disappeared into the women's side of the tent and I was left with a group of men. We sat there and after a few minutes I saw that someone was slaughtering a big sheep outside. I wondered if they were cooking it for me.

"Mahmoud," I called to him quietly, "what is your father doing?"

"This is your lunch." he answered simply.

"Oh no!" I thought, "This is a hundred dollar sheep they are killing and they are poor people." I looked at Mahmoud. "I am here for a purpose, not to eat."

"First," Mahmoud replied, "you must give us a chance for hospitality and then you can do whatever you want. It is the way of the desert."

That day I ended up drinking coffee and tea and eating a large meal. Finally, I had to go home without teaching my lesson.

It was completely dark when I left and I had to pick my way carefully along the rocky path back to my car.

I had come prepared to do the first Discovery Lesson but I ended up eating a large meal and wasting a day.

A few days later, I decided to call Mahmoud at his work. This time, however, he was very scared and he seemed very hesitant to talk to me over the telephone.

I was surprised. I wanted to invite him and his family to visit Amal and I. They had invited me and I wanted to return the hospitality. When I asked Mahmoud about it, he was not as friendly as before. After some prodding, I discovered that he was afraid to see me as he had been called in for having had me at his tent.

His family didn't know about it, but he was called into the Military Police. Mahmoud was in the military, and the Military Police could make things difficult for him or even fire him. I hadn't realized until then how well known I was to the various Jordanian security departments.

AROUND THIS TIME WE HEARD OF A CHRISTIAN WORKER in Egypt who seemed to be doing very well at evangelism. Chuck, one of the young American missionaries wanted to go and see what he was doing. "Abdalla, I want to go and learn," he said to me one day.

"Feel free; I am not your boss. Do as you wish. We can all learn from each other."

So Chuck went to Egypt, where he learned all about contextualization and how to be a Muslim for Christ. They taught him how to pray facing Mecca and how to act like a Muslim.

In the end, this young man came back full of enthusiasm and announced that he was going to go to the mosque.

"Chuck" I protested, "you are an American. If you go to the mosque there are fanatics here in Jordan that can eat you up."

"No, I'll be OK. I got an invitation to go through the Egyptian guard at my apartment building. I asked him if I could and he got me the invitation."

The Man From Gadara

"Chuck, what do you want to do there?"

"I can go stand there and pray with them, just like they do. I can tell them that I am a Muslim for Christ."

"Chuck, I think I should go with you. I'm afraid that something will happen to you. I can act as your translator. You speak English to them and I will translate. Don't use any Arabic. That way I can be in between."

"OK." He agreed.

We went to the mosque close to his house. It was evening during the Holy Month of Ramadan. There were about twenty men in the mosque. As we arrived, a young man came to greet us and welcome us at the door.

"Hello; my name is Abdalla and I am a translator for this man. I am not here for religious reasons. I'm here just to translate for him." He smiled and we were off to a good start. But it didn't last long. They had some tough questions for Chuck.

"So you think you are Muslim?"

"Alhamdulila." (Praise be to God)

"What about your Islam; what do you think?"

I did not envy Chuck that night. He was squeezed and squeezed. Slowly they backed him into corners. At one point I told him "Chuck, let's go."

But they kept pressing him. "Do you believe that the Qur'an is the Word of God?"

"There are many good things in the Qur'an," he answered.

"No, wait. That is not what we asked. Do you believe that the whole Qur'an is spoken by God himself?"

Then someone else interrupted us in English. "Hold on here; you don't need interpretation. I can speak better English than your translator." He had a good American accent. Perhaps he was a professor in an American university. I felt really humbled by my English.

"Tell me, Mr. Chuck," he continued in English, "what does Islam mean to you? Is it running to the light from the darkness of Christianity?"

"Oh my goodness," I thought, "this is very direct."

151

"Well, there are many good things in Islam...."

"Let's go back to that question that my colleague just asked you. Did you say that you believe in the Qur'an as a whole?" He spoke like a lawyer.

"OK, Chuck, enjoy it." I said to myself. "You wanted this; let's see if you can get out of it."

Then to my horror Chuck said, "Yes."

"Excuse me please." I interrupted. "Can I halt this talk? Let's get out of here, Chuck."

One of the other men suddenly spoke up. During the discussion, he had been looking at me and not saying anything. He just stared at me. When I told Chuck to stop, that man said, "Excuse me. Can I ask you a question, Mr., ah… what was the name?"

"Mr. Abdalla."

"Mr. Abdalla, are you two evangelists? Are you trying to reach us for Christianity?"

"Yes," I admitted, still wanting to run. "Look, I apologize for my friend. He just wanted to share with you his love, through an Islamic jacket, but it doesn't work. We are Christians and we are sorry to have offended you."

"Why didn't you just talk to us. Why not come and say, 'We want to tell you about Christ.' Talk plainly. Why do you come here and lie that you are a Muslim?"

"Look, I'm here as a translator." I protested.

The man scowled. "You're here as his boss." He spoke like he was an Intelligence agent.

"No, I'm not his boss. We both work at different companies.

"You both are evangelists, and he is guided by you because I watched you talking to Chuck in English. You really wanted him to say something different, and you added some things in your interpretation. We all know English here."

"Oh, who are you people?" I thought.

"OK," I said, "I apologize. I am an evangelist. We just wanted to share about Christ."

"Why didn't you tell us from the beginning? You could have sat here in front, and we would have given you time and listened to you?"

"Oh really? I'm sorry. Good night."

Chuck was really ashamed of himself. "Do you really believe in the Qur'an?" I asked him later in the car.

"No, no, I just didn't know what to say."

We went home with our tails between our legs but determined to learn better ways to answer questions when they were put to us.

THEN THE MUSLIM BROTHERHOOD FOUND ME. It is usually easy to identify members of the Muslim Brotherhood. They like to wear loose fitting robes with bare feet and sandals, and all of the men have beards. The women are always veiled, and often they wear a distinctive head covering. In most cases, the men try to resemble the prophet Muhammad as much as possible.

The Muslim Brotherhood are the fundamentalists of Islam. One of their goals is to bring Islam back to its roots. Their hope is placed on establishing true Islamic laws and government around the world.

In Jordan, the Muslim Brotherhood have entered politics, and they have successfully obtained seats in the parliament. Around the fringes of the Brotherhood are smaller groups of more sinister Muslims whose plans include any form of force or persuasion to establish what they feel is God's holy calling on Islamic nations. These small groups concern the Jordanian security departments. In the past, they have resorted to protests, riots, and even bombings. Despite these activities, many Muslims hold them in high regard and, consequently, the Brotherhood is capable of rousing the Muslim masses to support some of their causes.

One day six men from the Muslim Brotherhood came to my office and knocked on the door. "Mr. Abdalla Hawatmeh?"

"Yes?"

"Can we talk to you about a few questions that we have?"

"Sure; who are you?"

They introduced themselves as Munther, Mohammed, Suliman, Kassim, Basil and one other. Munther was the leader. He was a psychiatrist. Two of the men had long beards; the rest were clean shaven. These were the kind of men I feared. They were highly educated and they had goals and strategies. They didn't go to the mosque simply to pray; they went there to make up ideologies, think strategically, and plan.

We sat at the conference table. "What can I help you with?" I asked with a smile.

"We heard that you are a priest."

"What exactly did you hear?"

"We heard that you go after Muslims to make them Christians."

"Oh, what else did you hear?"

"We also heard that after they become Christians you teach Muslims how to be stronger Christians."

I was amazed at what they knew about me. I was not a priest, but they didn't understand the priesthood of all believers. I tried to witness to Muslims and build them up in the faith, but I wasn't that good at it. Most importantly, however, they did not know of my background. They thought I had been born a Christian, so that helped ease the tension a bit.

They had over 25 questions, fashioned after Ahmed Dedaht's teachings. Ahmed Dedaht was an Islamic leader who used the Bible to question Christianity and try to prove that Islam was true. These six men had questions about the deity of Christ, the genealogies of Christ and comparisons between the Old and New Testament. They picked on the Bible, but they were very polite and well mannered. This made me quite afraid. If one of them spoke, the others would stop. It was like they were in a team.

I found myself weak the first day. They spoke about the famous debate between Ahmed Dedaht and Jimmy Swaggart and how that debate proved the Qur'an was really the book we should follow.

I then offered them coffee and, while I was preparing it, I started to pray hard, "Lord could you please take over? This thing is really not going too well." It took me fifteen minutes to make the coffee. I needed this time so I could pray. I then called another Christian brother, George, to come and help me. His office was just down the street from mine. When I called him I said, "George, please come to my office."

"Abdalla, I'm busy right now."

"Shut up George and get right over here."

"Oh, you must have someone, eh?"

"Just come please."

He came. He knew something was up. The Intelligence Department was monitoring my telephone calls so I didn't want to say more and George understood.

Before our coffee break these men introduced their ideas to me, and they stated their questions and objections.

"Oh no," I had thought, "I don't know how to answer all these questions. I need time to research them and to ask others."

While I made coffee, I prayed. "Why don't I go ahead with my own agenda?" I thought. "Why should I be tied to their questions? They should also listen to me and what I have to say."

By that time George had arrived and I asked him to serve the coffee, get himself one, and sit down with us.

"And George, you pray."

George had worked with me before and he was a good backup man. He was very hospitable and could put people at ease. And he could pray. George often depended on me to talk, but I knew that in this kind of situation there should be two of us and one of us should be busy praying. In a moment, George was busy with hospitality, George's way.

"How many sugars would you like to have? Would you like cream? Where do you work? Have you ever read the Bible? Oh, what kind of Bible?"

George showered the table with kindness. I had been missing this because of the questions they had asked. I was still reeling from the fact that we were having this kind of confrontation but God provided, through George, just what was needed.

We started the second round and I took the lead. They sat there and listened. I was amazed that they didn't interrupt me.

"Now, can you allow me a few minutes to tell you who we are and what we are and what Christ is all about?"

"OK."

"And no questions, OK?"

"No questions."

During the first round, one of them men pinned me down with questions. I didn't know at that time that he was a lawyer. All I knew was that he was a smart man and that he knew how to corner me, and he did it many times.

During the second round, we saw them carefully listening and taking notes. I spoke for almost an hour.

At the end of the second round they didn't reply to my talk but simply said, "We think it is getting late and we need to get back to you some other time. But why don't you come to us at that time?"

"OK, where?"

"We meet in the mosque every Tuesday at four."

"Oh?" I was suddenly wary. Government agents had been watching me for a long time. They had warned me not to get involved with fanatical Muslims. I told them, "No, I don't want to go to them."

"Why, are you afraid?" I hated that lawyer's questions, but I loved his style. "Are you afraid?" he asked again.

"Yes."

"Why?"

"Well, Islam believes in violence and I don't want things to get violent."

"Were we violent when we came here to your office?"

"No, but you are not in a mosque; you are in my office."

The Man From Gadara

"Our office is the mosque. You can come there and drink Pepsi inside the mosque. We have offices around the mosque. We can sit there."

"Maybe later, but not this time. I want to see you again somewhere. If you don't want to come to my office, we can go to the church nearby."

"OK, next time the church." They were very polite, quiet thinkers and willing to do whatever I said in order to meet again.

A few days later, we met in the neighboring evangelical church kitchen. We sat around a table, and the Egyptian caretaker served coffee for us so George could sit with me.

We spoke boldly and we spent time looking in the Bible. Since I didn't have any other materials, I used the Discovery Lessons that we had been developing. When we had finished, they insisted that the next time we needed to meet in their mosque.

"Why?"

"We will not be alone," Basil, the lawyer said. "You are going to meet our leader."

"Oh, who is your leader?"

"Sheik Mohammed"

"OK, I'll go." I didn't care if I was beaten up or killed, I wanted to go. My father had taught me that if someone visits me, then I need to visit them. It is part of the Arab code of hospitality. These men had come to me twice, once to the office and once to the church. Why shouldn't I go to them? If they are coming with good hearts to us, why shouldn't we go with good hearts to them?

But I wouldn't take anyone with me.

If anything bad should happen, it would be best if it only happened to one person.

I invited George and George refused, "No, not the mosque." He protested.

"Then I will go alone."

"OK, but we will pray for you."

I looked sideways at him. "You'd better," I teased. "Don't you dare not pray."

157

The Man From Gadara

THE NEXT TUESDAY I HAD AN INTERVIEW with the Intelligence Department, and then on the Wednesday I went to the mosque. I drove and parked my car in front of the mosque. That morning I kissed my wife a very long kiss. Then I told her where I was going. "What?" She had cried out. "Why there?"

"I was invited and these people seem to be genuine, so why shouldn't I go there? Jesus went to all kinds of places and did all kinds of things, so why shouldn't we?"

When I arrived at the mosque they were very humble, quiet, and welcoming. As I got out of my car, there were six or seven of them waiting on top of the stairs. Basil, Munther, and their leader came down the stairs to greet me. "Thank you for coming to us," they said warmly.

"You're welcome. It is my pleasure. You came to me twice; why wouldn't I return the favor?"

Basil looked around, "Where is George?"

"He is a rabbit." I thought. He is a praying rabbit, and I am a rabbit ready for the slaughter."

When we got inside, I was very surprised. They led me up to the front of the mosque in front of more than 45 Muslims, all of them Palestinians.

"Oh my goodness" I thought. "Most of them have Qur'ans." The six men and the sheik were sitting in front.

Then Sheik Mohammed stood up. "In the name of Allah we sit and think and talk about issues related to God. Please know that this is your home. This is your family."

"Thank you." I smiled.

"We have just a few questions," the sheik went on. His voice was so soft and low I could barely hear him. "We have no political intentions; we just want to talk about God." I nodded and they asked me the first question.

"Do you believe in the Qur'an as the Word of God?"

I was immediately alert. That question had been asked of Chuck and he had gotten into trouble. Since then we had thought a lot about how to answer this.

"Look, the Qur'an is not my book." I started. "It would be impolite for me to give any opinion about it. I want to say the truth, nothing but the truth. I might say something about the Qur'an that is not true, so could you ask about the Bible please?"

"OK." The sheik replied. He seemed to accept my answer as logical.

The sheik then showered me with questions. The audience just sat there. These six men, Munther the psychiatrist, Basil the lawyer, and the others also just sat there. The sheik asked questions for the next hour, and I listened and sweated and tried to answer him.

"Why do you want us to say that the Bible is the Word of God? Why do you want us to confess this with our mouths?"

I thought for a moment. "Do you want me to think and believe that the Qur'an is the Word of God?"

"Of course."

"I do the same for the Bible."

"Do you really believe that Jesus is God?"

"Yes, I do believe that."

"Why?"

"Can I ask you a question?"

"Why don't you answer my question?"

"I will, but first let me ask one question. Before I answer, I need to know something."

"Go ahead."

"Describe God to me." I asked.

"Well, God is holy; God is mighty; and God is living forever, from ever to ever; He is alive and never dies; He gives life and He takes life," the sheik paused.

"Jesus is all of those things." I said carefully. "Tell me, can any human being or man have these features?"

"Of course not," the sheik retorted.

"What is the clearest feature of God?" I went on.

"He is complete."

"Jesus is also complete."

"How can you say this?"

"Don't you believe that? Is it not in the Qur'an that Jesus had no sin in him?"

"Yes, but what you say about Jesus makes him just a prophet, not God," the sheik protested.

"Let's talk about Jesus' works. What He did also announced His deity. He raised people from the dead. I don't care. He could have paid someone to get some loaves and fishes and to hide them somewhere on the mountain and then pretend to give them out. He could have done many tricks. But who can be alive again after being dead?"

"He never died."

"OK, I know you believe this. But he is still alive. Who can be alive forever? If you don't want Him to die, fine; but where is He now?"

"He is in heaven."

"I agree, because He is alive. And God doesn't dwell on earth, He dwells in heaven."

It took us a while to get through the questions. However, God had prepared me. During the previous two years God had provided many opportunities for input into my life and, because so much had been given to me, I could give to others.

When Dr. Ravi Zacharias, from Atlanta, Georgia came to visit Jordan, several of us formed a group to study apologetics. Three or four brothers and several sisters and I studied once a week during the afternoon for almost two years. We discussed how to "not answer someone" but "how to help someone find answers."

It was important not to offend. It was important to help them see the light of the truth. In the mosque, I was working hard to apply the principles that I had studied. Ravi Zacharias used to drum into us, "Abdalla, take the style of Jesus. Take question for question. Don't answer; give a question to open the answer. Help people to find their own answers. If they find something very obvious against their beliefs, at least they will not come against you. They will find it by themselves and it will seem more logical to them."

God gave me great peace inside the mosque. I had never experienced a peace like it before. I loved these people.

Sheik Muhammad had another question.

"If you studied the Qur'an, do you believe that maybe God might lead you to be a Muslim?"

"Look, I would follow God, even if He would lead me to be a Buddhist. I don't care where God would lead me. I trust in God. If He wants to lead me to be a Muslim, fine. He would find ways to make it clear to me. But at this minute, I am really led to be a Christian. Now, I would like to ask you the same question. If God led you today to be a Christian, would you do it?"

"Yes, but we are fully believing that Islam is the only religion accepted by God."

"Again, what if God led you to something else?"

"I don't think so."

"Are you sure?"

"Well, I would go with whatever God calls for me to do."

"Thank you; maybe God is calling you to do just that."

He was very patient but persistent in his questions. I tried to stay calm and cool and to give answers that would prompt the listeners in the mosque to think.

After some time, however, I grew tired and eventually I gave a negative answer to a question.

"Why do Christians drink a lot, divorce, and commit adultery in these western Christian nations?"

"Oh, Sheik," I said, "do you believe sin is everywhere?"

"Yes, but Christians do most of the super sins." he said.

"During the last few years, I have discovered many horrible sins in the society here. Some are done by Muslims. I've discovered a brother sleeping with his sister. In 1994, I found an 18 year old girl sleeping outside my doorstep at two o'clock in the morning. She was cold and shivering and she had run away from her father who was trying to abuse her sexually. This was in Amman, not New York."

"He must have been a Christian."

"I tell you, he was a Muslim. He had the same name as yours, Muhammad."

Suddenly the sheik got excited. He raised his voice and started to shout. "He could not be a Muslim. You are not here to slander Muslims."

"You also not are here to slander Christians. You wanted to know more about the Bible and then we stared talking about the Qur'an. I'm telling you that sin is everywhere and sin is not classified by nations. These standards are made by God and not by you and me."

"Mr. Hawatmeh, we hear that you go to the University of Jordan and that you turn Muslims to be Christians."

"How did you know that?" I asked.

"I teach there, in the College for Islamic Law."

"Oh no," I thought to myself, "he is a teacher of Islamic Law." Aloud I said. "People are free to study the Qur'an and the Injil. People are free to choose."

"Yes, people are free to think whatever they want, but they cannot choose religion."

I said, "God only decides that, not you."

I was very much at peace during this time. No one knew I was at the mosque except George and Amal, and I asked them not to phone anyone, as our phones were taped.

I answered many questions but before I finished, I asked, "Can I say something without anyone interrupting with questions?"

"No," the sheik refused, shaking his head. "You're here to answer questions and to ask some questions if you wish."

"Look, can I ask questions to the people here?"

"No, you talk to me," he glared.

Then I started to see him as he was. He was a very strong dictator. He wasn't really that humble and nice. His personality was starting to show and he reminded me of a serpent unwinding.

Whenever one of these people would call him *Siyadi* or Master, I thought, "My, imagine having a Master who leads you into darkness!"

"I don't care," I told him, "I will talk to you, but you others please hear me. I am here as a friend but that doesn't mean I will say anything but the truth. Only the truth will save you. I can flatter you and say that the Qur'an is the best, Mohammed is the best, you are the right people, and after I leave I can say, 'You bunch of jerks.' I can say that, but I don't want to say that. You are good people and I want to be truthful."

I spoke about ten minutes, until he asked me to stop.

"Excuse me, excuse me, there is a prayer time coming up and we want you to leave." He wasn't very friendly and he ignored me at the end. Several others walked outside with me.

"You should forgive him," they said.

"I have nothing but forgiveness for him. I would be like him if it wasn't for Christ," I said sadly as I left.

THE NEXT DAY I WAS CALLED INTO THE INTELLIGENCE DEPARTMENT. The authorities told me that the reason I was picked up was that I was meeting with fanatical Muslims and they were afraid for the security of the nation. I didn't deny it. We had done five Discovery Lessons with two of them and three lessons with the full six men.

Then the Intelligence Department asked me to do three things. First, I was to stop my ministry among Muslims. Secondly, I must stop meeting with the Muslim Brotherhood and fanatical Islamic clerics. Lastly, I was to act as an agent for the government among the missionaries.

The last one surprised me. I didn't know how to react. "How much will you pay me?" I asked, rather curious to know what informers got paid.

"We will give you enough," the officer smiled. He named a figure, but it wasn't much. I felt sorry for any informers working for the Intelligence Department. It seemed rather absurd. They were offering me so little to give up so much. I had discovered something far more precious than gold or silver, far more precious and important to me than even life itself. They thought I would give it up with a couple of threats and a handful of coins. They

The Man From Gadara

had a lot to learn. Little did I know how soon they wanted to start their lessons.

CHAPTER SEVENTEEN

And they arrested them... and jailed them. Acts 4:3

THE INTELLIGENCE DEPARTMENT REFUSED to accept a quick answer from me. They insisted that I return the following Thursday so I could give my 'yes' answer to them. They thought their three-point proposition was an irresistible offer.

The following Thursday, however, started rather poorly. Laura, our newborn was only five weeks old and I had been awake with her several times in the night. Then, when I awoke in the morning, I had a terrible stomachache. Amal fed me some herbal tea and she sent a mug along with me in my car. I had only drunk half of it when I returned to the Intelligence Department.

When I arrived, I was politely ushered into a room full of uniformed officers. They reviewed my case and then listed off their three points again looking at me as sternly as they could.

"No," I insisted shaking my head. "The decision is no. I won't do any of these. I am a free Jordanian citizen and I will do what I like as long as it is legal."

There was tremendous tension in the room. Then the highest ranking officer spoke to me. "By the authority of the State Security Court, we arrest you and want to search your home."

A bad day was about to get worse. I told Amal earlier that morning that I would be home for lunch. But I hadn't told her about the eleven uniformed police officers I would have with me. I also hadn't told her about the plainclothes men that would come along! I didn't even tell her we would all be early for lunch. And I certainly didn't tell her that my guests would refuse her food.

Despite the tension, it was kind of fun to be sitting in the back of a nice BMW. There were two officers on either side of me, plus the driver. We drove like crazy through the crowded streets of Amman.

"Look," I said to them, "I don't care if you don't like life, but I love my life. Please don't drive so fast. Be legal."

They didn't slow down. In fact, they simply ignored me and went on about their business like they did this every day.

As we sped through the streets of Amman, I suddenly realized that they were getting closer and closer to my office. Fear began to build inside of me. "Lord, don't let them go to the office," I prayed silently. In my office I had stacks of literature as well as records of names, dates, and appointments. If they found those things, a lot of other people could get into trouble.

They came closer and closer to the office. Just when I thought that all was lost, they sped right past and a block or two further pulled into the Jebal Hussein Security Center. The driver went inside and I waited in the car with two officers guarding me. They seemed like nice men. So far they had been very polite to me, so I decided to ask them some questions.

"Why are you arresting me?"

"We don't know."

"What's going on?"

"We don't know."

"Why are we here at this police center?"

"A policeman has to come with us to make the arrest legal."

I realized that they were going to my home. As I thought about this, it dawned on me that this could be an embarrassing scene. Police would be swarming all over our neighborhood and I would be arrested in front of everyone. "Oh Lord," I prayed, "please help us in this situation."

The Man From Gadara

A few minutes later the police officers started to gather. There were uniformed officers, plainclothes men, and the *muhtar*, who is a civilian contact for the government. His role is to act as the appointed person in a neighborhood to lead the government to people who are acting out of line. His role is also to act as a social witness.

The police then gathered a convoy of vehicles to transport us all to my home. In a few moments we were off to my house. When we arrived at our apartment building, I asked the officers, "Look, can you wait down on the stairs a moment so I can tell my wife what is going on? We have a new born baby and I don't want to alarm her."

To my surprise, they were very polite and agreed to stay. So I rang the bell. Amal was surprised to see me and even more surprised when I said, "Amal, there is a group of people, police, who are coming here to search the house and arrest me." She was very shocked and then afraid. I didn't know what to do so I turned and invited them in. "Welcome into your brother's house," I said as warmly as I could. "This house is your house. Welcome."

Most of them nodded and almost everyone said, "Thank you."

When they had all gathered in my living room, I addressed them all. "I would like you to do two things if possible. First, please don't smoke in my home and, secondly, please be nice to my kids and my wife." I paused. "Amal, could you please make some tea for our guests." Amal smiled and everyone had tea while they searched our home.

The police were very polite during the search. They started going through almost everything, but as I watched them I realized that they weren't searching very well. They would grab something and put it down without opening it. They would grab a video and look at it without checking it. I think they were just intimidating me.

At some point, they asked me what was in the storage space above the bathroom. I had been dreading this question but had resolved to answer as clearly and honestly as I could. "There are over 80,000 letters from 80,000 Muslims in Jordan who have written Middle East TV requesting the Bible." I announced. (It wasn't really the truth; there were around 85,000 letters in two big boxes.)

"Do you want me to get them down for you?"

"No," was all the officer answered, and he came down and started looking elsewhere.

"What's on this video tape?" one man demanded.

"It is a children's program."

"OK," he answered and set it down. It seemed amazing that they believed our answers. Whatever we said, they simply believed and they looked elsewhere. They were kind enough to come quietly into the room where Maria was sleeping. The man said he would be quiet and he searched very gently.

Maria woke up in the middle and I wanted to carry her, but the officers wouldn't allow me so Amal carried her until Maria went back to sleep in her bed. Up to that point, I was handling things well, but not being allowed to carry my little daughter hurt me the most. I didn't argue with them or even ask them why; I just accepted.

It took them around an hour to search our house. During this time, they received many telephone calls and messages on their portable radios. Someone higher up was making sure that they were doing things in a peaceful way. One of their calls was even for me. A police officer answered his radio and then said, "This is for you."

I took the phone and a voice said that he was from the Intelligence Department.

"Please understand," he said, "we have nothing against you as a person, it is going to be peaceful. It will be only a few hours and then you can go home, but we want you here."

I knew then I was going back to their office.

Amal asked me if I needed anything. Should I take my pyjamas, my toothbrush, or whatever?

"No," they insisted, "don't worry. He will be back here in the evening."

But I had my doubts. I knew I was being arrested.

We piled into the cars and drove off. Before we left, I asked them to leave me with my wife for a couple of minutes (The kids were both asleep.) I said goodbye to Amal and we held each other, not knowing when we would see each other again.

Then I stepped outside and was pushed back into the BMW and whisked off down the street. I remember sitting in the BMW, looking back at Amal's face anxiously peering out our window and wondering if I would ever be back to my apartment again? I knew that Amal was thinking the very same thing.

The amazing thing about my arrest was that no one was in the whole apartment building, except Amal and I that morning. The neighbors were out. No one on the street saw us. We came and left and not one of our neighbors knew. God had answered my prayer.

THE GENERAL HEADQUARTERS of the Jordanian Intelligence Department is located in a section of Amman called Wadi Seer. The building was so new that many Jordanians had never seen the inside, not that many of them wanted to.

I was very impressed with their new facilities but no one offered to take me on a tour. Instead, they took me directly to the jail section.

In one room, they took everything out of my pockets and spread it out on the table. They even took my wallet and spread out the contents. There were a couple of soldiers in the room and I noticed that all of them were younger than I was and less educated. One of the guards was a young man, and I could tell from his accent that he was from Irbid near my hometown. This young man seemed disturbed by my presence. He was talking to me in a rough way like he thought I was an enemy of the people. As he looked in my wallet, he saw a card with a few verses on it. He picked it out and read aloud John 3:16. He snorted and looked at me. "What do you mean, 'Son of God'? What does this mean? Are you crazy, having this thing in your wallet?"

The Man From Gadara

One of the other soldiers seemed annoyed and told him to shut up. "This is not your business. You remember what the officers told us; be kind to him."

When I heard this, I knew I was not in any physical danger. At least, not yet. Perhaps God had a reason for putting this young guard on my case. "Why don't I explain to him what is being said on the card?" I thought.

I was pleased when this young soldier was assigned to escort me as they took me through the various sections of the security building in order to prepare me for prison. First, we went to the finger printing room. Then they took me to a room to register my belongings. There they took my wallet, my money, my wedding ring, and even my belt. I felt in my heart that I was going to be staying for a long time.

While we were walking between the rooms, I said to the young soldier from Irbid, "You asked me a good question when I was in your room. You asked me why I say that Jesus is the Son of God. He is the Son of God. What do you think?"

"No, he is not the Son of God. God is powerful and mighty and He is good enough for Himself. He cannot have another God around."

"So you think if He has a son He would also be God?"

"Shut up," he growled. "Just walk; don't talk to me!"

"If I am staying here for a long time," I ventured, "feel free to come and talk to me about this while I am in your custody."

"Don't ask me these things!" he snapped back.

Of course I wanted to know if I was going to be staying for a long time or not.

"OK," I smiled.

"Just walk," The guard growled.

He led me down the corridors of the brand new Intelligence Department Headquarters. The building was full of rooms and halls. As we walked, I thought perhaps my guard was trying to disorient me, but in the process I got a nice tour of the new facilities.

Again, I broached the subject. "Are you a Muslim or a Christian?"

"Don't talk to me about that. I am a soldier."

"That's fine, but you are a human aren't you?"

"Just walk!"

Later, I ended up in a doctor's office. He checked me over and everything seemed OK. The only problem was that I had a cold sore inside my lip. The doctor sent my guard to get some medicine right away. I waited in the doctor's room for almost half an hour before the soldier returned.

As the doctor put some medicine on my lip, he said, "You can keep this in your room."

"No, doctor," the soldier told him, "he cannot keep anything in his room. We will give him the medicine whenever he needs it. If it is three times a day or whatever, just tell us."

"OK, that's fine," the doctor said. "All I care about is that he takes his medicine, and you are responsible for that."

So we finished with the doctor and headed off down the corridors and through doors until we finally stopped in front of a heavy steel door. The young man called another soldier to open the door, and then he said, "This is your room."

I knew this was a jail cell. The first cell I was ever to see was to be my own.

It was maybe 3 1/2 meters square. I had thought that jail cells were tiny, but this room seemed large to me. It also had an attached bathroom. There was a bed, a table and a chair, and some writing paper and two pens. There were even electric lights.

The window was barred and looked out at the back wall of another building. No sun ever came into that room, but I could see light.

The guards then left the room and the door clanged ominously behind them as they shut it and slid the bolt into place.

Later I heard someone in the hall and the door opened. A guard was there with a blue, two-piece jail uniform. Nothing else happened. I just had to wait. No one said anything and no one asked any questions.

The Man From Gadara

The first evening was the worst for me. I was used to a very busy lifestyle, meeting people each day and going to activities each night. Now I was in this room doing nothing.

That first night, I thought a lot about Amal and the kids. I was sad, mad and upset. Then in the middle of the night someone came and looked in the window of my door and said, "Get ready."

"OK," I thought, "I'm going to be released."

But I was not.

They took me back through all of those corridors and, finally, I met again with Abu Sayed, my old interrogator. I had met with this man many times over the years. It was always the same man. In my first interrogation years ago he had been the nice man who had asked polite questions and he never slandered me through all those years. But he was an Intelligence Officer. He was always trying to trap me with his questions, always trying to get me to say things. In this, he was my enemy and I was his.

"Abdalla," he said, "we don't want to harm you."

I just sat there. It was in the middle of the night after all.

"Why don't you call your wife and tell her you are staying here. Tell her to bring pajamas and whatever you need."

"Look," I protested, "I was promised that I would be back home this evening."

Abu Sayed looked at me evenly. "That was a lie. I never told anyone to say that. You are staying with us until you go to court, are sentenced, and put in a regular jail."

"If I go to court," I almost hollered, "you will be the one in jail. Right now you are breaking the law that King Hussein signed. He made it a law for this country. I am here as a citizen functioning within my rights and you are breaking the law."

Abu Sayed was very upset. "Look, just call your wife and tell her to bring these things. In court, you can do your best and I will do mine." He paused and looked at me. "I'm a lawyer," he stated, looking at me out of the corner of his eye. "I'm a lawyer and a prosecutor. I will be the one against you in the court."

"Fine," I said, "Of course you know who my lawyers are?"

"No." he said and his eyes flickered.

"Asma Khuder and Saleem Sweiss. They both represent me."

Abu Sayed looked physically sick. "Oh my God," he whispered. "How do you know these people?"

"Well," I thought to myself, "I've given them a lot of money, so far for next to nothing. Too much money. Perhaps now they will be useful. I just hope that they are still willing to represent me."

That night they sent me back to my room and I wasn't called again for several days. Other than the guards who brought my food, I was alone. It was like solitary confinement, only Jesus was with me.

CHAPTER EIGHTEEN
But the church was earnestly praying. Acts 11:5

ON THE FIFTH MORNING, the prison warden came to me. He was dressed in his immaculate uniform. I guessed he was a colonel. "Abdalla," he said, "tell me something. Everyone is talking nicely about you in this jail. Why?"

"Why not?" I asked. "Everyone should be nice. You should be nice to me and I should be nice to you."

He laughed. "Look," he said, "if you cooperate fully with your interrogator," he paused, "then I will definitely recommend that you smoke."

I looked at him in surprise. "What?"

"I said, if you fully cooperate with your interrogator, then I will allow you to smoke in your room."

Then suddenly it dawned on me. Most Jordanian men smoke. The last four days alone in my cell must have been designed to bring the average man to the edge of desperation, craving for nicotine. I smiled and looked at him. "What else can you offer me? How about chocolates?"

Now it was his turn to look at me in amazement. "Chocolates? No, we don't have any chocolates. Why?"

"I don't smoke."

The warden looked totally flustered. He seemed lost for words. "You should advise me not to smoke then."

"OK, don't smoke."

He laughed. After that he regularly visited me, sometimes for several hours at a time.

THAT NIGHT THE INTERROGATIONS STARTED. Sometimes my interrogator and I would sit for hours. He was always nice but always in control. I eventually learned that I had been arrested for being a threat to national security. They were going to have a court case. My interrogator was going to be the prosecutor. He was a lawyer and could act as a prosecutor in a court of law. They were holding me while they gathered their evidence.

"You went to a mosque. Why did you go there?" Abu Sayed said accusingly.

"When?"

"The day before you were arrested you stayed an hour and 16 minutes in the mosque."

"That's right. Is it forbidden to go to a mosque?"

"No, it is not forbidden, but when you lecture about Christ in the mosque that is forbidden."

"Maybe you're right. Perhaps I shouldn't do it again."

"Before that you took the American, Chuck, and went to another mosque. You had people gathered around you there. One of them was a journalist. He could have put something in the paper and you could be in trouble."

"I was only a translator."

"Oh, really?"

"Yes."

"Then tell us about your debate with the sheik in the mosque. Who did you meet? What were their names?"

"Ahh," I thought, "he probably wants to know the names of the leaders of the fundamental Muslims."

"I can't give you names of others. They are not my church; they are other people," I answered, trying to avoid discussing fundamentalist.

"OK, you don't want to talk?" He picked up his telephone and called someone. Two men came into the room. "Do you know these men?"

"I think I saw them at the mosque" I answered.

"Where was this man sitting?"

"He was in the front row at the debate and that other man was kind of behind."

The interrogator turned to the two men. "Why were you there?"

"I was there to guard him," he answered curtly, pointing to me.

"What were you carrying inside your jacket?"

"I had a pistol and an automatic machine-gun."

"What were your orders?"

"To attack anyone who attacks Abdalla and to arrest them."

He asked the same questions of the other agent.

"Oh," I thought, "they really are serious."

Several nights later, Abu Sayed told me that I could call my wife. I was delighted and he left the room so I could call home in private.

"Amal," I said, "they let me call you. How are you? How are the children?

"Abdalla," she said with emotion. "We're all fine. Abdalla, they had a meeting at the church—"

"Hang up the phone," someone hollered over an extension.

"—all the pastors in the country are united in supporting you."

"You must hang up now!" Abu Sayed screamed, as he rushed into the room and grabbed the phone out of my hand.

"I'm sorry madam, but I must cut the line now!" He glared at me angrily and we sat in silence, staring at each other.

"How did you manage it?" he growled. "How can you be a member in one church and speak in other churches? How can you meet and have debates with Christians in other churches about how to convert Muslims? How can you disagree with people and still have everyone supporting you?"

"I really don't know. I didn't do it, but I praise God if they are all behind me."

"This is becoming a really dangerous situation."

After a while, he calmed down and we got back to business.

Once during the questioning he suddenly said, "We know you are a nice guy. We have tried everything we could to trap you: counterfeiting, stolen goods, prostitution, everything, and you didn't fall for any of it."

That got me thinking. They must have wanted to use legal reasons to stop me. If they did this, then it would not raise flags in the human rights courts. If I were caught with a prostitute, for instance, then the whole church would collapse. The police would have to deal with me, and the Intelligence Department would not have to be involved. The community and even the evangelical churches would be against me. We had started something that the local evangelical church could imitate. Some of them were getting interested and were even supportive of what we were doing.

The secret police wanted to trap me in some way. The thought had crossed my mind before. After every interview or meeting I would start thinking, "What can they do to get me in trouble?" I searched my car many times for fear that someone would plant drugs or stolen goods on me.

I would not sit with any woman anywhere behind a closed door, not even in my office. I knew a man once who told me to watch out. He used to be with the Department of Intelligence and he told me that they would use dirty tricks. He said sometimes they even got government ministers in trouble and thrown out of office.

Consequently, I was half prepared when they sent a woman to me, a really attractive woman. My hair almost stood on end because she was so good looking. She came into the office and asked to see the director.

"Did you have an appointment?" my secretary asked her.

"No, but I want to see Abdalla personally." She spoke with authority.

"Who is this lady outside my door?" I thought. I looked out and said, "Oh, my goodness, help us, Lord!"

If Amal had seen her in my office, she would have had a heart attack or something. This woman then burst into my personal office without listening to the secretary.

"Good morning," she bubbled.

"Good morning," I said carefully.

"Do you have a light?"

I was caught off guard. "What?"

"My cigarette, do you have a light?"

"I don't smoke."

"Can you ask someone for a light?"

"I'm sorry, I don't smoke, and I don't like smoke in my office."

Silence.

"Don't you welcome investments into your company?"

"Oh, OK." I raised my voice. "Suzan, can you see what she wants."

"Isn't this an investment office? Isn't it called Gadara Investments?"

"Yeah," I thought, "but what do you think? We don't just invest money."

She sat down. "Look I'm a rich woman."

"Oh Lord!" I said. Then I smiled and tried to be friendly. "I'm married now. Why didn't you come several years ago before I got married?"

She laughed.

"Who sent you here?" I asked.

"The company next door. Do you know them?"

"Yes."

"They are related to me. They told me to come to you if I needed a trustworthy man to take care of my investments."

When she said this, I thought "You're a big liar, they don't know anything abut my work! Either you are after something, or you've been sent by the Department of Intelligence."

"Suzan," I shouted to my secretary. "Please keep all the doors open, even to the hall."

"Why? You could close this door."

"No, please, leave that open."

"To be honest with you, I want to partner with you in some way," she said, trying to look serious.

"Look, we are not a company you can partner with. What do you have to invest? Money?"

"Yes, I have thousands of dollars. We came from Kuwait."

"OK." I said tentatively. Perhaps she was interested in business after all.

"I am alone in my house. If you are not comfortable here, you can come to my house and we can discuss business there in a more relaxed atmosphere."

"Oh no!" I groaned to myself, but aloud I said: "No, ma'am. Not even in my house. This is a business place and these are business hours. Could you discuss it with me here?"

"Look," she said, "Why don't I make it clear. Let's be friends."

"What do you mean friends?"

"Let's have a relationship," she said with a smile.

"Are you married ma'am?"

"Yes. Aren't you married?"

"Yes."

"OK," she said brightly, "we can be friends."

I scowled, suddenly tired. "Madame, did you finish your coffee?"

After she left, I asked the neighboring business, "Did you see that lady?"

"What lady?"

"Yesterday she was here looking all fancy and cute."

"Oh, yes, she came here a couple of times and she asked us if we knew the office of Abdalla Hawatmeh. We told her we didn't know who he was but perhaps it was the man who has an office on the third floor. His company name is Gadara Investments."

"Did you tell her anything else?"

"No, we don't know anything else about you. We asked her what she wanted and she said that she was a relative of yours, but she didn't know where your office was."

Now it was clear. It really had been a setup.

ANOTHER TIME THEY GOT THROUGH TO ONE OF THE BELIEVERS. He came to see me from his job in the town of Madaba. I was eating at a fast food place with some friends when one of the new converts came and drew me to one side.

"Abdalla, I have some ancient mosaics. I have a small piece here and I have a very large piece in my possession. Do you want to buy them and sell them to the foreigners?"

"Muhanad, what are you talking about?"

"I have ancient artifacts for sale. This mosaic is worth a lot of money."

"What?" I exclaimed. I immediately thought of one of my brothers who had found a statue of a king and a queen on our property. He had sold it immediately for a lot of money. It was an easy way to make fast money in the Middle East.

"I have a large mosaic." Muhanad went on. "We could cut it in pieces and ship it to the west. People there will pay a lot of money for it. I have a sample piece if you want"

"Look, do you want to call the police, or should I?"

"No, don't do that," he protested, and he took off. Some time later I saw him again and he confessed that the Intelligence Department had approached him, threatened him, and told him to do this.

ANOTHER TIME THEY SENT A MAN WITH A BUNCH OF FAKE DOLLARS to my house. I was at home when this man, whom I had only met once before, came and said to me, "Can you help me?"

"What is it?"

"I have dollars. Can you sell them for me?"

"Dollars? You can exchange them anywhere. Any money exchanger or any bank will take them."

"No, we cannot go to the banks," he replied shaking his head.

"Why? Did you steal them?"

"No, it is not good money."

"What do you mean 'not good'?"

"It is counterfeit."

"Are you crazy?" I got up. "Look, wait a minute; I will be back in just a minute." I went into the other room and called the police.

"What is the name of this person?" they asked me. When I told them, they said, "OK, we will come and get him."

He must have overheard me. "Please let me go!" he begged when I returned. Then he ran out my door and off into the night.

When the police came, they didn't seem to care that much. I was giving them information, but they didn't seem in any hurry.

"What's your name?" they asked me. I told them my name and they wrote it down.

"Look," I said. "I'm telling you about the man carrying a bag of counterfeited money. Don't you want him? Go run after him!"

"It's OK, Abdalla; there are many people like that." The police officer said carelessly.

"What? Oh, now I get it. Maybe he's sitting in your car now, waiting for you to finish here."

NOW IT WAS CLEAR TO ME. When Abu Sayed my interrogator said "Look, Abdalla, we know you are a nice guy. We tried everything we could to trap you: counterfeiting, stolen goods, prostitution, everything, and you didn't fall for any of it." I had proof that all of these occasions were traps set by the Intelligence Department.

"You sure did." I replied. "But I knew it. Whenever you sent me something, I knew in my heart that it was you. Listen, I would act the same, even if I was in New York and these things were offered to me. I would do the same thing and call the police."

I then remembered another event that had taken place several years before. Only recently had my office landlord, Mr. Suheil, discussed it with me.

"Abdalla," Mr. Suheil said to me only a couple of months ago, "what is it with the Intelligence Department and you?"

"What was this?" I thought. "Mr. Suheil was only my landlord. I saw him if I needed some legal things for the office or to pay the rent. Usually the secretary went to pay the rent. So how did he know about me?"

"Can I tell you something?" he said, looking at me. I nodded. Mr. Suheil was a big businessman, some sort of banking lawyer. "A few years ago," he continued, "they came here to this office. At that time, you didn't have a secretary. Do you remember?"

"Yes, I remember." I always wondered about that. I had a secretary, but one day she came and said, "Brother Abdalla, I found other work."

"Is it a good job? If so, congratulations." I was always supportive of people finding better things in life. "Where is it?"

"It is in a government office."

"Of course it is better than Gadara Investments. Amen, go for it. May the Lord bless you." Yes, I did remember.

"You were looking for a secretary," my landlord continued. "During that time, two officers came to me. One of the officers was a colonel and the other one was a captain. They showed me their IDs."

My landlord leaned forward and then continued with his story.

"Look," they said, "could we as the Intelligence Department bring a secretary to you, and would you recommend that secretary to Abdalla Hawatmeh."

"Why?"

"We simply want a secretary from our department to be in his office."

"No," I told them, "I refuse. He is a good man," my landlord continued. "I've never seen any immoral things going in his business. They are quiet neighbors, and I have a very good relationship with him. Why would I do a thing like that?"

"We don't mean to say he is bad; we just want to be close to the information they handle."

"Well, if you want to know more about his business, you could just ask him."

"OK, thank you for your time, sorry we bothered you. Please don't tell this to Abdalla."

"Well, I can't promise you that. Maybe I can hold it for a few months, but I will tell him one day, 'cause I want to die with a clear conscience."

I really respected my landlord. The Intelligence Department could have placed the best secretary in the country, and she would have accepted my salary of $100 a month. Of course she would have taken another salary from the government. I was pleased that my landlord refused them.

During my interrogation, I joked with Abu Sayed, my interrogator. "How could you do that to me?"

"Oh, so he told you about it?"

"Yes. He told me a couple of months ago. How could you do that to me, to send a secretary to my office?"

"Ah. It's OK; it is all in the past."

IT DIDN'T TAKE ME LONG TO REALIZE that the reason for my imprisonment was simply to isolate me and to put pressure on me. They also wanted to frighten me. The questions they asked were not strange to me. I had heard all these questions in previous interviews. I would sit for three or four hours in the middle of the night waiting for them. Then they would act all friendly and say: "OK, let's talk. What do you want to drink?"

It was a friendly atmosphere. They would ask about people. They cared about the people that I knew, foreign or Jordanians. They asked about my connections with churches and whether I was linked with a mission or not. What was my position in the mission?

I told them.

They then asked if I was an official representative for CBN. I said that I had connections with them.

"OK, how much money do they give you?"

"Nothing, no money. If I buy books from the Christian bookstore to give out to interested people, then I can add it to their bill. They send letters to me and I pay from my own pocket to follow them up."

"OK, what is your position in CBN?"

"I'm just a follow-up person. I travel around and follow up with people who have responded to the TV broadcasts."

"Do you do reporting for them?"

"No, I don't do any reporting. I don't even write reports. I hate reports. However, every now and then one of them will come here and we go out for dinner. We talk about TV, what they produce, and what is aired.

Once they brought a group of engineers and we did a survey on the signal reception in Jordan. That was the heart of my work for them. At that time they paid me one thousand dollars for helping them. I did not ask them, and I did not have a contract with them. But after three days of running around, spending over $300 on food and renting a couple of cars, they gave me a thousand dollars and told me that whatever was left over after expenses was for my ministry. I simply said thank you. They wanted to have a conference in the city of Irbid to meet with people from their audience and I helped them book a place and get things ready. I did some translation for them, but I wasn't involved in the interviews other than that."

My interrogator went on to ask about the names of the churches in Jordan. What did I know about this pastor or that one?

"I don't know," I replied. "These people are Jordanians and they have been ministering in these churches for years now.

Who am I to speak about them? I cannot speak good or bad about them. Ask me about the people I am linked to."

So they went into detail about the various converts in our fellowship. What is the name of this one and that one? What are the names of their wives?

"I'm sorry, we don't know their wives names. We call people by the name of their first child; mother of Mirwan or father of Mohammed. This is the Arabic way of doing it, and we don't care to know all their family names."

"What is the real name of Abu Mirwan?"

"We just call him Abu Mirwan." I protested.

"OK, OK, you don't need to tell us, we will tell you. His full name is Zayid Muhammad Ahmed Husseini. His wife's name is Fatima Mahmoud."

"Oh, OK. I guess you know this and I don't know it. It is not important to me. I don't know all the names."

"How many conferences did you have in the last couple of years? Where did you have them and who spoke in them?"

I honestly forgot. "Ask me about something that happened in the last year and I might remember."

"No, I want you to tell me. Who spoke in the last conference? Who attended? How many people came? How many nights were you there? Who served you? Who sang?"

I couldn't remember all the details of that conference. I remembered a few things but I had honestly forgotten many details. This irritated them.

"If you don't cooperate with us we will do something that will make you remember."

"No, look I'm an honest man. If I tell you I don't remember, then I really don't remember. So take it as it is. If you beat me up all night..."

"Who said anything about beating you up?"

"You said…"

"No I didn't. Maybe I will bring you a cup of coffee to help you remember."

"Even if you brought me all the coffee in Jordan, I won't t remember."

"Oh."

Then he went back to asking about names. I was very careful about names. I didn't want to give any names from my side. If they knew about certain people, fine, but I didn't want the information coming from me.

When he tired of asking me about the names of converts he switched and started asking me about missionaries. "What do the mission names mean?"

"I don't actually know what they mean"

"I can't believe you don't know. You work with the missionaries."

"Believe me I don't know. All I know is the letters in the names. I don't know what they stand for. I don't deal with these things. I don't need to know."

Then he switched directions.

"We know you are now a team leader in a mission. Why did Bob Clark leave?"

"He got a better position."

"What position?"

"He is the leader of the field."

"What is the name of the leader of your mission?"

"It is publicly known. You can look him up in any phone book outside of Jordan."

He didn't like it, but he wrote my answer down.

After a few minutes, he drilled me about my last trip to Egypt. Where did I stay? How many times had I visited there? What was my relationship with my host? Why did I meet in a certain home? Why did I meet in certain churches? They bombarded me with all kinds of detailed questions.

One night, we simply looked at pictures taken from my home during the search.

"Who is this?"

"He is a colleague of mine."

"Where does he work?" I told them.

Some of them were pictures from our ministry. There were photographs of meetings or of me baptizing someone.

"Who is this? Did you baptize this one?"

"No."

"How about this one?"

"No."

"How about this one?"

"Yes, I baptized that one."

"OK," he said and he put that picture aside and started asking about the next picture.

The Intelligence Department never kept the pictures. Perhaps they made copies, but in the end they returned them to me when I was released. However, during this exercise I noticed that they were very interested in matching names with faces.

They then asked me about particular meetings I had attended or spoken at.

"Tell us about the meeting in the east of Amman. Did you teach about baptism?"

"Yes."

"Who attended?"

"I'm not sure who all attended."

"What did you teach about that night?"

"I don't remember."

"Then listen to the tape, perhaps it will remind you." He put on a tape recording. I was stunned. I felt weak. It was scary but sort of funny at the same time. They knew the answers to most of the questions they were asking me. It was all a big game.

"What is your strategy? What do you want to do?" The questions kept coming. "Do you want to change your papers to become a Christian?"

"Look," I said, "I don't discuss this, I have a lawyer and he discusses this with the court. I am not in a position to say anything about that."

"Do you want Christian papers?"

"Yes."

"Why? Won't you lose your inheritance?"

"Maybe."

"Perhaps your family will kill you."

"That also may happen, but when that happens then God will allow it to happen."

"We will never allow it to happen. But you will never get new papers. You have your Muslim papers and you should be proud of them."

"I am proud of them. Really, I'm not ashamed of my Muslim inheritance. I want my legal status as a Christian, however, for my daughters."

Abu Sayed ignored me. "What are your connections with the surrounding countries? What about Palestine? Do you have connections with Lebanon? Who do you know in Syria? Do you have contact with people in Iraq, Egypt, or Tunisia?"

I tried to tell him.

"Don't you think you were going overboard to visit Palestine?"

"I didn't visit Palestine," I protested.

"You did."

"No, I have never been to Palestine."

"Yes you did, and you met with Jewish people there."

"Look, If I went there, I would tell you, and if I met Jewish people there, I would tell you also. But I did not cross the River Jordan to Palestine."

"What did you do in Egypt?"

"I spoke in a church. I was officially invited to speak.

"OK, what did you speak about?"

"I don't remember. Maybe you have a tape you could play, to help me remember?"

"No, we don't have a tape of that meeting," he laughed.

Then he got serious. "Did you distribute Bibles in Jordan? How many Bibles did you distribute? Where did you buy them? Where did you get the money from?"

"Look" I said, "I'm not very interested in simply distributing Bibles."

"Yeah we know, but you taught people how to do it."

"Not that many."

"What is your connection with the Catholic Bishop?"

"He is just my friend, and I go there sometimes to visit. He helped us to get married. He loves us and gives us advice about life as a married couple. It has nothing to do with theology."

"What is your relationship with the human rights organizations?"

"Very little. I'm not a great supporter and I don't go to conferences or anything. I simply want to claim any rights that are mine. That's it. I love the law and try to keep it. I am a law abiding citizen."

"You are not obeying the law; you are far away from the law. We want to bring you back under the law."

"If I am away from the law, tell me, and bring me back. I would appreciate it." That is how it went, over and over again every night.

AT ONE POINT, THE RED CROSS SENT A WORKER TO SEE ME. There were two visits, one person each time. Since no one could get in from the outside to see me, Amal called the Red Cross to see if they could do something.

So, one night, during my interrogation, they told me that I would have a visitor the next day from the Red Cross. My interrogator looked at me sternly. "Don't discuss anything with them except your food and your living conditions."

The Red Cross worker was a woman from Europe. When she arrived, I said nothing about my food or my living conditions. We only talked about my case.

"Your wife called us yesterday and told us about you, so I am here to hear from you," she said by way of introduction.

The soldiers closed the door behind her and she was alone with me in my cell for about an hour.

"I believe that I am here because of a human rights violation. I am here because I believe in Jesus. I was born a Muslim, but now I am a Christian.

I looked at her carefully and wondered if the Intelligence Department had hired this woman. How could I know? They could hire foreigners to go around milking information as easily as they could hire Jordanians.

"I was born a Muslim," I continued "but I became a Christian in America. I then came back here, worked for the government for some time, and now I am here."

"Why?"

"Simply because I talk about my faith to other Muslim. I do not do this to propagate my faith. If someone asks me what I believe, I tell them."

"Why did they arrest you?"

"I think it was for doing that, nothing else?"

"Did you ever commit a crime?"

"No. If I committed a crime, I would not be in this jail; I would be in a normal police jail."

"What can we do for you?"

"Get me out of here, that is all I ask."

"Do you want to send a message to your wife?"

"Yes," I brightened. "Tell her I love her. If you can visit my wife at home and tell her that, then I would appreciate it."

She did that and she returned a few days later.

"I have asked the Red Cross Headquarters to act on your behalf, but that takes time. We are very limited here in this country."

"I know that," I smiled. "We are all limited, aren't we?" She laughed.

"Did they beat you up?"

"No."

"Is your food OK?"

"Yes." I smiled. "Don't tell this to Amal but it is better than at home."

"I'm sure that is not true because I ate in your home and it was delicious."

That evening, my interrogators were visibly upset with me.

"How do you know these Red Cross people?"

"I don't."

"Then why did they come and visit you?"

"They were concerned."

"How did they know you were here?"

"I don't know."

"Why did you talk about the reasons for your being in prison?"

"My discussion with the Red Cross is my business, not yours."

They changed tactics and started on a new line of questioning. I was sure they had recorded what I said. They treated me like a mouse in a laboratory, trying all kinds of techniques and tricks to see what would work. Thank God I am still alive.

After a few days, these periods of interrogation really boosted my spirit. I sensed the presence of the Lord and I started to think, "OK, I accept that I am here. Now, how should I act as a Christian under these circumstances? How should I function? How should I talk to people? I represent Christ in this place and I need to speak like him." So I started to speak as a believer. I started to reach out to those who worked in the prison.

One day the warden came to my door and stood for two hours, from ten to twelve, listening and talking to me. Every time they wanted to take someone else to or from their cell, they had to shut the door so I couldn't see what was happening in the hallway. But he would open the little window in the door a few minutes later and stand there and talk some more. On another occasion, he sat in my room for almost two hours and talked about different things.

"How do you see politics?" he asked one day. "What do you think of the situation the country is facing now?"

"Well," I answered, "I'm just a citizen in Jordan. I think what you think. I disagree with the wrongs and I agree with the rights."

His face twitched a bit. God had given me the right answer to sidestep another trap.

191

I think by the end of the first week I knew I was getting out. I knew it in my heart. It was just a matter of days. Why? Because there were no more questions when they interrogated me. We talked a couple of nights the first week and then we met again another four or five nights the next week. One day he asked me to call my wife again and talk to her.

By the eighth or ninth day, my interrogator told me that Amal was coming for a visit on Friday. "Would you like to see her?"

"Of course."

"Your brothers also want to see you."

"No," I replied, "I don't want to see my brothers while I am here."

"Are you sure you don't want to receive your brothers?" he asked again. Again I said no. So they didn't tell my brothers. They were that nice to me. I discovered later that one of my brothers came to the gate of the jail, but they did not let him in to see me. They told him that I was fine and that he should go and see my lawyer. They assured him that I was in good shape and would be getting out soon.

Then Amal came and she brought a Bible with her.

"I want to send this Bible to him," she told the guards.

"Wait," they told her, and they sent for a soldier to take the Bible to me. The soldier who arrived was that very same soldier who had befriended me. "Don't worry," he told her. "Abdalla has had a Bible from the second day." Amal didn't know if she could trust him.

"This is a special Bible," she insisted. "Can you send it to him?"

He agreed and he brought it to me. So from that day on I had two Bibles.

Later, Amal was allowed into a room to visit with me. A guard was present all the time.

Before I entered the room, they said to me, "Don't tell your wife about anything that has happened or what has been said here. You can only talk about the food, your health, or if you were tortured."

"No," I said, "I will answer any of her questions. I have nothing to hide. If you want to stop us, then you will have to stop the visit." They weren't too happy with that.

"Next," they said, "you have to shave."

"No." I said again, "I will not shave. You haven't let me shave up to now; I won't shave for this visit."

"You have to shave because we want you to look good for your wife."

"Look," I said, "this is like a vacation. Maybe I'll shave sometime afterward."

Next they arranged so I could wash my hair. When I was done, a man came with a hairbrush to make sure that I looked my best.

Then two men in civilian dress took me away. We walked down hallways and took elevators and walked down more hallways. It wasn't really like a jail; it was more like a castle. As I walked down the halls, I could see rooms and offices with desks, computers, fancy elevators, and door plaques. One huge room was full of men sitting at computers.

Finally we came into a big room with a thick glass wall down the middle. It was a very modern facility and there were microphones and speakers so we could communicate through the glass. An officer would be with us during our visit. I waited for a moment and then Amal came in.

"How are you?" I asked.

"I'm fine." she smiled. She looked tired and tense.

"How is Laura?"

"You know, after you were arrested I didn't have any milk anymore so I had to start her on a bottle."

Then Amal started asking me questions. "So what is happening?"

"I'm sorry," the officer said, "this question is forbidden."

I waited until the officer was finished speaking and then I told her, "Nothing is happening; they are just interrogating me."

"We heard you are going to court."

"Ma'am," the office insisted, "you cannot speak like this! It is forbidden."

"I don't care." I told him. I knew deep in my heart I was getting out. "Expect me home any time."

"Oh I hope so!" she sighed. "Abdalla, do you want us to report this to the outside media?"

"Oh my goodness, don't do this. But be prepared; if I am not home by the thirteenth day, do whatever you want to do."

I said this because under Jordanian law the police can arrest you and hold you for thirteen days without charging you. If they cannot charge you within thirteen days, then they have to let you go.

As soon as I said this to Amal, the officer shouted, "Stop, the visit is cancelled! Please go, ma'am."

"OK, OK." I tried to calm him, "can I talk to her about some personal stuff first?"

"Yes, but this is your last warning."

"Amal, do you have enough money at home?"

"Yes, your brother brought seven thousand dollars to the house to help with finances and to help pay for the lawyers."

"Does Maria know where I am?"

"No, of course not. But she looks around sometimes for her daddy."

In a few moments the visit was over. I missed my wife and children after that but I knew that they were safe in God's hands. Later I would learn that a Christian women came to help Amal. She stayed in our house day and night and helped Amal make appointments with the lawyers and the Minister of Interior, as well as helping with kids and cooking. Other sisters in the Lord also came by to encourage and help.

My brothers were also concerned about me. It soon became obvious to them that I was more than just a curious Muslim looking into Christianity. Several times when they visited Amal, various evangelical pastors and leaders were also in my home to try and encourage all concerned.

My brothers were surprised at what they heard. "Here Abdalla is in jail and he is a minister."

My brother was shocked, but people kept on talking about me. "Yes," they said, "we know his life. We all know his testimony, how he asked the Lord into his heart many years ago."

My brothers sat silently. They didn't respond at that time, but our close family relationship was affected. From that time on they started to become more concerned about my situation.

Two days later, I was called back to the interrogation room. Abu Sayed asked me to call Amal again and tell her that I was leaving in two days. It was a very happy telephone call.

The two days passed and still I wasn't released. Finally on the thirteenth day after my arrest I was called into the office of my interrogator. It was 1:30 in the afternoon. I had been arrested at two in the afternoon, thirteen days before. If they were going to get me out in thirteen days, they would need to hurry.

First they brought me my clothes and asked me to change. I put on my own clothes, but when I came to put on my shoes there were no shoelaces.

"Look," I said to them, "I can't walk in these without shoelaces." The soldiers started to search for the laces but they couldn't find them. Then someone rushed out to buy me some new ones.

By this time they were getting desperate. Time was running out. They needed to get me out of there before 2 p.m. If they kept me longer I would have a case against them for holding me longer than 13 days without my being charged. They would need an official statement from the court saying that they found some new evidence, so I could be held longer.

The officer said, "Let's go out to your car."

But we had a problem. Stacked on the floor were six or seven large plastic garbage bags full of the things they had taken from my home. There were tapes, books, and literature. Now it was only ten minutes before two and he was getting worried.

"Quick," he shouted to some soldiers, "Come on, quick. Bring him some shoelaces."

I took my time putting them on, making sure my shoes were tied up good. It wouldn't do to have them coming off while I was walking to my car, would it?"

"Come on" he urged, "Just sign this and then lets go." He threw a paper in front of me.

"What's this?" I asked. I sat down to read the paper. It was nicely typed and neatly prepared, all ready for me to sign. It contained some very interesting reading.

> *I commit myself to helping the kingdom's security by informing the Intelligence Department about any sabotage or actions that people are planning to do against the government.*

I read further.

> *I will report about any conflict or potential conflict situations that might arise because of religion.*

"Oh-oh."

> *I will report to the authorities about my activities and the activitiesof others around me.*

"Never. I'm not going to sign that."

"Sign it, because it is getting late," he protested.

"No, I won't sign it."

"You will go back to your room," he threatened.

"OK, let's go back," I sighed.

He grabbed the paper and tore it up. "Come on, let's get out of here."

We grabbed the bags and started out of the building. He looked at his watch and saw that there were now only seconds left. We started running towards the gate.

Then he couldn't find my car. It had been parked outside when they arrested me but now it was nowhere to be found. He called on his radio to find out where my car was. Some soldiers standing nearby said that they had moved it behind the buildings so that it wasn't sitting out front.

"Stay here!" he commanded me, "and I will get my own car." When he arrived we loaded up my things and drove around the building. To my relief, Amal and my brother were waiting beside my car.

After we transferred my belongings, he shook my hard, "It has been nice getting to know you," the officer said frankly. Then he turned and addressed my wife. "Amal, I'm sorry for the trouble we caused you. Your husband is a clean man. There is nothing against him."

CHAPTER NINETEEN
Strengthen the brethren. Luke 22:32

WE WERE WEEPING AND HUGGING ONE ANOTHER as we stood outside the car. It was a few moments before we felt we were ready to go. I must have been a sight. I had an ugly beard on my face so we discussed getting me cleaned up before I met people. Amal then commented that our house was full of people waiting to greet me.

On the way home we decided to get my picture taken before I got my beard shaved off. We stopped at a small photography studio and had some pictures taken. The pictures were priceless. Amal was standing beside her bearded husband, so glad to have him back. I was glad to be out of jail and back into the real world. After taking the pictures, we jumped in the car and headed for a barbershop to get my beard shaved off.

On the way, I told Amal how much I had missed her and how much the girls meant to me when I was on the inside. I asked about Maria and Laura and tried to imagine what Laura would look like now that she was two weeks older.

Amal had lots to say as well. My time in jail had been a good testimony to many people. I shared about some of my experiences in jail and Amal shared about the impact my internment had had on the believers, both in the churches and among the converts from Islam.

The Man From Gadara

I couldn't help noticing that Amal had developed in her personality as well. She had become much stronger. While I was in jail, she had stood by me and fought for me. I was inside like a rabbit and she was outside like a fox, running around on my behalf. I appreciated her so much that day and I could see she had tears in her eyes as we drove along.

Once my beard was shaved off, I felt ready to meet my friends and family. First of all, my brothers wanted to talk to me. So we stood outside my house and talked for a few moments.

My brothers were very glad to see me. From them I learned that one of my brothers had gone to the gate of the Intelligence Department with a gun in his belt. He had threatened that if anything happened to me, and he swore on the Qur'an, Muhammad and God, then he would kill the officer who hurt me. He took out his gun and added, "With this gun," and put it back.

The soldiers at the gate were amazed at his guts, so they told him, "Don't worry, your brother is fine. Just go home."

While I was in prison, my brothers became very upset. Abdul Karim flew back from Saudi Arabia and they all rushed to see Amal. "What happened?" they all wanted to know.

"He is in jail because of his faith." was all she told them.

Of course they were mad at Amal. They were kind to her but still mad. Somehow they believed that she was responsible for boosting my Christianity. When they confronted her with this, she told them, "Actually, he boosted mine."

They were even madder then.

"Look," she protested, "I've known Abdalla for only a few years. You should hear about him from others. Don't just hear rumors and think bad things about him."

Amal then took my brother, Abdul Karim, to a meeting with some of the evangelical pastors. He sat and listened quietly. To my brother, it was a disaster. To these Christian leaders, it was a powerful testimony. They all shared how I was trying to serve the Lord in Jordan. Abdul Karim was horrified.

"Abdalla has been a member of this church for many years." The church leaders said. "He is an elder and practically an ordained minister. Abdalla baptizes people in our church and he teaches people." Once started they didn't know when to quit. "Abdalla also preaches in many different churches."

"Oh really?" was all my brother could manage.

We Hawatmehs have always had strong bonds in our family While my brothers were shaken, these things really didn't shake our family ties deep enough to separate us. The day I got out of jail, we hugged one another and discussed nothing.

"You need to come home," they said, "You need to see your mother. Please come whenever you can."

I nodded.

"Is there anything we can do for you now?"

"No, but thank you," I told them.

They came in for a moment, had the customary cup of coffee, and then went back to the north. I could see tears in their eyes and I'm sure that on the way home they were crying.

My brothers also told me that my mother had been sick while I was in jail. They all knew about it but they didn't want to tell me until I was released.

Once I was inside, I greeted everyone who was gathered there. Our house was crowded with over sixty people. There was a mixture of relatives, believers, and church leaders. Everyone was beaming and smiling. It was a great welcome home.

I was happy to see everyone, but I noticed that our neighbors weren't there. I then discovered that the neighbors knew nothing. Amal had not told them a thing. They were Muslims and we didn't want them to get upset. Nevertheless, the house was full of people. Everyone was gracious and we hugged and kissed and talked. Around six o clock people started to leave, saying that I should have time with my family.

Once they were gone, Amal sat beside me. "When I was young," she said, "we heard about lots of Christians becoming Muslims. But we never heard of a Muslim who became a Christian. Then, when I first heard about you, I didn't believe that you could be a Christian. However, when I got to know you I started to think. Later, when we started our relationship, I knew we loved each other. It was then that I started to hope that more Muslims would become Christians. I think I now know why God worked so hard to get us married.

Around eight o'clock, the doorbell rang. I went to the door and opened it. Standing outside my door were the six Muslim fundamentalist scholars I had debated with.

"Welcome," I beamed. "Please, come in." They stayed for only a couple of minutes.

"Mr. Hawatmeh, we heard you were imprisoned. We now know your story. We went to the parliament and asked them for your release."

I was really surprised! Imagine these Islamic scholars who carry Ahmed Dedaht's books around asking for my release! During our time of debating, I had been really hard on them.

"We came here to show solidarity for you and to show how we care for you. You are a good man; we love you as a brother."

I really appreciated that they came. It was a miracle that these men who knew that I was working to see Muslims become Christians actually appreciated me as a person and supported me at that time.

The next day, Amal and I decided to take a week off and go to Syria for a vacation. I wanted to check the borders to see if I really was free and could travel. That afternoon, we passed through the border into Syria and we enjoyed a week together as a family. For years, I had rushed from person to person, ministering to their needs. Now, God had shown me how much I loved and needed my family and how much they loved and needed me. We worked hard to make up for lost time. The girls were young so we didn't have to worry about their schooling, and we just enjoyed each day as it came.

As we returned to Jordan, I came back with a new sense of direction. I had made a decision while in jail. Amal and I needed the time in Syria to talk it out. I had only two choices. I wished there was a third one, but there wasn't. Either I would continue the ministry to Muslims or I would quit and leave. I couldn't stay in Jordan and not be involved in ministry. Every day I would see people and would have to speak about Christ. I was ready to quit and leave the country or continue full speed ahead. It wasn't much of a choice. I knew in my heart that I couldn't quit.

While I was in jail, I made a promise to God. It was something like a covenant or an oath. I promised God that I would stay at it. I would not quit. I resolved in my heart that, with God's help, I would continue the ministry He had given me. I made that decision on my tenth night in jail. That night I knelt by my bed and poured out my heart to God.

"Lord," I had prayed, "I believe you want me here. If I want to close my mouth because the flesh is weak, then, Lord, you open it. You are mine Lord, and I am yours..."

When I explained this to Amal, she grew afraid. I could see it on her face as I talked with her. She begged me to cool down and be wise. As lovingly as I could I explained to her what really good times I had had with the Lord while I was in jail and she was encouraged.

"If you think that the Lord spoke to you about these things, then I am with you all the way," was her quiet response. And she kept her promise.

A NEW PHASE HAD NOW STARTED. Before I went to jail, we had a church that met regularly but now the church was gone. People would see me in the street and wouldn't speak to me. People I honestly loved as much as my children. People I lived for and cried for. People I had eaten with. People who had slept in my home, and I had slept in theirs. But now they were afraid.

The scare tactics of the Intelligence Department kept them from talking to me. Even to this day, some of them see me on the street and they stop to hug me. I may visit them in their homes, but they don't visit me. This is fine. I don't care. I visit and keep reaching out to them.

The Man From Gadara

Despite this, I left the prison with a new vision of what we should be doing. The plan was very simple. We would concentrate on developing a handful of key leaders. By training a few leaders, we could then multiply ourselves more easily.

When I was released I started looking among the converts to see who were the godly ones. I knew one or two; the Intelligence Department told me about them.

A handful of believers from Muslim background had kept meeting, even while I was in jail. Four or five would meet in a park. Under the trees they would sit and worship and fellowship.

One night, while I was in jail, an Intelligence officer suddenly said, "Abdalla, even today they were meeting. What is this? They are meeting in a large park."

In my heart I said, "Praise the Lord," but out loud I said, "How did you know?"

"We saw them. Look, we have pictures," he handed them to me.

"Oh? Is it forbidden to sit under trees?"

"Shut up. It has nothing to do with that...."

That night I said, "Thank you Lord. Thank you because they are still together or at least these few."

After I got out of jail, I followed the new vision. We stopped concentrating on gathering large numbers and started concentrating on a small group of godly men and women who could be trained for leadership.

I invited the ministry team for breakfast one day. After breakfast, I told them my story. "Look," I said, "we need more Abdallas. We need more leaders who are better than Abdalla. We need new blood in leadership."

They all agreed so I began with four or five believers. Out of the four or five, we had two who were older and who had been Christians for years and knew the Word of God. They had faith in their lives. They worked and had good testimonies in their work place and in their lives at home.

Then we started training. We taught lots of lessons and shared various kinds of ministry together. We ate food in each

203

other's homes. Amal and I stayed with them in their homes. They stayed overnight in our home, in order to learn how we functioned as leaders at night and in the morning. Did we pray or not? What time did we wake up? What time did we sleep? How did we deal with our children? Did we help our wives in the kitchen or not? (I don't. I don't like the kitchen, but I help with the cleaning. I'll clean any room, even the toilets, but I hate to go into the kitchen except to make coffee).

"Look," I told them, "in our culture we must respect our wives. If your wife feels it is her place to cook in the kitchen then let her run the kitchen and you stay out of it. If your wife feels it is her place to clean the house then let her do that and you stay out of it. You can respect your wife by helping her if she desires this. Or you can respect your wife by letting her have a share of the responsibility and doing some things alone."

We presented all these subjects to the new leaders to be trained. Then we switched them to a more academic level of training with others from the Christian community teaching them.

Through these leaders we started gathering more believers. When I came out of jail, we had just a handful of believers who we trained as leaders. Within two years, we had over thirty adults meeting together. However, we were not just adults. We were blessed with families and children. Suddenly, we went from zero to eighteen children in Sunday School. We had a new face. If we were going to have Sunday School, we had to get more organized. We met together to share our visions of what was coming.

During those days, we met in a local neighborhood church hall when it wasn't being used for church services. We had moved out from the main church into this smaller church so we could have our own identity.

Everybody was encouraged. The ministry was moving ahead. I was being blessed tremendously by these people. Now, instead of rushing into the church with my mind full of the things I had to do, I was coming and doing nothing. I would sit back and do nothing in a service. I enjoyed watching the new leaders teaching. I was thrilled as one shared about communion and another one led the meeting. I could just sit back and I enjoy what I saw.

"Thank you, Lord, for replacing me with others," I prayed.

I used to do most of these things by myself, but no longer. Even today, I have the same vision. This new phase of ministry was simple. I was never to be alone in the leadership or in whatever role I did. Others should always be in training alongside of me. This had been in my heart from the beginning but I hadn't known how to go about it. Now that we were doing it, I found it thrilling. This approach gave people a new trust in me, and it gave me a new trust in them. When an opportunity for ministry came, I handed everything over to them. At first, they were surprised.

"Oh," one of them said, "we thought you really wanted to control things."

I just smiled and thought, "No comments. You don't know what has been inside of me from the beginning. I would love to dump all this on you and go back to doing just evangelism. That is where my heart is. Over the years I have pastored and taught, but my greatest strengths are in evangelism and discipleship."

Yes, Satan tried to use the Intelligence Department and my time of imprisonment to crush the church, but the Lord used it to build and mature the church.

By 1995, the ministries in the church had grown. Everywhere there were new faces. We even had women ministering to women in Bible Studies. Some of these activities were new to us, but they encouraged everyone. That year we saw more than fifteen people come to the Lord and stay with the church. One family with seven children came to Christ. The father had been a weak believer but he was good enough to ask us to come and share with his family. We came one night and we talked and talked and, in the end, they prayed to receive Christ as their Savior. All of them! I was stunned. "Lord, we were looking for one and you gave us a whole family!" Now this family is in the group, which means that we have teenagers to minister to!

This encouraged me. I could see that the Lord not only cared for me as a person but that He also cared for this work. It was a work that He was doing. From that time on I had peace in heart about the ministry. I was no longer under pressure to see people come to Christ. I would like to see crowds of people. But if they don't come to the Lord this week, it's OK. The Lord is the Lord of our ministry, and it is He, not we, who shoulders the burden.

God had given us the plan to train new leaders, but very quickly God would test us with the very plan he had given.

PART TWO

CHAPTER TWENTY

If any man draws back I have no pleasure in him. Hebrews 10:38

ONCE THE LORD HAD SHOWN ME that we should concentrate on developing leaders for our group, I began to look for those who could be trained in leadership. One young man stood out and so I began to train him as a leader. In the following months, he would become my greatest encouragement and then, suddenly, one of my greatest discouragements.

Ahmed was in his late 20's and our meeting was quite a surprise. Years before, he had been one of my students in the Air Academy, but I had long before lost contact with him. Then one Sunday, as I was preaching in a church, I looked down from the platform and saw Ahmed walk in. I was so shocked I almost stopped preaching. Ahmed looked very surprised when he saw who the preacher was. Several times we caught each other's eye and I knew that we couldn't wait to talk to each other.

After the service, I stood at the back and greeted people. Ahmed came up, greeted me, and kissed me.

"Aren't you the Abdalla who used to teach at the Air Academy?" he asked.

"Yes I am. Aren't you the Ahmed who used to be my student?"

"Yes," he said excitedly.

"So, why are you here?"

"I was going to ask you the same question!"

I just smiled so Ahmed continued.

"I knew there was something about you. You were teaching in electronics one day, giving us a lecture in digital techniques. Then in the middle of your lesson you said, 'We as humans, if we look around, we can see so much of the glory of God.' That day I decided to seek something different, but I haven't found it yet. Today I was passing by and I saw this church, with a sign that said there was a meeting. I came in and I saw you!"

Amal and I took Ahmed home. We had tea and we talked. It wasn't long before I started studying the Bible with Ahmed. It was so encouraging to see that he was genuinely seeking. Eventually Ahmed was baptized and, in time, he even had meetings in his home.

When we started leadership lessons, Ahmed was one of those chosen and he went through most of the lessons.

Along with teaching Ahmed, we also tried to find him a job. Eventually a Christian businessman took him on. He didn't care if he was a convert or not; he just needed a good reliable worker. He talked to me and I confirmed that he was a good man. He was smart, prompt and worked well. His Christian witness was exemplary to the small fellowship and he was bold but wise in his witness.

ABOUT A YEAR LATER, I came back from a business trip in Germany and immediately this businessman's brother, who was also a close friend of mine, approached me.

"Abdalla," he said, "can I speak to you?"

"About what?"

"How much do you know about Ahmed?"

"I don't know that much about him. He's a good man, a good believer, and a good disciple."

"OK. Could we visit my brother sometime?"

"Why are you asking these things?"

"It's nothing; I just want to make sure we are serving this brother fully."

"Why do you want me to visit your brother?"

He then changed the whole conversation, but I knew there was something wrong. We set off to visit his brother, but first he called to let him know we were coming. I didn't hear what he said on the phone, but when we arrived at their business, his brother acted normally.

"Abdalla," he said warmly, "we just want to help you in this ministry if we can."

"Wait a minute," I said, "you hired this person. This is not a ministry. You and I are brothers in the church, but please don't mix business with ministry."

"OK."

We had coffee and a nice visit and then we left. In my heart I knew something was wrong so I prayed about it and thought about how I could meet with Ahmed. I couldn't ask Ahmed what was wrong, but I could ask him how his work was going.

"Yeah," he said when I asked him, "my work is going OK. Why?"

"Oh nothing."

One month later, we were meeting in a church on the north side of Amman and Ahmed came in. Right away I noticed something strange about him. He was wearing dark glasses like he was a spy. I knew he didn't need glasses and it wasn't sunny that day, so a strange feeling came in my heart.

After the meeting I approached him. "Ahmed, is there something wrong? You are not the same."

"No," he protested, "nothing is wrong."

"OK," I said, "tell me what it is."

"No, no there is nothing. It's simple."

"Oh no," I thought. "When someone tells me 'it's simple' and 'there is nothing' then usually there is a big problem. Maybe someone in his family had died."

"Look, you can tell me," I gently insisted.

"No, you don't need to know; it is very personal."

"No, I need to know," I insisted, "and I need to know now." I realized that I was really getting on his case, but something inside drove me on.

About then Bob Clark interrupted me and told me that he was playing baseball at the American School. He invited me to come and watch so I asked Ahmed to come with me. We drove over to the American School but when we got out of the car, I accidentally took my Bible with me. I don't know why I took it. I had been sharing that day at the church and I forgot to leave it in the car.

While Bob Clark played, I spent time with Ahmed. I asked him about his problem. Ahmed was one of our brightest up and coming new leaders and I was deeply interested in him and his problems. He was like a son to me, and I dearly wanted to share in his life and help him.

At first he insisted there was nothing wrong but after a while he broke down and confessed that he had committed adultery with his sister.

I was absolutely shocked. That day was a black day for me. I don't know how, but I threw my Bible away in disgust. Bob saw my reaction and came running off the field.

"Abdalla, what is it? What happened?"

"I don't want to minister in Jordan." I blurted out. "I don't want to deal with Muslims. I don't want to deal with this." Inside I was crying out, "How can I tell someone that this guy is committing adultery with his sister?"

I was so angry and upset that I told Ahmed to get away from me. I didn't want to see him again. Then in the next breath, I asked him, "How long have you been doing this?"

"For the last year."

I felt sick. It had started after he became a believer! And he was in training as a leader.

"Why?" I cried out. "Why did you do it?"

Ahmed looked helpless.

"OK," I said, "I don't want to see you anymore right now. Just go and we will check back with you later."

Ahmed left us.

A few days later, I asked Ahmed to stop coming to the meetings and told him that we would arrange for someone to meet with him for counseling. In the end, an elder from one of the evangelical churches started regular counseling sessions with Ahmed, and Amal, my wife, started to meet with his sister.

Several months later Ahmed came back to the fellowship. We kept his situation a secret from the fellowship and he kept his job with the Christian brothers.

Two months later one of the Christian brothers came back to me. "How much do you know about Ahmed?" he asked.

At that time I didn't know how to answer him. I knew a lot about Ahmed that no one else did. "Why?"

"We've been concerned about your health the last couple of months," he said, "and we didn't want to tell you what was going on."

"What is it?" I was ready for anything now.

Once again we drove across town to visit the other brother's office. They asked the same questions about Ahmed and this time I said, "Look I don't know. Ahmed is just a person. I don't care what you are going to tell me. What did he do, anyway?"

"He stole twelve thousand dollars from us."

"You're kidding."

"No, I wish we were. We didn't tell you because we were concerned about your health. We knew you were encouraged with him so we kept this news from you for the last two months." To my amazement, they hadn't fired him but kept him working.

"Today he did not come to work. We discovered that he has been stealing from the deposits he was taking to the bank. Each time he deposited money, he would write himself a fake receipt for the full amount and deposit a smaller amount."

"Who is your stupid accountant?" I asked.

To my embarrassment, I discovered it was another Muslim convert. He was a very smart man but he was traveling at that time with his wife, so the deposit slips had been piling up. They had all trusted Ahmed. Even I had vouched for Ahmed's integrity.

"Look at these false receipts," I protested. "Even I can tell they are not original. How could you take these receipts?"

"Abdalla, we just trusted him."

When I left their office, I went immediately to Ahmed's home. Sure enough, he was at home.

"Ahmed" I said, "One question. Did you steal twelve thousand dollars from the brothers?"

He looked down. "Yes" he admitted.

It was like the stamp of hell to me. I was so angry. Angry with Ahmed and angry with Satan. "Ahmed, I never want to see your face again," I shouted and rushed home.

I was sick in bed for almost four days after this. I refused food and drink. I was fasting and sick. Sick at heart. A doctor from the church visited me and forced me to take an intravenous drip. "You need to have this," he insisted. "If you don't want to eat, that is fine, but you need to have this."

I finally stopped fasting but the sick feeling in my heart and mind stayed with me for weeks.

Ahmed still goes back and forth as a believer. Sometimes he attends church and claims that Jesus is his Savior. Sometimes we don't see him for a long period.

Then one day he invited me to his wedding and I attended. A short while later his sister got married. They had taken two thousand dollars from the stolen money and hired a doctor to restore her hymen so she was a virgin again. Soon after this operation, she was married.

Then, two months after his marriage, Ahmed had a child. Still to this day he claims to be a convert and says that Jesus is Lord and that he wants to be back in the church.

He told his wife, "I am a believer and I am not a Muslim anymore." Since she was a non-religious woman, she didn't care. I occasionally visit with Ahmed and try to minister to him. He showed so much promise at the beginning and caused us so much heartache and pain in the end.

The Man From Gadara

Sometimes discouraging things can happen. I prepared a leader for the church and he ended up not being a leader in spiritual things but rather a leader in sin.

If this weren't enough, only a few months later we would have another discouragement.

CHAPTER TWENTY ONE
Some fell by the wayside. Luke 8:8

FAISAL WAS A PROFESSIONAL ACTOR. He wasn't very famous but he acted on the various stages around Amman. Faisal was also a believer. He had been baptized in a local church by the pastor and myself and was involved in many of our fellowship meetings. Faisal was also a teacher in one of the schools in the nice part of town. He was single and had a beautiful house. When he came to Christ, we were so happy.

"Oh Lord," we prayed, "thank you for giving us some rich people during these last days." It was exciting to have a home in the wealthy section of town open to us. Sometimes we would have meetings in his home and sometimes we would use it to teach Discovery Lessons to people who lived in the more wealthy part of town.

About this time, we had a very beautiful believer named Maha. She was a wonderful believer and we were very encouraged by her Christian life. She was a jewel to us. Over time, Faisal began to take an interest in Maha.

I didn't really mind this until one day when I took a couple of new young men over to Faisal's house to introduce them to Faisal. When we were driving away from his home, a neighbor motioned for me to stop my car. When I stopped he said, "Who are you?"

"Who are you that is asking us?" I asked back.

"Did you come to see Mr. Faisal?"

"Yes."

"He seems to be a nice guy."

"Why are we having this conversation?" I thought to myself.

"Look," he said, "could you please be careful?"

"Why?"

"Just be careful; that is all I'm saying." He turned to leave.

I left for home with thousands of questions on my mind. When I got home to Amal, I told her, "I want to go back tonight, late tonight, to visit Faisal." Amal didn't disagree with me. She has always been supportive.

So I came back to Faisal's home and knocked on the door. Faisal opened the door and seemed surprised to see me.

"Faisal," I said, "I want to ask you a few questions."

"OK," he said, "come on in."

When we were seated inside I continued with my question. "Why did your neighbor ask me to be careful if I dealt with you?"

"Which neighbor was that?"

I told him and he laughed, "Oh, that neighbor. He is with the Department of Intelligence."

"What? Are you sure?"

"Yeah. He's an officer in the secret police."

"No, he can't be," I said. "His car license plate has a 211 number. That means he is in the army. We have army officers all over the place. He is not in the secret police."

"No, Abdalla," Faisal countered. "I'm sure he is with the secret police."

"No, he is not Faisal. He has a Lancer car and a 211 number. That is army."

"OK, maybe you are right."

"Are you hiding something, Faisal? " I was still upset over the situation with Ahmed and I felt I couldn't tolerate darkness anymore. I wondered about Faisal. He was an actor and he used to tell us stories, wild stories, and we used to believe him. One day, he told us that three guys with cloth wrapped around their heads attacked him at night. He said that he could only see their eyes, and he showed us the blue and red bruises.

"Wow, that's terrible." I had exclaimed. "We should pray for you. Have you called the police?"

"No, don't call the police," he said shaking his head.

Sitting in Faisal's house, I suddenly remembered these stories and was suspicious. Ahmed had put some bad seeds in my life and now I was suspecting everyone. I didn't want to argue, so I left Faisal's house.

Several days later, Chuck, some others, and I were in Faisal's home, practicing for a play about the prodigal son. It was to be performed at a retreat that was soon coming up.

Abdalla," Faisal said to me, "can I talk to you for a moment?"

"OK," I said, and we stepped a bit apart from the others.

"Abdalla, I want to marry Maha."

Suddenly I became defensive. I felt like a father to Maha.

"Don't even think about it." I told him. "Don't even dream about it."

"Why not? I am a teacher. I have a master's degree. I have this home."

"Yes, I know that, but you haven't got a strong faith. Faisal, she is too good for you. You don't deserve her at all."

After dealing with Ahmed, I had trouble tolerating any sin. Something about Faisal made me uneasy.

"No," I told him, "the answer is no. Don't even start to proceed."

The next day I told Maha about our conversation.

"Look," I told her, "if Faisal approaches you, can you say no to him?"

"Whatever you want, Abdalla," she said simply, "I will do as you wish."

Of course, this was asking a lot. Faisal was a nice good-looking guy with an education, a house and a job as a teacher. He was about to buy a new car and he was everything that a girl might be looking for.

Maha also had a master's degree and her family was pushing her and persecuting her. They desperately wanted her to marry a good Muslim. Faisal looked like a good match for a girl who desperately needed to get married. Despite this, Maha agreed with me. She was a faithful sister.

NOT LONG AFTER THIS, I had something to discuss with Faisal about the upcoming retreat. The retreat was only 48 hours away, and there was very little time to waste. It was about two a.m. and I needed to see him. We discussed very little over the telephone as we were afraid that they were taped. I drove over to Faisal's house to talk with him.

It was late and it was cold. I knocked on the door until Faisal opened. I looked at his eyes and he was wide-awake. He had not been sleeping. You could see if someone was sleeping or not. Faisal was wide-awake and he seemed ashamed to see me.

I wanted to come into the house but Faisal blocked the door. He wanted to talk on the doorstep.

"I need to get in," I thought to myself, so out loud I said, "Hey, how is your house?" and I pushed my way in.

"What would you like to drink?" Faisal asked when I was inside. "Should we have coffee or tea?"

"No," I said, "let's talk first and then we can drink coffee or tea."

"OK, what do you want to talk about?"

I mentioned the things that we needed to go over, about the upcoming retreat and the play.

"OK, I got that." he said, "Coffee or tea?"

"Coffee."

Faisal went to get the coffee and I went to see the other rooms in the house. When I came into Faisal's bedroom, I found a young boy about thirteen years old. I always found it strange that Faisal had a double bed. Perhaps it was just that he liked to spend his money. But that night I smelled sin in that house and I knew something was wrong. When I came to his room and put on the lights, there was this child in his underwear. He was just a child, but you could see terrible shame on his face.

Faisal burst in behind me and he was outraged. "This is my brother's son!" he shouted. Then he started yelling at the boy. "Why are you here in this room? I asked you to go home."

"Shut up, Faisal," I said. "I don't want your coffee; I want you to·tell me the truth. What did you do with this child? Tell me!"

"I swear by God, Abdalla, there is nothing."

The boy tried explaining things, but he only contradicted Faisal. In the end, I realized that they were just working hard to make up excuses. What hurt me so much was that the next day Faisal needed to be on the stage playing the part of the prodigal son in our church play. Faisal played the leading role and the whole play was written around his acting ability. I had to make a decision and I needed to do it right there and then. Should I let Faisal proceed? This was to be our largest conference yet. There were people invited and things were all planned. He had done the prodigal son play before. This was the second time and now the script was far more developed.

Suddenly I decided. I didn't care about the conference. I had been confronted with what the Bible clearly called sin. I would not let him on the stage. I told him so and then left.

I was so upset that I couldn't sleep. In the middle of the night I called one of the other brothers to talk and pray.

Faisal left us on his own accord. No one kicked him out. I told him that he couldn't perform in the play at the conference; he decided that he couldn't face the group. He had often been the center of attention in our fellowship and he was interested in marrying Maha. Only God spared Maha.

The church doesn't know about a lot of these things. Amal and I carried most of these burdens ourselves. The church is precious to us, but we stand against sin. If someone is sinning, we must say, "Excuse me, this is sin. Stop it or leave." I love the people but I hate the sin.

The Man From Gadara

It always saddened us when someone loved their sin more than they loved God. It was almost as sad as finding out that someone was an informer. And that is what happened next.

CHAPTER TWENTY TWO
Woe to that man who betrays him. Luke 22:22

BY 1995, THE JORDANIAN GOVERNMENT had still not fully registered my children. I discussed this problem with my wife and the lawyers, and we decided to take all the family to Germany to try from there. There was a human rights organization related with the United Nations in Frankfurt. We had a lot of discussion with them and then we decided to sue the government of Jordan for not recognizing the Christianity of my daughters.

During the discussions, they asked us, "Do you want us to move legally in the courts, or do you want us to move personally with the king, or what?"

My lawyers reacted very strongly. "Look," they insisted, "we don't advise you to move legally. In Jordan, the government could turn around and hurt you. The government of Jordan, and especially King Hussein, are so smart that they can crush you."

"OK," I responded, "Let's try and reach the king personally."

One German members of parliament who was participating in the discussions put forward an offer. "I will talk to the king personally about your daughters and you when he comes here for vacation." he promised.

We decided to take that approach and we returned to Jordan. Unfortunately, to my knowledge, this man never spoke with the king on our behalf.

Other people and organizations from the outside have since offered to intervene in our case, but we are now afraid that it might bring danger to the believers here in Jordan. These people offered to come to Jordan and make a big fuss over us, but we preferred that we move quietly through the government without a big fuss. If a big fuss is made, not only will we as a family be drawn into the public view, but many of the converts here might also be exposed. Once public view is focused on us, then the Muslim fanatics will have new targets.

So, in the end, we returned to a quiet role, ministering Jesus to those who were seeking Him and trusting God to provide the needed papers when we really needed them.

ONE DAY THE INTELLIGENCE DEPARTMENT CALLED ME, as they often do, and tried bargaining with me. "If you will stop your ministry here we will give you all the papers you need," they offered proudly. "We will write in your family book that you are all Christians."

I wondered if this might be the break we were looking for. But after a short pause they continued, "Of course, you will have to leave the country."

I almost laughed at them. "Look," I said, "if I leave Jordan, I don't need your family book. In other countries, no one cares what religion I have."

We then threw ourselves back into the ministry, and the next few months were a real encouragement. In fact, there was such a good atmosphere that one day we said, "Let's do a retreat for everyone in the country. Let's invite everyone together, but not just our small group here in Amman. Let's invite others from neighboring countries as well."

Suddenly, everyone was excited about the possibilities. A committee was formed and they immediately got to work booking a conference center, lining up speakers, and inviting guests.

The Man From Gadara

We had our best retreat ever in 1996. We had had three retreats in the past, but this retreat was special. Previously, I did almost everything. I invited the people, booked the conference center, arranged transport, and decided who should bring what. It seemed that during those retreats, everyone was saying, "See Abdalla... Ask Abdalla...Go see Abdalla about it. Abdalla this... and Abdalla that...." I was getting sick of hearing 'Abdalla' at that time.

However, in 1996, I was just invited like anyone else. I wasn't in charge and it was a wonderful experience. Because I was considered the pastor, I was on the committee, but we also had two sisters and three brothers on the committee. They took care of the food and how it was to be cooked and served. They discussed who would teach, and they gave me part of that responsibility.

"Abdalla," they said, "can you do this?"

"OK, sure," I replied, "whatever you would like."

"Could you also bring..."

It was so nice to be simply a part of something that was happening. It meant that whatever was happening was now bigger than I was.

We had our forty eight hour retreat at a Christian retreat center on the edge of Amman. We stayed there two nights and we had a lovely time. People came from all of the cities in Jordan. We gathered over 75 converts, but what was dear to all of us was that there were also converts from neighboring countries. We had a marvelous time together.

The first evening, I was so happy when I saw the host and hostess in their best clothes standing at the gate. "Welcome here!" they greeted each person warmly. "It's so good to have you with us." They meant it. Each one was special. The whole retreat was special.

The committee had asked me to come up with a theme and the Lord gave me the verse, "They come from the east and the west and they sit in the lap of Abraham." An artist even made banners and posters from this verse. The meetings were wonderful as well, as the Lord provided wonderful music and speakers. Our play, "The Prodigal Son" was enjoyed by all; even though we had to switch actors at the last minute, God stepped in and helped make the play a wonderful success.

Before the retreat, I had searched for a suitable music group. The best group seemed to the one headed up by a young Christian man. His father was a local minister and the entire family was very musical.

When I tracked down the young man he told me that they couldn't possibly come. "Look," I implored him, "we want some worship music in our meetings. We need good music. The committee has asked me to get you and your Christian music group to provide us with music."

He shook his head. "It's impossible; we've been around for only two years and everyone is spread all over. It's so hard to get us all together that we don't even go to churches if they want us. It's impossible."

"Good!" I smiled, "I love impossible things. You've given me more appetite for this. You are going to come. I won't take no for an answer."

"But Abdalla, it's really hard!"

"I love it!" I beamed. "I love it because it's hard. Look, we don't need the whole team…"

"But it takes time to gather these people."

"And you have a week."

"Abdalla!"

"Look, give me their phone numbers. I can call them."

In the end, he agreed and we had eight people from his group, singing and sharing.

When it was time for them to start, I told him, "In my heart I want to see a Muslim woman free to sing with full freedom and joy. I want her to sing in the presence of her husband, with no shame. I want her to worship without fear of what her husband or others will think of her." I looked him in the eye. "I want Muslim women to get out of the Islamic prison and discover freedom in Christ."

"OK," he smiled warmly, "we will do our best."

They did better than that. As the group sang we saw heaven touch earth that day.

After the singing, I saw Um Mirwan going forward to the stage without anyone asking her. Her husband never asked her. She just came forward carrying her child. Amal slipped up beside her and took the child into her arms so Um Mirwan was free to share.

Um Mirwan gave a beautiful testimony. We didn't ask for testimonies at that time but she came. She raised her hands and said, "Hallelujah!" As she shared with us, she was in the Spirit and the Spirit was in her. We were all blessed.

That day we had three speakers. One of them was the musician's father who pastored a local church. I will never forget the tears in his eyes as he said to me, "I have never ever seen anything like this. To see Arab Muslim women standing on the stage and praising God in front of us all, this is a miracle."

"Our God loves miracles." I responded warmly, not knowing what else to say.

"How did my son and his group get here?"

"That is another miracle."

That weekend was a wonderful experience. But unknown to us, we had an informer among us.

As a committee, we had discussed security and we decided that when everyone was in, we would lock the door and not open it until the conference was done. This way, those inside could relax in safety, knowing that no one could come in and disturb us. We didn't want people coming in from the outside, and we didn't want information from the inside going out.

The very first night, however, we had visitors from the Department of Intelligence. They knocked and knocked until finally we answered them from the inside and told them that we would not open for anyone.

They threatened to bring a bulldozer, but we refused. They said they needed to talk to Abdalla Hawatmeh.

I came and told them, "Look, this is private property. Come in the morning. We cannot open for you. Have a good night."

"We have to talk to Abdalla," someone shouted.

"No." I shouted back.

"We can break the door in!" they yelled.

"Be my guest." I yelled back, "It is not my door anyway."

Then they left. We didn't say anything to those in the conference, as we didn't want to frighten anyone.

Later in the evening we all moved to the large flat rooftop to have a time of sharing. It was a beautiful night with thousands of stars shining above our heads. We sat, squatted and laid around on whatever we could find, listening to testimonies. We especially enjoyed listening to the testimonies of our guests from neighboring countries.

They really were our guests. To my amazement, members of our small group had offered to pay for tickets for our non-Jordanian guests. "I'm paying for this ticket." one man argued. Another thrust $200 in my hand, "For someone to come from Egypt." Their love, concern, and warmth for other converts from Islam was amazing. This too was a miracle.

Around one in the morning, members of the Intelligence Department returned. This time they did not call for us. They simply forced the Egyptian guard to open the gate for them. I was then called down from the roof to meet with them.

"What is this conference?" they demanded.

"It is about the church, the Bible, and Christ." I replied.

"We want the names of everyone who is here."

"I can't give you names. We are just a group of families having a nice time here. I think you should just leave in peace."

Surprisingly enough, they left. We continued our meetings, but soon we noticed that one young man had disappeared. We looked around and then started searching for him, but he was gone. He was a certain young man whom we had long suspected of being an informer for the Intelligence Department. He was different from most young Jordanian men. He didn't have a job but he could afford a telephone. He wanted to be especially close to me, and he called me many times during a week. Sometimes he was even seen on the street going towards the section of town where the Intelligence Department had their offices. Many mornings he would be waiting for public transport going in that direction. Finally, we knew for sure that he was an informer.

So about three in the morning, two of the leaders and myself went to this young man's home. He was there.

"Why did you leave?" we asked.

"I came home because I was tired. I walked all the way."

Of course he was lying. He had a bed at the conference. Besides, he didn't look like he had just walked for miles. We were sure he had left with the other officers from the Intelligence Department.

"Look," we told him, "we know you are an informer. We don't care. We all know what is going on."

He broke into tears, "You knew this?"

"Yes we knew this," I assured him. "We have used you to pass some information on to the Intelligence Department. We made sure you knew that we were praying for the King and that we loved the government and so on. We made sure that you knew the things that needed to be known. You did pass it all on to them, didn't you?"

"Yes," he admitted. "OK, I'll never be back in the meetings."

"No, no, please," I insisted, "Please stay with us. You're a faithful man. You don't have to leave and we won't tell the others."

But he didn't return.

Since that time, God began to give us a spirit of discernment. Many times God showed us the truth about situations and people. We never had that before, but God knew we would need it in the days ahead.

CHAPTER TWENTY THREE
Bearing one another in love. Ephesians 4:2

SOMETIMES MINISTRY CAN BE PAINFUL. I'm not talking about pains for myself, but pains for others. I discovered this as I tried to help one brother in the Lord. His name was Arif. Before he got married, Arif had some debts. Most of them came from passing bad checks. Arif had been around since 1989, and by 1996, he still hadn't gotten his debts paid off. I hadn't realized the extent of his problem until he came to me one day to get a loan from the church. He had asked me several times before, but I had always managed to shrug it off. This time he asked very directly.

"Arif, you are still young and single," I told him. "You live with your parents and you are working. You should be able to save money. How much do you need anyway?"

"I need $9,300.00."

I was shocked. If Arif worked hard he might make $400 a month. At that rate he would have to work for two years and not spend a penny to pay it off. I was sorry I had asked.

"I'm sorry. I thought you needed a hundred dollars or something and I was going to give it to you. But $9,300.00 is an awful lot of money."

"I'm sorry too," he answered, "but I have large debts to pay off."

"Look, the church won't give you money for debts," I told him. "Debts are debts. I can't care for your debts. You need to care for them. Your family should care about them as well."

"My family is poor," the said; "they can't help me."

"No, I think they can. They own a home. Your family should sell it and pay your debts." I challenged him.

Then I got an idea. "Let's go to the people who are holding the checks you signed. Since you can't pay, maybe they can reduce the amount you owe."

We visited each of Arif's creditors and we managed to get the total lowered from over $9,300.00 to around $4,000.00.

The creditors wrote out new bills and asked him to sign them. I was going to tell him not to sign but he signed and they tore up the old checks.

Then they gave him three months to come up with $4,000 or they would raise a legal case against him. I was happy. $4,000 is much easier to handle. I felt that Arif could go to a bank and take a loan. Then he could pay a hundred dollars each month from his salary until the loan was paid off.

But Arif chose another route. He took his passport and disappeared. Then people started telephoning me. "Where did you go with Arif? Why did he disappear?"

I really didn't know where he was or why.

A long time later, I got a phone call. I could hear someone speaking in a very soft voice from far away. It was Arif, calling from Egypt.

"This is Arif."

"Arif! How are you? Where are you?"

"Alexandria."

"Oh? What are you doing there?"

"I want to go to Libya."

"Why Libya?"

"I want to stay away from Jordan until I get some money. Then I will come back and pay the debt."

"Look," I responded, "call your creditors and tell them yourself. Don't call me."

I told Arif's family that he was in Egypt and they were very frustrated. "Why would he call you and not call us?" they wondered.

"I'm sorry, but I don't know."

Two months later I received a letter from Arif. He was living in a mosque in Libya, praying five times a day. He had a genetic disease which caused inflammation of his skin and affected other organs. The doctors told him that there was no any treatment for his ailment. The letter went on to say, "Please send me $200 so I can eat.

As soon as I read the letter, I called together the brothers in our fellowship. We prayed around the letter, and we cried.

After praying and asking God for wisdom, I sent back a reply. I knew I was being very strong in what I said, but it was what I felt I should do. I wrote:

> *I can book you a plane ticket from Libya to Amman, but I will not send any cash.*
> *You need to come back to face what you have left."*

In the end, Arif came back on his own. As soon as he arrived at the border, the police picked him up and put him in jail. We visited him in jail and I hired a lawyer for him. In the end, his family paid his debts and he was set free.

Not only was he set free from his financial debts, Arif found freedom from his sins. We saw a change in Arif as he faced up to who he was and what he was in Christ.

Sometime later Arif came to me and told me that he was going to get married. When I asked him about the bride, I discovered that she was only sixteen years old.

"Why did you do this? She is not a believer and she is very young."

"Abdalla, I've waited many years and haven't been able to collect the money. Now my family is pushing me into this marriage."

I tried, but I could not persuade him to break the engagement. After several weeks, the family married him and his nephew on the same day. They were a poor Palestinian family and they wanted to host one party in order to keep things cheaper; so they had the two weddings on the same day.

On the wedding day, Amal and I drove Miriam, the bride, in our car. We helped with the wedding and said, "Congratulations." We supported the marriage, because they were set on getting married. This was a believer entering a marriage and we needed to support him.

After the wedding, we started praying for Miriam. We asked God to bring her to Himself. Amal started visiting Miriam and in the months that followed, she spent many long hours on sister to sister visits. Amal taught her how to cook, wash dishes, and please her husband. Amal counseled her and pointed her to the Scriptures. Many times Miriam was in our home. Sometimes she would spend the whole day with Amal until Arif would come from work to take her home.

During these visits, Miriam would share with Amal that her one desire in life was to have a son. As a good Muslim young woman, she had been trained that her role in life was to love her husband and bear him children. This was her destiny and she wanted to fulfill it.

But there was no pregnancy.

One day I asked Arif if he would consider having a doctor do tests on him. "Start with yourself." I encouraged him. "Go to a doctor and see if he can help."

Usually, Arabs send the woman to the doctor first, but I told Arif to come with me and I would take him to a doctor. I suspected something was medically wrong with Arif. He had no hair anywhere on his face except on the top of his head.

The doctor decided to do a physical examination first. It took him two minutes. While Arif was putting his clothes back on the doctor took me aside and asked, "Abdalla, who is this man?"

"He's just a friend."

"I'm sorry," the doctor said, "I think he will never have children."

"Wow. OK. What should we do? Can we do anything?"

"I think it is a waste of money, but if you want you can go ahead and get a sperm analysis."

Because it had only been a simple check-up, the doctor refused to take any money. Perhaps he felt badly for Arif.

The following day, we went to get a sperm analysis. Arif prayed fervently, "Oh Lord, I want a son. Oh Lord, help us to have children."

The next day, I went to the lab to get the results. They gave me a piece of paper with something written on it.

"Can you tell me what is on this report?" I inquired.

"Is it you?" they asked cautiously.

"No, it is someone else. A friend."

"They can't have children. There is a problem with his chromosomes. The doctor can tell you all about it, but he will never have children."

"What?" I gasped. "All the hope this woman has to have a child, and now I had this news! What about all the hope Arif has?"

Amal and I were upset. I could not give that report to Arif. I called several more doctors and talked with them. They all said the same thing. I called to America and talked to an American doctor. "Can you fix this case?" I asked eagerly. "If you can, I will fly him over to you. He is a believer and he needs help."

"Send me a copy of the report." he said, so I faxed it. A short while later the doctor called back. "I'm sorry," he said, "nothing can be done."

I was deeply troubled when I talked to Arif. "Arif," I said "Pray for children." I could not bear to give him the report.

"Did you get the report?"

"You just need to pray for the children." I replied sadly. I couldn't bring myself to tell him.

He so badly wanted to have a child. Whenever they came to my home, they would play with my kids. Miriam, Arif's wife, would take Laura and play with her. She loved Laura.

After we discovered that they could not have children, it began to affect our relationship. We felt we couldn't visit them a lot and that they shouldn't visit us a lot. We didn't want to expose them to our children so they would become discouraged.

It was a very tricky subject. Adoption is not an alternative in our country, and Miriam was young and wanted a son.

Slowly she started to turn bitter against Amal and I. She started to say all the lies she could think of about our relationship with them. We knew that she was just frustrated about not getting pregnant.

Arif would say to her, "You are still young. You will get pregnant. Don't worry; you are still young."

He didn't know that it was completely impossible. I didn't want to release the information that soon. I said to Amal, "Let's hide it for a while and let them try. Who cares. They are not going to have children without a miracle. Let them try. Maybe we will be surprised with a miracle and we can throw the report away." I hid the report in my office for two or three months.

One day, at two in the morning, I received a telephone call. I've learned long ago that phone calls in the middle of the night are seldom good. I got up and answered the phone. It was Arif.

"Abdalla," he said, "I need to see you now."

"No, I want to sleep. What happened?"

"My wife is crazy."

I went to Arif's house. It was a long drive across the city but Arif was waiting for me.

"Arif, what happened?"

"Abdalla," he said, "I woke up around two o'clock, and my wife was sitting on my chest trying to choke me. She had her hands on my neck trying to kill me. When I woke up I gasped, 'Miriam, what are you doing?'"

"'I'm not Miriam,'" she said, "'I want you dead.'" Arif stared at me. "She spoke just like that."

"Oh my goodness," I thought, this was a different kind of attack. I wanted to get out of there. I had never faced this before. "Arif, are you saying the truth or are you dreaming?"

"Come see her."

They had two rooms and I was afraid to go in. I am an Arab man and I cannot see another man's wife in the middle of the night. But he insisted. So I came in and saw her. She was all bloody and she was in her night robe. I was embarrassed. I was a married man and it was wrong to be in this room at three in the morning.

"Arif," I said, "be patient." I didn't know what to say. So we prayed, "Lord, if this is Satan, then we pray in Jesus name against it." We really started praying.

While we were praying, Miriam came into the room. She was very humble and meek. She came up to Arif and said, "Please forgive me." Then she said to me, "Please pray for me. I don't know what I did. I woke up and I was choking Arif."

That night I drove home very quickly. Amal asked me what happened and, when I told her, she was scared again.

The next day, I got out the doctor's report and I told Arif and Miriam about it.

"Look, you are not going to have children according to the medical experts. This is your report, please take it."

Oh, how Arif cried. He cried hard for almost an hour. "I want to leave Jordan," he said. "I want to get away from this country." They were so sad that I could hardly take it.

During the next year, Arif woke up at least five times with Miriam sitting on his chest wanting to kill him. Once she had a knife.

The last time it happened he wanted to divorce her and I argued with him against the divorce. Prayer was better than divorce and we banded together to see Miriam delivered. God answered our prayers and Miriam seemed better after that, but to this day, she hasn't accepted Christ as her Savior. Despite this, we continue to work with Arif and disciple him and see him grow in the Lord.

In my years of ministry, I have seen many Christian workers who see evangelism as the focus of the work, and they fail to do discipleship. Many people have come to me to learn about evangelism. Few come to ask about discipleship. I find this imbalance very puzzling. If someone I am ministering to is not fed and well respected by me, that means I don't love him. I may look at him in a loving way, but I really don't love him. I may love the attention I get from being known as someone who has led a Muslim to Christ, but it is equally important to persevere in discipleship.

Helping someone take the first few steps in their Christian life is exciting. The rest is just hard work. After a short time, you come to the bad smell of sin and the real issues have to be dealt with.

Evangelism and discipleship are like a funny bicycle with a huge wheel in the back and a very small wheel in the front. You spin the small wheel, it seems so easy, but the big one is going very slowly. Evangelism is fun. It's wonderful to see results, but the big wheel of discipleship turns very slowly. Few people want to be involved in this kind of ministry. A lot of prayer, sweat, and tears go into every godly man, woman, or couple. That is why we persevere, even with those we suspect as being untrue from the beginning. You just never know how someone will turn out.

CHAPTER TWENTY FOUR
One of them shall betray me. John 13:21

ONE DAY I RECEIVED A LETTER from a man by the name of Birhan. He originally wrote to CBN television and his letter was passed on to me. I wrote back to him and gave him my phone number. A while later he called me and we met to do follow-up. He was a young Muslim man in his late twenties from the border town of Ramtha.

I started out teaching him the Discovery Lessons, after which we moved on to the Growth Syllabus. After some months of this, Birhan started to attend our meetings in Amman. Since he was a diligent young man, we got him enrolled in The Program for Theological Education by Extension. Birhan was too good to believe. He was perfect. We weren't used to these things. We usually got mixed up people who needed a lot of help and encouragement. Birhan, however, was good in his studies. Actually, he was the best in his class. His homework was done on computer and he was always there on time. He never asked the church for a penny, and he didn't have work.

I visited Birhan's family several times and each time they offered us a good meal. They had a good home and seemed to be doing well. One time, Birhan came with his mother and they stayed overnight with Amal and me.

Whenever Birhan and I were alone, Birhan would start talking about his desire to work with a mission organization. He always requested information about mission organizations. What could I tell him about this one or that one? Were they a good organization? What about other organizations?

"My goodness," I thought, "How in the world does he know about these things?"

At one point, he worked with a Canadian businessman. I introduced him to this man for follow-up and, later, when he needed money, this businessman hired him to work in his business.

But he didn't last. He left his job and came to Amman. I warned the businessman, "Don't give him too much information. There is something about him that I'm not sure about."

After a while, Birhan became fed up with me and how loyal I was to Jordan.

"I want to go to Canada," he said.

"Why Canada? It's better here in Jordan." I protested. Of course, almost everyone in Jordan dreams of going to Canada, except me. After that Birhan changed and he started going to others to get more information.

"Maybe now," I thought, "he is connected to the Intelligence Department. Perhaps he was called in and they found a weak point. He is not working, so perhaps they could use that."

Those thoughts stopped me from baptizing him. Some of the others came to me and rebuked me for not baptizing Birhan. Every time I was confronted I replied, "I don't know why, but no! Even if it is un-Biblical, the answer is still no. I know I need to baptize him, but in this case I will be against the Bible. I don't want to do it."

I was really adamant. Whenever his name came up, there was a dark cloud in my mind. Even Imad Shehadi rebuked me, "Abdalla, if you don't baptize him, then we will baptize him."

I said, "Fine, if you want to baptize him, it's OK with me. It's your business, but I will not."

"But why?"

"This guy is… I don't know, but I have a feeling I can't express."

Then Birhan stopped seeing me. He used to come by every two days, but in the end, he came only periodically. After he met other Jordanians in ministry, he seemed to gravitate to them and away from me.

One day, he went to another organization and announced that he wanted to go to Beirut. "Help me," he requested, "I want to study the Bible in Beirut."

"OK, let's talk," the director said, "but first, please excuse me. I want to call somebody." Guess who he called? Abdalla Hawatmeh.

"Abdalla, I have someone here who wants to study in Beirut."

"Who is this guy?"

"Birhan"

"OK." I sighed, "Send him over to my office."

He came. He wasn't too happy that he had been switched back to me.

"What do you want, Birhan?" I asked him.

"I want to go to Lebanon."

"OK. Go to Lebanon. Why do you want us to intervene? Lebanon is not Australia. Just jump onto public transport and go."

"No, I need a reference to go to school in Lebanon. I need a letter from you to introduce me so I can study theology."

"I don't think I can give you this letter; you are not baptized yet."

"Look," he said, "you are the one who won't baptize me."

"The time will come."

"But I need a letter now," Birhan protested.

In the end, I agreed to write a letter for him. I addressed the letter to a friend who ministered in Lebanon. In the letter I also made a special trick. I had used this before with him. If the letter was opened beforehand he would know it had been changed from how it was originally sealed.

The Man From Gadara

Inside the letter I wrote:

Here is Birhan from Jordan. We believe he is a believer, but he is not baptized. My concern is that I have some suspicion about his mysterious ambition. He wants to go somewhere but we don't know where he is going.

I signed the letter and then sealed it in my special way. Birhan didn't notice what I did to the envelope.

"Here," I said. "Give this to my friends in Lebanon."

Birhan left and several days later I called my friend in Beirut.

After the customary greetings I asked him if he had gotten my letter.

"Yes, Birhan is here and he brought your letter."

"Did you find that it had been tampered with?"

"Yes." The envelope had been opened! I had sent envelopes to them before and none of them had ever been tampered with. "Yes it's been opened," he confirmed.

"OK. Ask him sometime why he opened it."

Birhan was placed with a good believer from a Muslim background. Everyone watched Birhan closely. He started to move around the believers in Lebanon asking all sorts of questions. The folk in Lebanon, however, saw more. They began to notice a car coming by almost every day and picking up Birhan. After an hour or so, it would bring him back. They thought it was someone from the Jordanian embassy, perhaps someone with the Intelligence Department.

One month later, Birhan walked into my office and surprised us all.

"Birhan, what are you doing in Jordan?" I asked.

"Thank you for giving me that letter," he said. "Those brothers are angels. They tried to help me a lot."

"Praise the Lord," I responded. "I'm glad that you are encouraged."

"Yes," he responded enthusiastically, "I want to be baptized today."

"Oh," I said, a little less enthused, "let's take time to discuss this."

"Birhan," I said, changing the topic, "did you open the envelope I gave to you?"

"No," he said, rather abruptly.

"But you did, I know you did. Why did you open it?"

"I'm sorry, Abdalla, I did open it, but I just wanted to see what you wrote about me."

"Yeah? OK. Can I ask another question?"

"OK."

"Would I be surprised to see a photocopy of that letter in my file at the Intelligence Department?"

"Abdalla," he protested, "Why are you saying this about me?"

"Who was in the car that used to pick you up from the church in Beirut? Who are they?"

"Oh, those were relatives of mine."

I knew he was lying but I let him go.

It took me another twenty days to work things out. After a while, it stared me in the face and I was worried. Birhan knew us all. He knew everyone in my ministry, everyone linked to Imad Shehadi, other ministries in Jordan, and even the people in Lebanon! He knew us all!

"Lord," we prayed at our next team meeting, "if he is an informer, please make it clear to us. We don't want to judge him if he is not."

Several weeks later an evangelistic team arrived from Lebanon for revival meetings. My friends were among those on the team.

"Abdalla," they said to me, "Birhan called us yesterday at the hotel. How did he know where we were staying?"

"What? I don't know!" I replied.

"Birhan called us in the hotel," they repeated.

"Did he? That's interesting. He lives in the city of Ramtha. How in the world did he know that you were staying in the Shepherd Hotel?" The more I thought about it, the more concerned I became. I got my car and drove straight to Ramtha. As soon as I arrived in Birhan's home, I asked him. "Did you call the team from Lebanon at the hotel?"

"No," he said, "why do you say these things about me?"

"Oh Lord," I prayed. "What is going on?"

I returned to Amman and went to see the team. "You guys!" I said angrily, "you're crazy. It wasn't Birhan who called."

They looked at me lovingly and said, "Abdalla, it was Birhan; he called us three times. The very minute we entered the hotel, Birhan called. He said, 'Welcome to Jordan.'"

At that point we got on our knees and committed this situation to the Lord.

When the evangelistic team returned to Lebanon, we tried to stay calm. It all seemed to be over, until one night, around two in the morning, I got a telephone call.

That night my youngest brother was staying with us. Around 2 a.m. the phone woke us all up. Who would call us at 2 a.m.?

Birhan was on the line. "Abdalla, can I meet with you now in the Tyche Hotel."

"Why the Tyche Hotel?"

"Just come and don't tell anyone."

"Even my wife?" I asked.

"If you can, yes, don't tell her."

"What room should I come to?"

"Don't worry. Just come to the lobby," Birhan said. "I will be there."

Of course I told Amal. "Wait until five in the morning and if I am not back call the police and tell them I went to the Tyche Hotel."

When I arrived at the hotel, Birhan was not there to meet me. As I looked around, I was approached by a strange man.

"Abdalla Hawatmeh?" he said quietly.

241

"Yes."

"Birhan is in room 301."

"OK." I tried to smile. As I headed up the stairs, I was very afraid.

Amal had begged me not to go. "You don't know what is going on." She said fearfully. "Perhaps it is because you devastated this man's life spiritually. You've refused to baptize him and perhaps he is angry with you."

"No, I didn't do all that." I said reassuringly. "All I wanted to know was the truth."

When I came to room 301, I discovered the truth.

Room 301 was a fancy suite. I knocked and Birhan was waiting for me. When I was seated in the plush sofa, he started to talk. "Abdalla, I am here to confess to you that I am not a believer," he began.

"Why are you saying this?"

"Because I have never been a believer."

A sword pierced my soul. "What about the PTEE courses you took? You were the best student. What about studying the Bible in Lebanon? What about the church services you led? Why? You even wanted to be baptized!"

I paused. "Ah, no wonder I never wanted to baptize you."

I looked at Birhan, the pieces slowly falling into place. "I don't want to ask you why, but how did you dare to have communion with us? How did you dare ask to go to Lebanon to study the Bible? How did you dare ask for baptism? Didn't you get fed up lying to me?"

"Yes. That's why I am telling you the truth now. No one knows that I am here with you tonight."

"You are a liar," I said quietly. "I bet there are a couple of Intelligence officers hiding behind these curtains listening to us right now." I paused. "If they are there, then I know you are nothing in the Intelligence Department, perhaps only a corporal. If there are other officers here who want to handcuff me, let's go, I don't care."

"No one is here," Birhan said quietly. "I am alone here."

"Who is paying for this room? Is it you?"

"No, it's the Department of Intelligence."

"Why do they have you in this room?"

"I'm here on another mission."

"There is something fishy about this," I thought.

"Abdalla I've written many reports about you. I have copies of them all here with me." He pulled out a large stack of papers. I was so surprised I started laughing.

"Give me some of these," I joked.

"Take them all." Birhan was serious.

"No, forget it. I know what happened in my life, I don't want to be shocked that you wrote lies about me."

"No, please take them and read."

"No. I'm not going to read them. If you want to give them to me, then give me only a few. A random few." At this, Birhan selected a couple of reports at random.

"Lets go back to question one." I heard myself saying. I felt like someone in a dream. I didn't care what Birhan was at that time. I only cared for Birhan the person.

"Let me go back to the basic question. Do you want to accept the Lord as your Savior?"

"No," Birhan said sadly, "no, I can't."

"That makes me sad, Birhan. I don't care what you watched and reported. I know my life; you don't need to remind me about it."

"Abdalla," he replied gravely, "I was given a mission to follow you for five years. It is now four and a half years, and I can't finish. I was in your home and I went with you to churches. Everywhere we went I tested you."

"Thank you for saying that. OK. What do you want, Birhan?"

"Nothing. I just don't want you to have something against me. Forgive me."

"I forgive you, Birhan." I paused. "Now do you want to accept the Lord as your Savior?" He shook his head. "Do you have a copy of the Bible or should I give you one now?"

243

"No," he said. "I don't want one now. I had one but I destroyed it."

"God bless you, Birhan, for being truthful. Is there anything you want me to do?" I inquired.

"No."

"Where are you going now?"

"I am leaving now and going to the Department of Intelligence."

"Can I give you a lift there?" I asked him this because I wanted to test him to make sure he was from the secret police.

He begged me not to take him but I insisted.

I drove my car right up to the soldiers at the gate of the Intelligence Department.

"Please open the gate," I told the officer, "I want to give Birhan a lift inside."

The guard took one look at Birhan and brightened. "Welcome," he said, and he opened the gate. Birhan was known and recognized and, because I was with Birhan, no one questioned who I was. The guard must have thought that we were both from the Secret Police. Who else would come at three in the morning?

"Birhan," I said as he got out of the car, "someday, if you want to hear more about Christ, you know my home. Please come." He nodded. "Have a good morning."

I noticed that the reports Birhan had made about me were on the back seat, so I insisted that he take them. "Abdalla," Birhan said, "I have one more question." It felt strange sitting there in the parking lot of the Secret Police. "What can I do for you here in the Intelligence Department?"

Ah ha! I was immediately alarmed and paused. This could be a trap.

"Nothing, Birhan. But I'm going to do one thing for you. I am going to pray for you. You do nothing for me. Do things for yourself. Seek the truth."

He left me then.

Our fellowship had some sad days afterward. It really broke our hearts. Many had regarded Birhan as a good believer. He had

244

been doing well. Imad Shehadi was stunned. Many people were surprised, but our senses were sharpened through Birhan's interaction in our lives. Since then, we have seen a chain of informers coming and going. Some lasted two weeks, some two years. Sometimes we even asked them to lead meetings. I mean, he is there, so let's get him to help in the ministry! One day, we asked an informer to pray for us in public.

"Ah, no." he replied sheepishly.

"Perhaps you could lead a meeting next week?"

"I really don't know how to lead music."

"That's OK; I will help you. You just stand there in the front."

We really wanted people to feel the freedom that Christ had given us. "We know you are an informer but...who cares?"

Once we realized that the Intelligence Department was regularly sending us informers, we learned how to spot them. Having them in our midst gave us a boldness and openness that we did not have before. We were being watched. Everything we said and did was being passed on. We couldn't hide anything. If we couldn't hide anything then we didn't need to hide anything. We didn't care if they call us in for an interview. It no longer mattered. We simply told the truth. True, our hearts may beat a bit faster, but there is no fear.

After that, our relationship with the Department of Intelligence changed. We now go to the Department of Intelligence for our appointments, and if they are running late, we insist. "Can I go in right away? I don't want to be delayed. I'm busy today."

Other people may sit there for hours, waiting in fear, but those days are over for us. We know we haven't done anything wrong. We are there for something that is wrong in their understanding. They are the ones who are all worked up, but we have peace in our hearts.

It was the beginning of a new wave of boldness that God would give us. While we knew there would be troubles ahead, we were confident that we could face the Intelligence Department.

The Man From Gadara

That's why we were caught off guard with what would happen in the not too distant future.

CHAPTER TWENTY FIVE

And more were added to the church. Acts 11:21

HE CAME TO MY OFFICE. I was sitting at my desk, and I could hear his conversation with my secretary.

"Could I see Mr. Abdalla Hawatmeh?"

"Do you have an appointment with him?"

"No, but I hope to have one now if it's possible."

"Who are you? Are you a client, a company representative, or a friend?"

"No, just tell him I'm Abdul Hadi."

"Oh," I thought to myself, "Abdul Hadi? I have a friend named Abdul Hadi, maybe it is him." But it wasn't him. The voice wasn't right. My secretary came to the door and announced that Mr. Hadi desired to see me. I told her to let him in.

Moments later he was standing in front of my desk. "Good morning. My name is Abdul Hadi, and I'm a captain in the Intelligence Department. This is my ID."

"Oh, good to have you." I was surprised at how boldly he flashed around his badge. "Can I get you anything to drink?"

"Do you have coffee here?"

"Sure, we can have coffee." I called the secretary and we had coffee together. For many centuries, Arabs have used coffee as a sign of friendship. Tea is often offered to strangers, coffee to friends. When a business deal is struck, coffee is drunk to show that both sides are committed to the deal. Now I was drinking coffee with a captain in the secret police, and we were making small talk and wasting my time. Mr. Hadi had a master's degree in law, and he was young. I had a master's degree in electronics and I was getting nothing done this morning. Soon the coffee was finished.

"Well, Abdul Hadi," I said, "I have work to do. You've had your coffee now let me work." I was being rude, but he was wasting my time. I had reported to the Intelligence Department countless numbers of times. When I was called, I responded. I was a good citizen. I did not appreciate this new tactic of visiting my office.

"Can we walk outside the building for a while?"

I looked at him carefully. "No, I have work to do."

"I'll wait for you to finish."

Of course, the Intelligence Department's offices were only two or three minutes walk from my office. He could get angry and call for help. I changed my mind. "OK, I'll walk with you." On the way out, I told my secretary, "I'll be back in a few minutes."

Then Abdul Hadi and I took a short walk around the neighborhood.

"Look," the secret police captain said, "I've heard a lot about you, and I want to be your friend."

"OK, what else?" I said seriously. "Come out with the truth. Do you have a tape recorder in your pocket or a bug in your bag?"

"No, please" he protested. "I've read your file, and I know all about you." He paused, "I want to be your friend."

"I already have many friends I don't really need another one, especially from the secret police."

"Are you a Christian?" he said, and then he started digging talking about spiritual things. "How did you become a Christian?"

"Oh," I thought, "thank you for this question!" I smiled at my fortune, and then I gave him my testimony. He listened carefully as I talked. Maybe he was recording, I didn't know.

"Now what if the group in Jordan gets bigger?" he asked. "What are you doing about marriages? Do you have a plan to handle tribal inheritances? Where are you going to bury people? Where are you going to be buried Abdalla? In a Muslims graveyard or a Christian graveyard or alone?"

"Well I'm still young, Mr. Abdul Hadi." I smiled. "Don't ask me these kinds of questions yet." I paused. "Look Abdul Hadi, if your name really is Abdul Hadi, I have work to do. But before I go, remember that we are a growing number of a new society in this country, whether you like it or not."

"No, I'm here as a friend." he protested gently.

"I know who sent you. Tell him, we love the country but we love God also. Go home and let me work. God be with you."

He left.

Six months later, I had moved my office to a new location. As I was coming into work one morning, I saw Abdul Hadi.

"Abdul Hadi," I called to him. "What are you doing here?"

I must have surprised him. His eyes met mine and then he turned his face. It was obvious that he didn't want to speak to me. I smiled.

"Come Mr. Hadi," I called to him, "come sit in my car."

He came and sat in my car.

"I'm going to the courthouse," he explained.

"Oh?" I teased, "are you going to testify a false testimony against somebody or what?"

He laughed. "Shame on you. I quit working for the Intelligence Department."

"Really? You made it to captain and then you quit? That's pretty strange!"

"I swear it is true."

"Well, that's neat, but how can you prove that to me?"

"I'm telling you the truth. This morning when you saw me I felt ashamed. That's why I turned my face from you." He paused. "Abdalla, I'm talking to you as a friend now. Keep doing what you are doing. You have nothing to fear, nothing to hide. I read all the reports about you and I was genuinely impressed. When I came to you I was seeking some friendship with you. They never knew about my meeting with you."

He was looking me straight in the eyes. "It's not that I resigned because of you Abdalla, but I think you are one of the reasons why I resigned."

"OK, God bless you. Where are you working now?"

"I'm working in a regional office of a foreign off-shore company as their legal counsel." He gave me his card.

Several days later I visited his office and talked to the manager of the company. "Yeah, this guy was in the secret police, but he left and a relative of his asked us to appoint him here, and now he is our legal counselor."

I was convinced that it must be true. I went to Abdul Hadi's office to visit him. Abdul Hadi visited me several times afterward, and we talked about nothing except the Bible and spiritual things. We never talked about the secret police or human rights.

My meeting with Abdul Hadi encouraged me. Even the secret police were being affected by their contact with us. The Bible says that a little leaven leavens the whole lump. Oh, how much we wished to be a gospel leaven that affected every strata of our society.

A SHORT TIME AFTER THIS, MAISOON, A RELATIVE OF MINE, CAME TO THE LORD. Like all the rest, she came to the Lord after studying the Discovery Lessons. Amal and I were very encouraged to see that even family members were responding to the gospel.

As with most new believers, Maisoon had been interested in the gospel for a long time. She had asked many questions at different times in her life. One of the secrets of Muslim evangelism is to sense when a person ceases to be just interested and really starts to seek. When that happens, we usually ask them to spend time going through the Discovery Lessons with a teacher. During these sessions the Christian teacher takes the seeker through the

Bible, starting in Genesis, and explains in detail who and what the Messiah was and how Jesus fulfilled the role of the Messiah.

The Discovery Lessons are not something magical. They are simply a set of notes to help guide a teacher as he or she takes the seeker through the plan of salvation. Over the years, we have tried to improve and hone the lessons so that the materials we use communicate effectively to someone who is coming from a Muslim background. Many Christian workers from other countries are starting to use the Discovery Lessons. Several times a year I am called on to take a group of new workers through the material and show them how to teach it.

Shortly after Maisoon came to Christ, a young missionary came to me for a short talk. He was struggling with ministry and he was not seeing many results. I sensed that he was getting quite discouraged. "Look," I told him, there is this girl. She is a relative of mine. I think she is ready to study Discovery. Would you and your wife like to teach it to her?"

The young man brightened. It sounded like I was entrusting him with a real ministry opportunity. They would be happy to teach her. It was good to see him so encouraged already. After the young man left my office, I quickly called Maisoon.

"Maisoon" I asked, "Could you do us a real favor?"

"Sure uncle," she responded positively. "What can I do for you?"

"Maisoon, could you accept the Lord as your Savior again?"

A few days later I met the young missionary. "Abdalla!" he was almost bouncing as he talked. "Abdalla, she accepted the Lord. It was so easy." I was smiling now too, but for a different reason.

"When we got to lesson five," he said excitedly, "I asked Maisoon if she wanted to accept the Lord?'" The young man was so happy. "She said 'Yes,' and she prayed with us."

I was encouraged that this young man was so encouraged. Now that he had led one person to Christ, he was excited and ready to lead another. I never told him about the joke. I think he suspected it, but I never told him. I don't think God minded my little joke. I'll do whatever I can to encourage Christian workers who are discouraged. A short while later we baptized five new converts, including Maisoon.

God has never given us big numbers, but every month people come to Christ. Each person who comes is a precious jewel. Many long hours of sharing, teaching and praying go into each soul who comes to Christ. Sometimes, it takes years of witnessing, and other times God has already prepared people.

ONE DAY I GOT A LETTER VIA CBN from a man who lived in the same area where Kamal had been from. Since Kamal's death I had made very few visits back to his village. I wrote the man back and several weeks' later two young men came to visit me. When they heard my testimony and saw what God was doing, they became very excited.

"Where have you been?" they asked in amazement. "We have been looking for people to help us for years."

"What?" I said. "I go down in the Jordan Valley once or twice a month. Where are you?"

"We are there!" they said excitedly, and then they described how to get to their home.

"Why don't you come this week? You are invited for supper in our home," they said excitedly.

"I would be glad to come."

I came the following week. To my surprise, they gathered over 16 neighbors. All of them were watching Christian television every single day. These people met in two groups of eight for the specific purpose of watching Christian broadcasts.

To my surprise, five of them were open believers and, to my biggest surprise, they wanted me to share about communion that evening. They said, "We've had communion together before, but we want to know if we've done it in the right way."

"Lord," I prayed, "this is Acts Chapter Two all over again. The Holy Spirit has raised up this group."

The Man From Gadara

I shared that night, and I returned many more times. As time passed, these young men dispersed to other places. Two left Jordan to study at a foreign university. Two others emigrated to Germany. Only one believer is still there to this day.

The encouraging thing about this group was that we didn't do anything. Once we knew they were there, we endeavored to encourage them and support them. Not only did we make regular visits, but one time we had a day of praying and fasting in the Jordan Valley. About eight of the believers from our groups in Amman went to the Jordan Valley, and we spent the day just praying and fasting. At the end of the day, one of the local believers invited us to his home where he slaughtered a sheep for us. Our fasting turned into feasting.

Truly, God was building his church, and the gates of hell could not stand against us. Little did we realize, however, how difficult the next testing would be when it came.

CHAPTER TWENTY SIX
They will be divided... Luke 12:53

THE HAWATMEH TRIBE WAS ALWAYS IN MY MIND. Originally, only my immediate family knew that I had become a Christian, but slowly the information started to move through the tribe.

In the very beginning of my life of faith in Jordan, I tried to show deeds, not words, to my immediate and extended family. But I was never clear in explaining the gospel to them in the early days.

They realized that I didn't pray in the mosque and that I didn't fast during the Holy Month of Ramadan.

But I didn't hinder people either. I respected their attitudes and faith. I would never discourage someone from praying the Muslim prayers and I didn't eat food in front of anyone during the month of Ramadan.

If it was prayer time, I might slip into another room or sit by myself while others prayed. Usually, whenever I was around, there were only a couple of individuals going to pray anyway.

However, when my father died, I was the only son living in Jordan and available for his funeral. So I went into the mosque and stood with the men. I really wanted to be close to my father. I was very lonely for him. He had been my example in life. At first I was quite hesitant. I am a Christian. How can I go into a mosque? And then I thought, "No, I am a Christian, and I have ministered in many different places. I can go and stand. I don't have to say what they are saying. I can simply be with them during this time of sorrow."

So I stood with them and I sat with them. I didn't have to say anything. It was enough that I was there. I knew that if I didn't go, there would be a scandal in the village.

During my early days as a Christian in Jordan, I had many chances to explain the gospel to my family, but I never did. Some of the young men, mostly cousins or more distant relations, showed some interest in where I stood. They would ask questions about what I thought of the Qur'an or Islam.

I always expressed my answers in a gentle way. Usually I directed the conversation towards God. It is better to talk to Muslims about God than it is to talk about religion. But these young men knew there was something wrong with me. Perhaps I lost my religion in the west and I had become a non-practicing Muslim. I don't think it ever crossed their minds that I had actually left Islam for another religion. While I didn't practice Islam, it was evident to them that I didn't lie and I never cheated. I was always careful never to cause trouble and I would always try to make peace between people. My 'yes' always meant 'yes', and my 'no' always meant 'no.' That somehow puzzled them. They often said, "You've become like a foreigner." They didn't know that it was because I was a believer in Jesus.

Then God did an amazing thing. Even though I was quite different from the others in my tribe, God gave me grace and mercy. During my days at the Academy, I was elected as the chairman of the Hawatmeh community. Although I was not a practicing Muslim, the family looked up to me. My father was respected, and I had a university degree and a good position with the government. For several years I was well known and respected in my tribe.

During the time that I was the Community Chairman, I noticed a young boy in our tribe named Fouad. I wanted to encourage Fouad. He was a good boy and his marks in school were very good. So I took a hundred dollars from the community fund and gave it to him as an annual gift. It was a lot of money for a young boy. It was equivalent to the membership fee of four people. I would just throw it in an envelope and give it to Fouad every May or June when he finished school. In a way, it was a reward for his good marks.

I always prayed for Fouad. "Father," I would pray, "I really want Fouad to be yours." I don't know why I singled out Fouad, but he was on my heart. He was and still is the finest boy in his family. His father has many boys, but Fouad shines above them all.

Fouad's father, however, became an enemy against me and my faith. One time, in the presence of my father, he attacked me. My father rebuked him and asked him to leave the house. He glared at my father, and then he stormed out. He was a big police officer, and he didn't want me to shame the tribe.

I prayed for Fouad for eleven years. Sometimes I was able to share a little with him, but it seemed that Fouad was not ready yet. Then one day he came to me and said, "Uncle, I want you to adopt me and teach me about Christ."

I was surprised, but I shouldn't have been. That very night I had been praying for Fouad. It was a funny prayer. I prayed like I was negotiating with God. "Lord," I had prayed, "what is wrong with you? I've been praying for Fouad for the last eleven years and nothing has happened. You'd better do it soon. And Lord, I don't want to approach Fouad; I want him to approach me."

That night, we had a family gathering. Fouad was at that time in his second year at university and he often looked up to me to encourage him in his studies. After I stepped down as Community Chairman, I continued to give Fouad a gift every year from my own pocket. Fouad treated me as his older brother and not someone who just gave him gifts occasionally.

When he finished his high school, he asked me what university he should go to, what subject he should take. Whenever I saw him I would ask about his studies and quiz him to see how well he was doing.

Not long after uttering the prayer, we were standing at a gate receiving condolences for someone who died. It was on that occasion that Fouad came to me. "Uncle," he said. "I want to talk to you."

"OK, go ahead."

"I want you, Uncle, to adopt me, and teach me, and I will learn whatever you teach me about Christ." I had tears in my eyes that night and, whenever I remember that night, I try not to cry.

"Sure." I told him, trying to control the emotions that welled up inside of me.

DURING THE YEARS THAT FOLLOWED, I had many occasions to defend the Bible in front of my family. Each year Muslims celebrate two main religious holidays. There is one at the end of the Holy Month of Ramadan and another when Muslims remember the day when Abraham took Ishmael (according to Islamic beliefs) to the top of the mountain to offer him, and when God provided a sheep as a sacrifice. On this occasion Muslims sacrifice a sheep and eat the meat.

During these feast days, all of the family would travel to the north of Jordan to celebrate together. During the holiday season, groups of Hawatmehs would come to greet my father. He was an old Hawatmeh, and in many ways, he was the patriarch of the tribe. Not only that, he was grandfather to many people.

After the formal greetings, we would have a gathering and sit outside.

Often during the conversation someone would ask, "What's up with *Father Abdalla*?" They used the word 'father' to jokingly call me a priest. Some would laugh, but it wasn't really a joke any longer. Then I would have my opportunity to talk. As I shared, people would think I was only giving my point of view in things. They didn't know that I believed and strongly confessed the Lordship of Christ.

In time, especially after I was imprisoned, they started to think seriously about what I was. After I was released from jail, two young men from my tribe came to me.

"Abdalla," they said, "we wanted to kill you one day. We really wanted to kill you to protect the honor of the tribe. We talked about where we should meet you and how we would kill you. It was all planned." They looked at me. "Abdalla, we really wanted to do this. The plan was all set."

"So what happened?" I asked.

"We don't know why we didn't do it," they said sheepishly, "something would always stop us."

"Boys," I said, "nothing falls from heaven to earth without the will of the Father." They nodded and took that as an explanation.

I was always amazed how the Hawatmehs could respect my faith but at the same time never agreed with me. They would sometimes call me a lover of foreigners. Many times I explained to people that it was not the foreigners that changed my life. True, I learned many things in my studies in America and my English language did improve. My attitudes also changed towards some things that are done here, but all this had nothing to do with my faith.

My faith came because I met with God. God planted something in me. Yes, some people ministered to me, but it was the testimony of their lives that affected me.

Did my relatives understand that? I don't know, but the years have shown that some of them didn't understand. Usually they just shrugged it off. "Tomorrow he will get married and have kids and forget about it."

After I got married, I was still the same. After I had kids, I still didn't change. Then my children spoke about Christ! At that point, family members started to strike their palms together and say, "My, this is serious."

They didn't know how serious it was. My brother-in-law came to Christ and, some years later Fouad came to the Lord. Then a few months later, his brother also came to the Lord. Now we were four, and a short while later Maisoon and others joined us.

I really cannot say what it was that kept our family from rising up against us, other than the Lord's mercy. Perhaps it was the lives that we lived as believers. Perhaps it was the quiet peaceful way we conducted ourselves, never returning their anger with anger but always showing as much love as we could. Perhaps it was my father's name that protected me. Whatever it was, God worked a miracle in the Hawatmeh tribe, and our lives were spared.

Then an amazing thing happened. Some of the Hawatmeh families started to visit me, and we began to rebuild relationships. These people wanted to know me better and to learn more about what I believed in.

The Hawatmeh family is not very religious. People are educated and the men often travel outside of Jordan to the Arab Gulf states to find jobs. We are a hard working tribe, and it is well known that Hawatmehs stick together.

But there was something more than this happening. Whenever there was a death or a marriage, there would be a gathering of all the Hawatmehs. During these times, people would talk to me and I found that they were looking up to me for wisdom. "This is really strange," I thought. "They should not come to me to ask my opinions or to help with peacemaking. Islam teaches them not to talk to me. According to Islam, they should kick me out of the tribe or kill me."

But no one harmed me at all.

There was another thing that may have helped. The original Hawatmeh tribe was made up of Christians. Most tribes in this part of the Middle East used to be Christian many years ago. The Hawatmehs are one of those tribes. Almost 50% of the original Hawatmehs are Greek Orthodox Christians. Today, the Muslim side and the Christian side are on good relations with each other. We have a community center and a committee that works together between the two tribes in the city of Zarka. They say it is the first time in the history of Jordan that this has happened.

The Man From Gadara

Tribal historians tell us that my eighth grandfather back on my father's side lived about 500 years ago. At that time, the entire tribe was of Christian descent. A fight broke out between two brothers. One brother ran away from his father, went to a Muslim family, and stayed with them. Eventually he converted to Islam and married a Muslim woman. This family had children and the Muslim Hawatmeh tribe descended from them.

In the last few years, many Christian Hawatmehs emigrated to America and other western nations. Consequently, the population of the Christian tribe in Jordan has been severely depleted. Still they are almost equal in number with the Muslim Hawatmehs today. There are many types of Hawatmehs. There are Christians, Greek Orthodox, Catholics, Muslims, Communists, and even Sufis in the south. I was amazed to discover that whole villages of Hawatmeh were Sufis. I like Sufis. They are very tender and non-violent, but still they are Muslims.

It helped that there are many different kinds of Hawatmehs. I believe that we have learned to be a bit more tolerant of each other.

But it can also hinder. One day, we had a time of condolences after a funeral for a Muslim Hawatmeh. He had lived in the city of Zarka where most of the Hawatmehs are Christian and was well known and involved in the upper crust of society.

In the middle of the gathering, a group of Christian Hawatmehs came to share their condolences. I went over to greet one of them, a lawyer. When we sat, people turned their faces away from him and the other Christians.

I saw this, so I took a few educated men from the Christian Hawatmehs and said, "Let's go and greet the Muslims."

We sat down with them and the two groups eventually got around to talking about the possibilities of their becoming more united in the future.

Then, one Muslim lawyer stood up. "We want to have a word with you Christians."

"OK," the Christian lawyer responded, "what do you want?"

"We don't want you to come to our condolences, knowing that when you come here, you want to have shoes on. Come with respect. Take off your shoes, sit, and share our condolences. But then leave. Don't ever think that coming here is becoming part of us." He was very aggressive.

Then one from the Christians stood up. "We are one family. We have nothing against loving you more. What is it? Do you want us to become Muslims? We could go tomorrow and become Muslims, if all we wanted was to get closer to you."

Then I stood up. "Now Mr. Adib, you speak for yourself. They should know the truth and they should come back to being Christians like you and I."

Boy oh boy, had I ever opened my mouth! I wasn't sorry, but many of the Muslim Hawatmehs looked at me and muttered under their breaths.

Later, one of them approached me. "Aren't you afraid we will kill you?"

"No," I smiled, "you are too nice to do that. If you were not my relatives, I would never say this, but I depend on you. You are my tribe and I lean on you as my tribe."

That night, many people approached me to ask me about Christianity and Christ. As the meeting was breaking up, the head of the Hawatmeh Christians came to me and told me that what I had said made them think twice about their relationship with Christ.

In a wonderful way, God has given me a relationship with both Hawatmeh tribes. Since then, I have been asked to speak in the meeting hall in Zarka on four occasions. Usually only Christians attended, but a few times some of the Muslim Hawatmehs came. They all know me because they knew my father and my brothers. To my amazement, several people came up to me afterward and said nice things about Christ. Some even mentioned the possibility of their becoming Christians.

God was truly at work in protecting me. The Intelligence Department had been willing to guard me with soldiers. The Muslim Brotherhood tried to get me released from prison. My own tribe had reacted quite neutrally. Surely, God had given us the green light to move ahead in actively building his church among people from a Muslim background. All the roadblocks seemed to be removed! As a result, the next time of testing caught us completely off guard.

CHAPTER TWENTY SEVEN
The people shall be oppressed. Isaiah 3:5

BY 1996, WE STARTED THINKING OF OURSELVES AS A CHURCH. We weren't an officially registered church, but we had pastors, elders, and deacons. We met regularly in a church, and the local believers knew about us. Most people considered me the pastor. I was certainly there from the beginning, but our fellowship is a group that God has raised up.

One day, I was preaching from the book of Revelation, and we were studying the Church at Philadelphia and the love of the brethren. After I finished speaking, a man stood up and announced that we should consider giving our group a name. He felt that our church should be called the Philadelphia Church. Everyone seemed pleased with this, and so I replied, "OK, let it be. I don't mind."

Within 24 hours, I was called into the Intelligence Department.

"What is this Philadelphia Church business?"

"Good night," I exclaimed, "that was fast. How in the world did you hear about this?"

"Don't worry about it," they replied. "What is this Philadelphia Church stuff?"

"It is just a name. Philadelphia was the ancient name of our city of Amman. That is what the Romans called this city. And Philadelphia is also mentioned in the Bible."

"Who elected the name Philadelphia?"

"We didn't vote on it."

"Did you choose this name?"

"Oh," I thought. "What should I answer? Which is more harmful to say: I chose it or someone else?"

"Look," I said, "I didn't choose it. I was just teaching about Philadelphia from the Bible, when someone responded enthusiastically and said, 'Let's call our church Philadelphia.' Then you guys picked it up when it got to your ears."

"But you taught about it, right?"

"Yes, but I didn't teach about us becoming a church. We are already a church. I talked about how to live for Christ by loving one another. We were studying how we should function as a church."

He hated that. He fumed for a while.

"That is the reason. When you teach about something, they stick to the teaching." He really wanted to bang the table. He was afraid that I was like Ahmed Yasein of the Hamas. I would sit and teach and the people would do. I wish I was like that but, on the contrary, I used to sit and teach and also do.

Our dream was to see a church come into existence that was made up of converts from Islam. We wanted to build a fellowship that was attractive to people. We were not interested in a church that would attract Christian tourists but one that would attract non-believers.

They asked a few more questions, and then they advised us not to declare ourselves and announce that we had a name. If we did that, then the government had some rules against us.

The next day they called Imad Shehadi into their offices. Imad was now the president of the new Jordanian Evangelical Theological Seminary (JETS). Right from its founding the Seminary has had trouble with the Intelligence Department. Imad has always been sympathetic to those from a Muslim background, and the secret police did what they could to stop new believers from attending the seminary.

So they started their regular line of questioning with Imad, but in the middle of his interview, they suddenly asked him, "What is this Philadelphia church?"

He was very surprised "What? Which Philadelphia?"

"The Philadelphia Church."

"What church?"

"Abdalla Hawatmeh's group."

"I didn't know they went by that name. It's the first I've heard about it."

I don't know if they believed him or not, but as soon as they released him he called me up. "Abdalla," he asked me, "what did you call your church?"

"Philadelphia."

"I didn't know that."

"Yeah? The secret police told you, right?"

"Yes, how did you know?"

"I didn't know, but they seem to be the only ones bothered by it."

After this, the Department of Intelligence began to move against us again. They called Imad back for another interview and they asked him not to have any cooperation with us. Then they told him he was not allowed to have any Muslim converts in the Seminary.

For several weeks after this, whenever any Christian got called in, the Department of Intelligence would ask him somewhere in the interview "What is your relationship with Abdalla Hawatmeh and his group?"

Then things started to take a strange twist. We decided to hold another retreat. Our last conference had been a great success, and we again wanted to gather believers from across the Middle East for several days of worship and fellowship. We decided to move to a larger facility owned by one of the church denominations. Our committee was excited. They had drawn up a list of over 150 converts whom they wanted to invite.

Committees were put in place to prepare the food, the worship, and to take care of the children.

Everything was in place, and everyone was excited when a pastor called me and simply said, "I'm sorry, but you can't use the Retreat Center."

"What do you mean we can't use it? Didn't we reserve it?"

"Yes, I know, but please forgive me. This decision is not from me. It is from the committee."

I was shocked. I hadn't expected this. There was no technical reason why we couldn't use the Retreat Center. The only reason they gave was that we were all converts from Islam and they were afraid that this might have repercussions against the church.

I called a meeting of our leaders and we discussed and prayed about this development. We realized it was the Intelligence Department. It seemed that their new strategy was to try to work through the church against us.

Apparently, some church leaders were threatened by the secret police. The police said that they would raid the place if we held the conference. Personally, I don't think they would ever do this. In Jordan, we have very clear laws. The place could not be raided without the Intelligence Department going through the police and the criminal department to lay charges. We were confident that they wouldn't raid us. Nevertheless, these church leaders were frightened.

A short time later, the Intelligence Department moved again. This time they started rumors that created a division between Imad and myself. It took prayer and some hard work to straighten out the misunderstandings.

Then the leaders of the church we were meeting in started to get phone calls. They became frightened and called a meeting with us. Obviously, the government was getting concerned about our growing numbers and our emerging identity. These church leaders had developed a plan. They wanted us to split our church into small groups and send them out to be merged into the various local churches around Amman. They meant well, but we realized that this would spell the end of our identity and the end of our ministry together. I reacted angrily, telling them that this was like killing an infant. We were an infant church and, as one of the parents of the infant, I would not stand by and see my child killed. I looked around the room at the denominational executive committee. I loved each one of them and they loved me. We had never ever had any problems before. I had spoken in their churches and they had spoken in our meetings. Now we were clashing.

"Brothers," I insisted. "It seems to me that by stopping our church, I feel you are saying 'yes' to the government and 'no' to God. It seems very clear to me."

"No," they all protested, "we are not against a ministry."

"If you do this, then you are." I took a deep breath. "If I become a step closer to Satan and his friends then I am a step further from God. If I am agreeing with the secret police against a church, what does that mean?"

In the end, they asked us to reduce our meetings to twice a month.

I refused. I wouldn't negotiate.

"Abdalla, why couldn't you make it two meetings a month?"

"No, our meetings are a weekly thing."

We didn't get anywhere in that meeting. I left the committee meeting with a heavy heart. I told the brothers what had transpired, and they decided that we should start meeting twice a week instead of once a week. We would refuse to negotiate one little bit with the secret police.

After that meeting, I was still in shock. I was aghast at the revelation that the registered churches were cooperating with the Department of Intelligence. It made me sad and quite mad. I felt the churches didn't realize what was going on.

The secret police had placed a number of stumbling blocks in front of people. They were feeding information to various church leaders, and I didn't want to bow down to them.

The executive committee met with us again, and again I resisted.

"It seems that you are telling me to let this church die!" I protested. "I am not going to leave the church to die. It's not your church. The people in the fellowship are the church. They should decide their own destiny. I am also part of your congregation and, as a member of your church, I have asked if we can use your facilities for our meetings. So, I won't leave. Go jump in the lake." I wasn't smiling.

"I have an idea," one man said. "Why don't you meet every week in a different church?"

"Look, we are not a choir. We can't move around all over the city."

"OK, I have an idea." someone else said. "When we ask Muslim women to come to church, why don't we teach them how to take off their veils?"

"Get behind me Satan." I said, looking at the pastor. I loved him and he loved me but I had to confront him. "Your wife should have a longer skirt and a heavier thing on her head." I paused. "They are more biblical than the way your wife dresses now."

"Whoa," the chairman said. "Wait, we are not getting anywhere. Abdalla let me give you the decision."

"Keep the decision and put it in water and make it soup and drink it." I growled. I was getting angry. I was like a mother lion wanting to kill everyone in order to keep my children safe.

Sadly, I got up and left the meeting and refused to listen to their decision. They sent me a letter asking us to stop the meetings in their church. I sent the paper back to them with a note:

Dear committee: We discussed your decision and have rejected it. The brothers here all want to keep meeting. We believe this is the voice of the Lord, and we are going to follow it. Signed Abdalla. Thank you.

We had no relationship with the committee for almost eight months. I still had a key and we kept on meeting in the church. Finally, in 1999, I grew tired of it all and wanted to make peace. I was sure that the church did not mean to do something bad. At the same time, it was another success for the secret police. Somehow they managed to work through the church. They didn't succeed through the converts from Islam, but in the end they managed to divide the Christian community. Feelings were hurt, but through prayer and meeting face to face, we worked at healing our hurts. I had to apologize for the things I had said, and God began the healing process in our hearts.

Some months later, that same church leader was visiting in our home for Easter. "Do you remember that meeting, Abdalla?" he said with big eyes. Our hurts had been mended but the issue was still in my mind.

"Yes," I replied with a smile, "And if you do it again, I will react even stronger!"

I then gave his wife a gift. It was a scarf for her head. She put it on and smiled. I saw her twice after that in church with that same scarf on her head.

"Abdalla," she said to me, "I never realized that ministry could be that dear to someone. And thank you for the scarf." she smiled. "I'm from the village of Mafraq. I am not from the wealthy areas. I am used to wearing these things."

THE INTELLIGENCE DEPARTMENT HAD SCORED A WIN. Their success made us upset, we started to refuse to have anything to do with them.

Once they called me for two weeks in order to arrange an interview.

"What about Monday?"

"Monday is an Easter holiday."

"OK, how about Tuesday?"

"Tuesday is also an Easter holiday."

"OK, what about the Saturday before Easter?"

"Oh no, I want to finish up whatever business I have in the office before the holidays."

"OK, what about Wednesday?"

"Believe me, I have work to do that day."

"Thursday?"

"No, that day is impossible too."

"What is this? We want to have a meeting with you."

"OK, leave it with me and I will try and find time in a couple of weeks."

"OK," he said and he hung up.

They couldn't get to us. We stood firm together, but somehow they seemed to get in through the church. In the end we made peace with the church but we agreed not to meet in their buildings. So, if the church was denied to us, where could we meet?

To answer this question I took several days vacation away from the ministry and the office. Amal and I fasted, prayed, and sought the Lord's face. Then I asked three of the Philadelphia leaders to join us. We gathered in our home and I unplugged the telephone. We still had some contact with normal life (the kids had to go to school), but no one knew we were there, especially my secretary, who would have flooded me with phone calls.

Then we sought the Lord's face. Should we rent a hotel conference room for weekly meetings? How could we finance this?

When the question comes around to financial support, I don't like it. We are not dependent on the west for any money now, which is good. No one has called us a western church. No one has accused us of being people who are influenced from the west. Most Muslims see Christianity as a western thing. We are not western, we are Jordanian, and we want to keep this identity. Building our own building or renting a big hall was out of the question.

Some of the brothers were very interested in the cell church concept, so they asked me to sit back for three months and let them try it. If it didn't work then we could go back to meeting as a group again. But back to where? We had no church to meet in. We were not a registered group, so we did not qualify for the rights to put up our own building. So we figured if church buildings were closed to us, then perhaps we could split into cell groups. We prayed about it and decided to try it.

The first cell meeting was in a nearby village. The next day the secret police called the head of the house.

"Why did you meet in the village? What did Abdalla ask you to do? Do you have a new strategy?"

"Look," the cell leader simply replied. "This is just my house and I want to invite people to my home. Is it forbidden?"

"No."

"So that is what I am doing. I am inviting them every two weeks, to sing and pray and whatever. It is a way to bless my home. If it is forbidden, tell me."

"No, we are just worried about the neighbors."

"The neighbors are fine. Just mind your own business."

The secret police officer hung up the telephone. God had given boldness to this house group leader and God gave him the right things to say.

Once again we started a new phase of ministry, this time using cell groups. Some of this was good, but we missed many things. Our meetings were smaller so we didn't see each other as often. Once a month we still booked a church hall so we could hold a celebration service and have communion all together. Other than that, we met in small groups.

These small groups had their advantages. In the cells, people came to know one another better because there were fewer people to relate to. In the cells, there was more room for the spiritual gifts to function. The church leaders got more experience and homes seemed to be blessed. This was the best part of it.

However, once we met in cells, we missed the blessings of corporate worship. In two homes, we could not raise our voices and sing. When we worshiped, it was like a funeral. I visited once and saw it and I was frustrated. I joined in but didn't want to say anything to discourage them more. They sang very slowly and very quietly, with sad faces. Can you imagine yourself singing a good song, with a very quiet voice? You end up crying. I stopped singing. I couldn't worship this way. I was not free to worship. Not far away was a registered evangelical church building. We were not free to use it. Instead, we sang as softly as we could in a tight little circle. Everyone was afraid that the neighbors might be offended.

I was trusting the Lord to take this cell church and multiply it. However, there was also pain in my heart. The secret police had accomplished something. When we were meeting in a church building we had large meetings. As new people came, they felt that they were joining something that was moving and reaching out. We had been bold as believers. We were actively praying and evangelism was something we were all involved in.

Our church had been busy discipling others and we had even considered sending a couple to the country of Yemen. We started thinking about which family to send. We also considered sending two single men to the Arab Gulf states. We had dreams then, but once we started meeting in cells, our dreams collapsed.

When we divided into cell groups, we formed what we called a board and I was a member on the board. They asked me to stay on as the pastor of the church, but in many ways, I pastored from afar. I removed myself from the group to see if I was the one hindering the blessing of the Lord. Each small group had its own leaders, and I simply encouraged the leaders. I met with the leaders, and they occasionally dropped into my office to discuss different issues. This way I could hear more of what was in their hearts. I started hearing grumbling. "Why don't we meet in a church? Why can't we worship? Why don't we have children's programs any more?"

Even though I was not leading any particular cell, I still had much to keep me busy. There was never a lack of things to do. Amal and I taught Bible Studies and we helped arrange marriages. We also did a lot of pre-marriage counseling. The men came to me and the girls went to Amal. We would talk and have lunch in our home or go out for something. Then we would open the Word of God and compare social marriages with the Word of God. What does the Bible say about a believing wife or husband?

Along with this, we encouraged the new leaders and tried to build them up so they could build up the brothers and sisters in their cells. We praised the Lord that there were some good results.

The Man From Gadara

Wherever there are results, however, people seem to gather to take credit. Sometimes they take credit for something they haven't done. That is why I hate writing reports. It is so easy to say that we have this many believers and this many groups but God looks at the hearts and sees what the true results are. Reports and prayer letters can be used wrongly to impress people with what we think we have done rather than giving glory to God. Little did I realize how many Christian people would be attracted by our ministry just so that they could be identified with something successful.

CHAPTER TWENTY EIGHT

I don't have any money…but I'll give you what I have. Acts 3:26

IF SOME OF THE LOCAL CHURCHES WERE AFRAID of being too closely identified with us, the opposite was true of many missionaries and Christian workers who were trying to raise money.

It never crossed my mind that missionaries would want to visit me in my office simply so they could say that they knew me and were helping my ministry.

During one visit I made to the west, I came across the prayer letter of someone working in the Middle East. While I was in a church, someone pointed out to me that my name was in this prayer letter.

"Really?" I replied

"Yes, in the middle it says, 'Please pray for us, we are cooperating with Abdalla Hawatmeh.'"

It was a complete lie. I had never been in this person's house and I had never been in his church. He had never attended any of our meetings nor had he ever sent anyone to our ministry. We knew who each other were but that was the extent of our relationship. Yet our group of converts from Islam had attracted his attention.

He wasn't the only one to do this. Other people used our ministry to obtain whatever attention or support they could get from the west. Churches sometimes want converts from Islam in their congregations to enlarge their capabilities for raising support. I know one church that takes pictures of all the new converts who visit and reports them to the west. One organization I know has a camera in their office. If you are a Muslim convert, and visit their office you get your picture taken. Then they take that picture, make copies of it, and pass them around like soup. They feed the pictures to the outside and sometimes tell supporters that they have this contact or that convert. Usually it is done in the guise of raising prayer support, but many times it is a very thinly cloaked effort to raise money.

I felt very sick when I realized why this one organization had a camera in their office and so I rebuked the man who was responsible, but I think they still do it.

I don't take many pictures and there are no pictures in this book. I have some pictures but I have never shown them to anyone. We've taken pictures at baptisms, marriages and retreats, but I never ever show them to anyone. Sometimes even the people I took the pictures of, never see them. "Your wedding? Oh, forget it." I say with a smile. "You are married now; that is enough. You have each other, why do you need a picture?"

"Your baptism? Brother, you are now a good believer; you don't need pictures of your baptism to prove it."

I hide any pictures that we have in my house or my office. Perhaps some day they will be safe to use, but right now they are better kept locked away. I have pictures and the secret police have pictures, and we both keep them under lock and key.

Sometimes people use my name in other ways. Once, someone used my name to borrow money. Hussam, an Arab Christian, was once talking to me, and we dropped into a local jewelry store together. I knew the shopkeeper, and so we all had tea and chatted about things. I am not much of a shopper and I don't really like jewelry. The only things I've ever bought in a jewelry store have been a wedding ring and a hair band. When we finished our tea, we left and I thought nothing of it. However, Hussam returned to the jewelry store a short while after we had left.

"Abdalla Hawatmeh sent me back here. He needs $200 and was wondering if you could loan it to him." The shop owner tried calling me but I wasn't home yet, so he decided to give the man the $200 anyway.

The next day I got a message to call the jewelry story owner. I called him, and he started with the Arab way of introductions. "How are you? How is your family?"

"This is kind of strange," I thought. "He wanted me to call him." So I started joking that I wanted to return the wedding ring I bought for my wife and exchange it for something much bigger for only five or ten dollars more. The owner joked back and said sure.

Then he said, "Abdalla, please forgive me, but I just wanted to check with you about the $200 loan for Hussam."

"What?"

"The $200 debt that you owe to me because I paid Hussam, and I just want to make sure that you know about it."

"What?"

"Oh, my God," he said, "You mean you didn't know anything about this?"

"About what?"

"Oh, OK, Abdalla, thank you so much for calling. I'm sorry I bothered you," he said, and he hung up.

Then I knew! So I visited Hussam myself and asked him. "Did you take money by my name? Or did you mention my name to that store owner?"

He hesitated. "Yes." He admitted slowly.

"Why did you use my name?"

"Because I thought he wouldn't loan me the money if I didn't use your name."

It was as simple as that. People sometimes use your name to get what they want, whether it is a loan, or support, or prayer or simply attention.

ALONG WITH THIS, THERE ARE PEOPLE WHO GENUINELY WANT TO HELP WITH FINANCES. This is fine, but finances are not the most pressing issue. I would far rather have a million Christians drop to their knees and offer a prayer for the Philadelphia Church in Jordan than I would have a million dollars sent to me from the west. I have often said something to this affect, but recently the Lord has put me to the test.

The first time I was offered money was about two months after my release from prison. A man called me on the telephone.

"Abdalla," He spoke like a gentleman, "Mr. Abdalla, I would like to meet you aside from your office, maybe in your home. I would like to meet your family as well."

"Now who is this?" I thought.

"I flew in from America last night just to see you. I didn't want to call you and bring attention to you. I was advised to use as much wisdom and discretion as possible."

I was surprised. "You must have been reading those warning notes on the top of some mission reports or something."

He laughed. "Don't worry, just let me know when I can visit you."

We had him over to our home.

I never asked him who he was or what he did, but he asked me a lot of questions that night.

"Can you tell me about your ministry? What do you do?"

I thought he was just another missionary, who wanted to know more, so I told him what we were doing at that time.

"Are you expecting to be put in jail again?"

"I don't know; I hope not, but maybe yes."

"Do you want to stay in Jordan?"

"Yeah." I wondered where this conversation was going.

He then got serious. "I am here to offer you financial help." My mind shifted into high gear. My car was getting older and needed repairs. "Are there any needs that you have?"

"Not really." It was true; my car was running well that week and we were still meeting in a local church.

"If you had money, what would you do first?"

"To be honest with you, I would buy a new car." I was joking. I really meant nothing by it. Most believers in this country cannot afford a car. Already some had made comments about my car, and I certainly didn't want anyone thinking that I was taking money from the church to pad my own pocket!"

"OK," he said soberly, "I am willing to buy you a new car."

I was suddenly sad, and I felt bad that I had said something.

"Really, to be honest with you, I don't need a new car. It is running fine right now, and it is already a stumbling block to many. If I buy a newer one, maybe I won't have any believers around me or maybe the wrong type of believers will be attracted to us."

"But whenever you need a better car, call me direct." He gave me his card and his telephone number and then he left. Several years later I did buy a new car, but I never called him.

SOME TIME LATER ANOTHER MAN CALLED ME FROM CALIFORNIA.

"I want to speak to Mr. Hawatmeh."

"Go ahead, I'm Mr. Hawatmeh."

"We've heard about you having troubles with the security there."

"Yes."

"We've been praying for you but also I have some news to tell you."

"What is that?"

"There are many families here that are ready to jump in anytime and defend you."

"Thank you very much."

"What is this I hear about you not having a place to meet?"

The question that was burning in my mind was a rather rude one: "Now who in the world told you about us?" I didn't dare ask.

"Sir," I said, "it's not that we don't have a place to meet it is just that we don't agree with the government and we don't agree with the churches."

"So you are now without a place to meet?"

I was sure this man had money that he wanted to give, but he was talking to the wrong person. There are many other ministries in Jordan that would have gladly taken his money.

"Look," I told him, "It's not that we don't have a place, but we do have a difficulty to overcome."

"If you had your own place to meet, would that be better for you in ministry?"

"Of course."

"Well, here is the news. How much would the church cost?"

"Man, it is very expensive to build a church here. Any small building is expensive. You first have to buy the land."

"How much is that?"

I couldn't see this man, but I could imagine him sitting in his chair with a phone, his checkbook open and a pen in hand.

"I don't know," I said, "it depends where you buy the land."

"Just roughly." I could imagine him wanting to get rid of the money.

"Any piece of land would cost you, not less than $60,000 around Amman."

"OK," he wasn't fazed at all. "What about the building?"

"Oh my goodness. Another sixty! That makes $120,000."

"That's easy. We are ready to pay that. Whatever it takes to build you a church."

"I wish it was that easy." I said. "Believe me, at this stage we do not need any money for building any church. We are fine. Thank you for calling."

I told this story to some of the other Christian leaders in Amman and they told me, "You were stupid not to take the money. Give me the man's address."

I didn't remember who it had been.

ONE TIME A CHURCH SENT ME $4,500 to buy myself a new car. Someone told them that the car I used for ministry was giving me trouble. It was true. We were even thinking of buying a van for the fellowship to use. This church collected the money, and the mission that handled it deducted 10%. Then they told me they had the money ready for me.

"Who asked this church for money?" I asked the mission organization. They gave me a name, and I remembered meeting him. He had said to me, "You are an extra-ordinary missionary. How do you question money? If money comes, just take it! Use it. They know you are genuine."

"Can you keep the money?" I asked the mission.

"No it was collected for you."

"But you deducted 10%."

"That was for processing and handling."

"Why not keep a hundred percent for that?"

"It's not ethical."

"Then send the money back."

"We can't. We've already deducted the percentage."

"Maybe I could pay that percentage and you could send the money back?"

"The church has written tax deductible receipts for those who gave the money."

"I don't care, send the money back anyway."

A while later the pastor of the church called me directly.

"Abdalla, we received the money back from the mission. If at any time you need that money, just call. That money has been donated by individuals in the church. It is $50 from 90 members. Do you want us to send it to you?"

"No. I am fine. I feel free without taking such money. If I take this money I will feel obliged to do something."

"I don't want you to feel obliged," the pastor said warmly. "I want you to feel free."

"I'm fine, pastor." I said, suddenly relieved that I had found someone who might be able to relate to me. "Pastor, I'm safe in the hands of God. Thank you for your concern for us."

Some people find this kind of weird. I would love to own a brand new van. I need a brand new van for ministry. However, there are many believers who don't even have good food in their homes. If I took the money and fed them then it would spoil them because they would get used to receiving handouts from the church.

The real need of our church is prayer. I find it so frustrating that Western Christians reach for their check books so easily and find it so hard to drop to their knees and stay there for any length of time.

The need of our church is not financial. The Philadelphia Church needs unity. We need to know the mind of the Lord and to stand together under the Lord's direction. The Bible clearly says that the people who know their God shall be strong and do exploits. Pray that this will be true for our church. If you are a Christian and want to help, take this book and pray for the believers mentioned here, even though their names have been changed. Pray for the officers in the Intelligence Department. Pray for the registered churches in Jordan that they will know the mind of the Lord and that we would be able to move together in unity. Unity is far more important than money, buildings, and meetings.

I feel free in the ministry when there are no financial strings attached. I like to be teachable when the Lord wants to teach me. I like to be open and to share with the brothers about any weakness I may have.

In the Arab world everyone covers whatever is possible to cover up. Christians even cover up sins and look shiny and nice on the outside. They cover up the real truth, and try to look nice and presentable. I don't want to do that. All I want to do is to please the Lord, and I don't care who doesn't like to see me as I really am. The burning question in my soul is, "Is the Lord happy with me?"

In my own life, I have always worked and earned my own income. The apostle Paul was a tentmaker and when he was in financial need he made tents. I too work at my job and I also trust God for the money I need day by day, especially when ministry crowds out work. Finances are important and we must think about them. We need to have cars to travel in and houses to live in. But finances shouldn't limit us in our ministry and shouldn't be a stumbling block to others. Along with this, the new church emerging in the Middle East needs to learn to tithe and care for its own financial needs.

CHAPTER TWENTY NINE
God will meet all your needs. Philippians 4:19

OVER THE YEARS I HAVE SEEN MY WIFE SACRIFICE MANY THINGS because of marrying me. The biggest sacrifice she made was losing her own family. Because they consider me to still be a Muslim, they have very little to do with us. Our children have grown up with very few connections to their aunts and uncles. Along with this, Amal lost her part in the family inheritance.

One day, Amal's brother called her and told her that the family had decided to sell their farm in Palestine and to distribute the money among those family members who would inherit. In order for him to sell the land, he needed a letter giving him power of attorney over her inheritance. Once the land was sold, he would return and give her almost $70,000.00

"Abdalla," Amal asked me, "should I do this? They might trick me. If I sign this, then he has complete power to do whatever he wants."

"Look," I told her, "I don't want to mess with this. This is your inheritance. You do whatever your heart tells you to do. I have some land, and I am fed up with owning land." I looked at her. "If you want to give it to them, that is fine with me too."

I didn't really care about the land or the money, but I cared about my wife. If something went wrong, she might become bitter or depressed. Together we sought the Lord and found freedom in Him. We would accept whatever would happen.

A few days later, Amal went to the court and signed over the land. I called her that day, and she told me that her family was very loving, and kind and full of respect.

One month later, they started calling her and telling her not to ask for any penny. They called her; she didn't call them.

"Forget that you have a family," they said. That really hurt her a lot. "Forget that you have land. We took it because you don't deserve it." They hurt her because she married Abdalla Hawatmeh. We were prepared to lose the money, but losing the family hurt very deeply.

ONE DAY I VISITED AMAL'S BROTHER. Amal didn't know I was going to do it. I surprised him by visiting him in his office. I walked in and closed the door. He was a big man, much bigger and stronger than I was. He was very surprised when he saw me and started to get up. I motioned for him to sit down.

"Hani," I began, "we love you. One thing I want you to know is that I never ever intervened in the land thing till now. Listen, I have land. All my land has been given to your sister, Amal. I have put it all in her name. Your sister was going to give her land to you anyway. She told me this. Why are you hurting her now? Why do your sisters call my wife with such hard words?"

Hani looked angry. "I promise you one thing, Hani. You and your sisters will always look up to my wife. Remember, finances, property, status and standards, are all junk to us. But even in the junk I want you to look up to my wife. I am sure God will help me in this.

He offered me tea but I refused and left.

Shortly after this, my own brother, Abdul Karim, told Amal that he no longer wanted to see her or the kids in Um Qais. "It's fine for Abdalla to come, but we don't want to see his wife and kids."

I called my brother back. "If you don't want to see my wife and kids, I don't want to see you either!" I was very sour at that time.

"No, you can come; you are our brother."

"Fine, but she is my wife. Listen, she is now closer to me than you are."

"Look," Abdul Karim said, "you don't want to give her the house in Um Qais, do you?"

It was then that I realized that the family was afraid that Amal might move to Um Qais someday and be their neighbor. Her presence would be an embarrassment to the family. It was then that I decided to buy a house in Amman for Amal.

"I think I will buy her a house in Amman."

Abdul Karim didn't believe it. He thought I was joking.

A short while later I sold a piece of land so that I could have a down payment to buy a house. "What if something happens to me?" I thought. "If I die or am imprisoned for a long period of time, or if something unexpected happened, where would Amal go? Would she go to her family or mine? She was caught in the middle. Our kids were young. Who would stand with Amal? Where would she be safe? Would she have to move from house to house?"

I decided to seek the Lord's face in buying a house in Amman for her. At least she could have her own house.

Sometime later, I found a suitable house, and I decided to make it a surprise gift to Amal on our wedding anniversary. First, however, the house needed a lot of work.

Everyday I tried sneaking out of the office a bit early, so I could drive over to the house and supervise the renovation. Before long, Amal started to wonder if I was seeing another woman. I would come home from the office, eat, kiss my kids, and do devotions with them and then leave.

"Where are you going?"

"Well, I have work to do."

"Where?"

"It's OK, don't ask any questions."

I would come back at two or three in the morning, and she would say, "Where have you been?"

"Well, I was just helping someone."

I hated to be deceptive, but our wedding anniversary was coming up and time was running out. During the daytime, I would go to the house to make sure the workmen were doing things right, and at night, I would get on my work clothes and do as much as I could myself."

Then one day, when I was driving with her down Mecca Street, where the fancy shops are that sell kitchen cabinets, I remembered Amal saying "I wish one day..."

"That day will never come" I had joked back.

"I wish one day I would have oak in my kitchen."

We laughed and continued on our way.

"Oh," I thought, "that might be a possibility. The new house has a bare kitchen."

A few days later I drove past the shop again, this time with Amal. "Let me introduce you to someone who is working in kitchens." I told her. It was true; I did know someone who was working in kitchens. I had met her the day before and I told the lady, "Don't you dare tell her what I'm doing. Just shut up and answer her questions. OK?"

I introduced Amal to the lady and I started looking at something else.

"What kind of color might you dream of having some day?" I heard the lady say.

"We don't have money for a new kitchen," Amal said, "but I've always dreamed that I would like oak cabinets."

The lady took her around the show room and they talked, and the lady took note of everything Amal said.

Later Amal said to me, "Why did you bring me there? Was it just to give me a hard time?" I laughed and told her that we were just driving by and that it didn't do any harm.

A FEW DAYS LATER I TOOK AMAL TO OUR NEW HOUSE. She was stunned. She couldn't believe it was true. It was a brand new house, complete with the kitchen she had always dreamed of. I told her it was my gift to her.

That night, we had a romantic dinner in our new house, complete with roses. As we ate, I told her why I had bought the house. "First of all, it was because your family took your property. This is my gift to help make that up to you. Secondly, I am giving you this house, because my family doesn't want me to give you the house in the north. So here is a new house in Amman." I paused. "It is for you and the children. If I die today, I will know that you are in a house, and you don't have to beg my family or your family for a place to stay."

It was a night to remember. A man doesn't often get to give his wife such a gift. We had a wonderful time moving out of our old apartment and into our new home. Truly God had been good to us, but God had another wonderful surprise in store.

CHAPTER THIRTY
And they ordained elders. Acts 14:23

SALEEM CAME TO US FROM ANOTHER MINISTRY. He had been raised a Muslim and like all the others in our fellowship, he had found Christ. He attended a local Christian church until he heard that there was a fellowship of people all from Muslim backgrounds and he came to find out if he might fit in.

I didn't like Saleem at first. He asked too many questions, and I don't like people who ask a lot of questions about the ministry. I guess it is because everyone always has the same questions. "How many people come to the meetings. How many foreigners attend? How long have you been meeting there? Is everyone there a believer? Are any of them not baptized?"

"What is this?" I said. "Are you trying to investigate me? If this is an investigation, call the secret police and get a copy of their reports."

"No," Saleem said, "I'm sorry if I offended you."

"You did not offend me, but I am getting upset with all the questions you have."

We had lunch that day, and as I talked with Saleem, I felt something very positive about this man. He was a believer and knew the Word of God.

Although he was young, just six months old as a believer, he was more mature than many. Later that night, I told one of the missionaries that I thought I might have found a future pastor.

We were all waiting to see what the Lord would do. After the bad experience with Ahmed, we were all very cautious. At the same time, we were always looking to see who the Lord was anointing as future leaders. Anything could happen to me at any time. I might be thrown back in jail. I might be killed or forced to move. If something like that happened, we felt there should be leaders able to step in and handle the group.

So we had our eye on Saleem and we watched as he grew in grace and faith. His heart was very warm and loving to the brothers. When he would visit someone who had not been in a meeting for a while, he would always pay his own taxi fares. He never asked the church to help him cover his costs.

Whenever I asked him to do something, he always responded in an obedient, humble way. In all he did, he was sincerely true and honest.

Saleem would visit the weak ones and encourage them. He would never judge somebody. He was always on the side of people, encouraging them and building them up.

One day I asked him to become an elder under training, and he said, "Brother Abdalla, I don't want to be an elder, I just want to serve."

"That is what an elder is all about, serving."

"Oh?"

"Yes, you should be on a team of elders. That way you can be accountable to me, and I can be accountable to you. And we can all be accountable to the Lord." I smiled, knowing what his answer would be. No one ever turned down an invitation to be an elder.

"Can you give me time to pray about it?"

I liked that. I was so happy that day. Many people had approached me about being an elder, and when they did, I was sad. I didn't want people to come and say, "I want to be an elder." I wanted someone who was called by the Lord.

None of them came saying, "I think the Lord wants me to be an elder." That would have been harder to answer, because if I didn't feel that way, then it was my feelings against someone else's feeling.

But this man said, "I want to take some time and seek the Lord's face."

That same day I had a telephone call. Saleem was sitting with me in my office.

The phone call was from one of the brothers in our congregation. His son was sick and in the hospital. Through some contacts that we had at that hospital, they had given him a discount. Despite this, he couldn't pay for the rest of the bill. We gave him some money from the church funds, but still he couldn't cover it.

"Abdalla, could you please ask the hospital to lower the price some more, or at least to give me some time to get the money and bring it to them. I think they needed another fifty dollars." He had personally paid almost $400, and the church had given him another fifty. Now he needed yet another fifty to pay the bill.

I then talked to the hospital accountant and explained that he was poor and that he had already paid four hundred and fifty dollars. Surely that was enough."

"Abdalla, listen to me," the accountant said. "We gave him discounts. The bill was originally over six hundred dollars. I cannot go down any more."

I accepted that but started arguing that the hospital should give the man a couple of days to come up with the money. The hospital was not being very nice about it. So I called the brother back. I was trying to explain this to him when I looked over at Saleem. He had his hands over his head and he was praying. When he raised his head, I could see he was crying.

Saleem just reached out and pressed the button on the phone, cutting off our call.

"Saleem? What is it?"

"Just hang up the phone," he said. "Why didn't you ask me for money?"

"You were not here, and we already gave him money from the offering."

"I don't care about the offering," he said. "I'm ready to give from my pocket." He reached in his pocket and he gave me two hundred dollars. "Here. When he calls, tell him to come pick up the money, or give it to me and I will go and tell him, 'This is from Abdalla and from the church.'"

"Saleem, this is not from me, it is from you. You tell him that."

"No, don't tell him where it came from."

This was a completely non-Arab, non-cultural way of doing things, and I was very encouraged. When the man called back, I told him we were coming to the hospital to give him the money.

When we arrived at the hospital, we gave him the two hundred dollars.

"Wait!" he said, "all I needed was fifty."

"Well," I said, "I think you need more. Here is two hundred dollars from somebody."

He took it gladly. I'm sure some of the money he used to pay his share of the bill was borrowed.

One week later, the church discussed appointing Saleem as an elder. That same brother, to whom we gave the money in the hospital protested against appointing Saleem. He didn't say it directly to Saleem, but it was shown in different ways to him.

Saleem was humbled. "Abdalla," he said to me afterwards. "I don't want to be an elder." I knew the reason why. If someone stood against him being an elder, he did not want to offend them.

I knew then that I had some work to do. I went to visit that brother and told him, "Look, I need someone like Saleem who can at least love the brothers." The man looked puzzled. "Do you know who it was that helped you in the hospital?"

"I know it was the church."

"No it was Saleem. He cried when you were talking with me on the phone."

"Really? Saleem did that?"

"He cares for you. If someone cares for you, it means he is a good, godly man. So use your judgment."

Later, that man went to Saleem and hugged him. "Saleem" he said, "I didn't know. I never meant to hurt you. I've been in the faith longer than you and I felt that you were so new."

Saleem took more than one month to pray it through. Then he came to me and said "Abdalla, I don't want to be an elder, but I am forced in it because we need to serve one another." That day was a very remarkable day in the history of our church.

Saleem has been a great blessing. We were looking for someone who was humble, honest, and caring about people, and God gave him to us.

Not long after this, God proved him to me in another way. One night Saleem called me.

"Abdalla," he said. "I need a thousand dollars."

"Saleem that is a lot of money. I don't have that."

"Abdalla," he said. "If you can find it, I will pay it to you in nine days."

"Nine days? This is very close. Why, nine? Why not, ten? Why not in 2 weeks?"

"Nine days. Today is the 21st. On the 30th I will pay you back."

"Saleem, where are you going to get the money to pay me back? I can go to the bank and get the money and give it to you; it's no problem."

"No. Don't go to the bank. If you don't have it then it's no problem. Banks mean paying interest."

"OK, don't worry," I told him. "I will get you the money."

I went to the bank anyway and got him a thousand dollars. In nine days he was back in my office. "Here is your money," he said.

To me that is a greater miracle than raising Lazarus from the dead. In this culture and ministry, if someone pays you back what you lent him, it is a miracle. Saleem accomplished that miracle.

CHAPTER THIRTY ONE

Finally, be strong in the Lord. Ephesians 6:10

WHEN WE BROKE THE CHURCH INTO CELL GROUPS, we had hoped that the new structure would work for us. The brothers and I had carefully researched cell groups. We had read a number of books, talked with people, and I had even flown to Singapore to see a cell church in operation. Christian workers around us were excited about the possibilities of seeing a cell church emerge in the Middle East. So we changed our structure and broke into a number of small cells. The first cell didn't go for more than one month and then it fell apart when the leader said, "I don't want you to meet in my house; it is too risky for us."

A second cell lasted longer. It lasted four months and then problems started to happen. The group was often struggling with leadership issues. Who was permitted to lead? Who was allowed to do the teaching? Where did the offering of this cell go to? It seemed strange at first, but eventually several sins came to the surface. We were surprised to discover that one member was an alcoholic. We were disturbed to discover that another was a practicing homosexual.

When we found this out, we were devastated. If you have these problems among a hundred member church, you can handle it, but when you get two or three people among eight members, that is about forty percent.

So our ministry team met and re-thought. When we were one group meeting together in a church I used to see most of the members on a regular basis. Once we started meeting in cells, the cell leaders were to take over pastoral care. After that, I ended up dealing with all of the hurt people. I would only see everyone when we had our monthly Celebration Meetings. At these meetings we would gather everyone together, have communion, pay our tithes, fellowship with each other, listen to teaching, and often have some food afterwards. As time pasted, however, the numbers at our Celebration Meetings started to drop. Once we had only seven or eight, this included Amal, another American couple, and myself.

We realized that it wasn't working. If we were dying, then we didn't need cells.

The Intelligence Department was delighted. Abu Sayed called me and told me, "What is this? Your people are dwindling. You know, this is actually better for the nation."

"I guess you have the right to say so," was all I could reply.

So our ministry team met and we decided that we wanted to go back to having one meeting.

We then called a general meeting in our home and invited everyone. Almost everyone came. We packed them all into our home and we were very open and honest with people. We opened the meeting for sharing. We said that we didn't want to study the Bible or sing in this meeting. This was a meeting to hear from each other. What had happened to us? Did we want to be a church or not? If someone didn't want to be part of a church then we told them to feel free to leave. We wanted to talk about how to better run and build our church. We were serious.

Almost everyone spoke, and almost everyone was encouraging. A few wanted to meet in an actual church building. I was against this; not building themselves, but against the feeling that we should have a building so we can be like everyone else.

I would rather people say, "I want to follow the Lord, I don't care where I meet."

We agreed that we would set aside at least two months and perhaps up to one year to have a weekly prayer meeting in our home. We chose Thursday at 7 p.m. to meet and to seek the Lord to show us His direction. We really wanted to hear the voice of God.

People were in tears, "This is our church; we really want to get a hold of it." I heard them say. No one was bitter or angry with anyone else in the group. Our problems did not stem from inter-personal relationships. Everyone was encouraged with this step forward. We thought people had stopped coming to the meetings and were upset with someone or something, but when we talked we discovered that they were still following the Lord, but they had some reservations over different things. They wanted to have an alternative to meeting in cells. They enjoyed meeting in larger groups.

So we started again with one group, based in our home, like the old days. People crowded together, being themselves. Perhaps it is our culture, but we like to be in crowds, boisterous, loud, and happy. No one enjoyed small cell groups where they had to be quiet.

Being in cell groups for a few months was helpful in demonstrating to people that I didn't want to control everything. I was happy for them to take over leadership. Others were free to lead meetings, teach, preach, and administer communion. Others were free to exercise gifts of pastoring, hospitality, and encouragement. Whenever I visited a cell group, the leaders would insist that I be the speaker and I had to argue with them each time. In the end, I would sit with the others, take notes, and be one of the cell members. However, even though people were exercising gifts, we were not happy. Somehow, we needed to be in a larger group.

When we decided to meet as a larger group again, the elders reaffirmed me as the senior pastor. They felt that since they had jobs, families, and responsibilities to their wider families and tribes, their time was limited for ministering to people. They did what they could, but they couldn't be available all the time.

On the other hand, Amal and I have tried to make ourselves available to people. If I got a phone call to come and help someone, I went. That person might be in a neighboring city, but I would always go. I have been able to structure my life and my occupation in such a way that I can put my business aside when necessary in order to be available for emergencies.

In our culture, one person is usually set aside for leadership. A tribe has only one sheik. He leads by consensus, not dictatorship, and this is what people desired in our own fellowship meetings.

THEN ANOTHER MIRACLE HAPPENED. It started at the retreat where Faisal was to play the prodigal son. At that retreat, we had visitors from some of the surrounding countries. Friendships were established and relationships started. Over the months and years that followed, our links with converts from Islam in surrounding countries grew. They visited us whenever possible and we tried to visit with them.

Eventually, we made an agreement with a group in a neighboring country that they would join with us on a monthly basis in our larger meeting. They were not a large group, only eight or nine believers, but they have been meeting for the last seven or eight years.

The leader of their group was a well known believer in his city and from a Muslim background. He was well educated and worked as a medical doctor. He and I became very close friends. This leader came to a couple of retreats in Jordan and then one day he called me.

"Abdalla could you come and visit us tomorrow? We are having a gathering."

I drove up the following afternoon and stayed overnight with them. I had the opportunity to fellowship with the group and to help them in resolving some issues that had come up.

The Man From Gadara

While I was visiting with this brother, we took the opportunity to telephone the leader of another group of converts in another country. Soon we started planning meetings between us.

The members of our Philadelphia church were very encouraged when they discovered that there were fellowships similar to ours in surrounding countries. We would often hear what God was doing in distant countries like Indonesia or the Philippines. That was nice, but when we heard that there was a group like ours meeting in a neighboring country we all got excited. Over time, I was able to visit other groups, learn from them, and share our experiences with them.

In one country, I visited a group of nearly forty. I was one of the speakers at their retreat. I was thrilled to see how other groups operated. I was curious to learn how they functioned, where they met, how they worshipped, and how they followed up with one another. Was it on a monthly or weekly basis, or more often? I don't care much about meetings. You can call a meeting anytime. If someone misses it this time, they can always come next week. But the real issue is the pastoral care of new converts. How often does someone meet with them? Who eats with whom? Who stayed overnight with who? That was where we failed in the cell groups. Our leaders were too busy with their jobs and their own families and tribes to concentrate on pastoral care. They would spend time preparing for a meeting, focusing on preparing something to teach to the cell. It takes a lot of effort, however, to provide discipleship and pastoral care of six or seven converts. It can be almost a full time job.

Now, when we meet as a larger group, only one person has to prepare a talk and only one person has to lead. We as elders can go back to our old role of visiting and providing pastoral care for people rather than preparing for meetings.

When we visit with believers from other countries, we learn from one another. In some countries, we encourage the believers to gather and form groups. Often they are amazed how much they benefit from the meetings and how much they learn when

297

they listen to someone who has gone through the same process as they themselves.

What a blessing it has been to see how God is working on a much larger scale than just the Philadelphia Church in Jordan.

One country I visited twice. The first time I discovered a weak group of new converts. The leader there was acting like a dictator. It was the only form of leadership he knew.

"Brother," I told him in love, "you need to step down. Don't try to be up high. Everyone has to reach up to you. Come down now or you will be forced to come down later. Please, don't be a dictator. Do this by your own choice. Go to the brothers and tell them you want to share. Can you do that?"

He agreed and he did it. We then appointed a group of elders and he was just an elder among the other elders. True, he was a senior elder, but the leadership was now shared. They each had full authority to make decisions.

The second time I visited with them, things were completely different. As a group, they had a broader vision and the leadership was now working together.

These elders followed our example of trying to know their people. They eat with them in their homes, see how hospitable they are. They see if there are any changes in them and see if they show anything of Christ in their homes. Are their lives changing? Are they growing spiritually? Are there any outward demonstrations of their love for Christ?

When I visited one man, I thought I was visiting one of the bishops in Amman. He had a picture of Jesus in his living room. He had a plaque that read, "May God bless our Home." Psalm 23 was also on the wall. I looked on his small bookshelf, and there were at least seven books and Bibles. And, this was the room that people would visit in!

I was very happy. I didn't want to say, "Oh, he is not wise." People told him, "Be wise, and don't display these things." But he didn't listen to them.

Other books by Roland Muller

Missionary Leadership
By Motivation and Communication

How does one go about leading a team of missionary volunteers, drawn from a variety of cultures and denominations? In his new book, Roland Muller examines the differences between secular and biblical leadership, focusing in on the two main aspects of leading multi-cultural volunteer teams: motivation and communication.

This book includes a wealth of resources, work sheets, and more. It is illustrated with cartoons drawn by Jon Clime. A must for every missionary leader.

Missions: The Next Generation

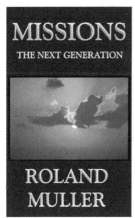

Are evangelical missionary organizations ready for the next generation? Is it possible to pour new wine into old wineskins? Roland Muller surveys the younger generations and takes a look at some of the new and radical organizations that are emerging. Will these be the patterns for new missionary organizations, serving a new generation of young people?

This book promises you probing questions and challenging answers.

Roland Muller on the Internet
http://rmuller.com

The Messenger, The Message and the Community
Sharing Christ in a Muslim Context

book and expressed their appreciation for its message. Missionaries have also responded enthusiastically, some reporting that this book has challenged and transformed their ministry.

The Community

Muslims view Islam as a community of faith. Believers from a Muslim background often face major hurdles when seeking to join a Christian community. Muller takes us through a number of important steps and issues that must be considered when trying to build a community that includes those from an Islamic background. If you are seeking to share Christ with someone form a Muslim background, Muller tells us that first the messenger (you) must be accepted as a valid messenger. Second, the message you share must be culturally valid for it's audience. And third, you must present a viable community that the seeker can identify with. But don't be surprised if seekers check out and test your community. Discover many of the checks and tests that your community may face. The material in this section has never been published before.

Many of Muller's readers express their appreciation for his original and thought provoking material. Discover why so many people are excited about the new concepts and challenges this book presents.

SEMINARS

Roland Muller also teaches seminars. You many contact him through the website listed below.

Roland Muller on the Internet
http://rmuller.com

Other books by Roland Muller

The Messenger, The Message and the Community
Sharing Christ in a Muslim Context

This book has been described by missionaries and national workers as being one of the best on the subject. Now you can purchase three Muller titles in one book:

> 1. Tools for Muslim Evangelism (The Messenger)
> 2. Honor and Shame (The Message)
> 3. The Community

The Messenger

What does it take to be accepted as a valid messenger to a Muslim audience? Muller surveys a number of successful evangelists in the Middle East, discovering some of their secrets to success. He then introduces us to the concept of 'teacher based evangelism' and demonstrates how it can be used in conjunction with or in place of friendship evangelism. Much of this material was previously published under the title Tools for Muslim Evangelism and was highly acclaimed for it's usefulness and practicality.

The Message

Muller moves on address the message that we endeavor to share. He begins by introducing us to the concept of guilt, fear and shame based cultures, showing their development over the years, and their influence on our understanding of the gospel message. He then examines the way we traditionally present the gospel, and the difficulties this poses for those from a shame/honor background. Much of this material was previously published under the title Honor and Shame, Unlocking the Door. Christians from a Muslim background across the world have welcomed this

Roland Muller on the Internet
http://rmuller.com

he was the last one to take food and the first one to clean up afterward.

"Brother," this university professor said, "Can I visit with you every two weeks?"

There were tears in that brother's eyes when he agreed. We never had to ask, but God answered our prayers. That brother e-mailed me a couple of weeks later.

I never ever felt I was part of a church before, except during the last few weeks. The professor now visits with me. When he comes, we go to a cafe, sit, and pray and read the Bible together. He stays overnight with me and then goes back. I am so happy.

These things give you hope. God is building his church. He is building His church in all of the countries of the Middle East. Our little Philadelphia Church is simply one example of what God is doing on a larger scale. Here and there, God is gathering together Christians from a Muslim background. As we grow and mature, we are discovering other groups that God has brought together. When we meet, we have a common identity. We have all come from the crescent to the cross. Our God is truly a great and awesome God.

THE END

We had no address and no telephone number. We also had no knowledge about the background of the family. How in the world can we trust someone who is just coming to the meetings?

"Look," I told them, "Don't send him to Poland; go and visit his family." It took them one visit to find out that the story was different.

When you visit people in their homes, then you will know how to counsel them and what Bible Study materials to prepare. Repeatedly I encourage elders to see their main responsibility as pastoral care, which is done through visiting.

In one country, I met with a group of elders who administered a large group of Muslim converts. Before our meeting, I had lunch with a brother who was from the distant city.

"Abdalla" he told me, I live far away and no one visits me. What can I do?"

As we talked, I discovered that the believers had never ever visited him; not just in his home, but even in his city. When he wanted to visit other believers, he had to take the train for seven hours in one direction to attend a meeting. He would spend a weekend or two days with the group and then return. For two years, he had done this.

"Look," I said, "Maybe we can talk to the brothers about this at the meeting this afternoon."

At the meeting, I opened it up for discussion. Did anyone have any recommendations or anything to share?

One of the elders stood up. He was a young university professor. "I have one little request please." We all waited for him to go on.

"I want to go and visit one of the brothers who comes to every event that we have, but we never visit with him." Wow, God was answering our prayer without us even having to ask! Sometimes you see little miracles like this that encourage you.

We had prayed at lunchtime, but we never expected a quick answer like this. I am convinced that that professor is one of the future Christian leaders in his country. When it came time to eat,

The Man From Gadara

When I saw those pictures and plaques, I thought, "If he likes it, let him do it. It is his home; he can have any pictures or decorations he wants. He is free in his home."

He then told me, "Abdalla, because of these pictures and plaques, many people have said 'What is this? Are you serious, that Jesus is Lord? Prove it to me.'" It had led to many positive discussions.

Some, however, said, "You are a blasphemer. You are a bad person. Don't display these things in your house." But they were a small percentage out of the whole.

So when an elder visits people's homes he is seeing what their lives look like. When people come to a meeting, it is just a meeting. They have to sing, they have to open the Bible, and they have to listen. They have to say "Praise the Lord" when you ask them how they are.

When you visit a home, however, you see reality, especially if you meet other members of the extended family, like a father or brothers or an aunt.

When I meet family members, I often ask them how the believer is doing. Then I usually hear the truth. "Oh, he is the best of my sons. I have six sons but he is the best one. I like to visit the others, but I like to visit this one the most. He is more loving; he has been changed and I don't know why."

When you hear something like this, you respond inside, "Thank you Lord." Then you trust the convert.

If you do not know the convert very well, you may wonder if he is telling the truth or not. Once we had an elder call us about a believer. This believer was in a lot of trouble and needed to get out of the country. The believer said he had some friends in Poland.

As church leaders, we had questions. We then asked who had been in the convert's home. No one. Who knew the family or tribal name of these people? No one. We know him as Brother Ali everyone said. No one knew the family name.